A HEMORRHAGING

OF SOULS

A light dazzled off her side mirror. Tempest glanced back. Headlights blazed close behind her. She punched her foot and the Pig shot forward. Her eyes flicked down to the speedometer. One hundred thirty kilometres an hour. About average for her.

The side mirrors glowed again. The trailing vehicle was within thirty feet, suddenly twenty. She swept the bike right.

Tires screeched and the headlamps followed. She grinned. This was what dulled the rage: an adrenaline charge electrified by cutting too close to the edge.

Tempest could make out the boxy silhouette of a truck's cab, a shadowy figure hunched over the wheel. The truck's bumper shot up to the Pig's rear, missing it by centimetres. The fun dissipated, replaced by terror...

"...a gripping story of death and family secrets...The characters are quirky and sympathetic."
—Tony Pascal, Editor, The Paper Chase

To John & Edith,
My delightful
ghosts from the
prairie past.
Enjoy
[signature]

A
HEMORRHAGING
OF SOULS

=

NICOLA FURLONG

Salal Press, Victoria, BC, Canada

First printing: September 1998
Second printing: December 1998

Canadian Cataloguing in Publication Data

Furlong, Nicola
   A hemorrhaging of souls

ISBN: 1-894012-01-1

   I. Title

PS8561.U9H45 1998   C813'.54   C98-900892-4
PR9199.3.F874H45 1998

Cover Photo and Design: P.A. Richer

Author photo: Bizzo

Printed and bound in Canada
by Transcontinental Printing, Inc.

Salal Press
P.O. Box 36060
Victoria, BC, Canada
V9A 7J5

Acknowledgements

The author particularly wishes to thank:

Jeffrey Ouellette, opera cognoscente; Paul Richer, for the cover photograph and design; Jane Bishop and Lydia Willis for libretto translation, and Glynne Turner, for always being there.

Also, thanks to:

Marsha Lalande; Patricia Gray; Patti Abela; Maureen Branch; Selena James; Margaret Stubbington; Sister Patricia Dickinson, S.A.A.; Sister Audrey Beauvais, S.S.A.; Elizabeth Laken; Dorothy Tubman and the Society of Friends of St. Ann's Academy; Constable N. (Nedge) Drgastin, Sidney/North Saanich Detachment, RCMP; Corrine Hurst; Clare Thorbes; and Alexandre Brisco, whose hand graces this cover.

The synopses of Giuseppe Verdi's *Rigoletto* were paraphrased from *The Trials of Rigoletto*, translation by Quita Chavez.

Dedicated, with love, to my siblings:

Allannah
Patrice
Kieran
Carla
Shauneen
Kilian
and Siobhan

For a life seven times enriched.

PROLOGUE

Tragedy strikes
local family
once again

Thirteen-year-old Nathan Winsloe died yesterday at his Metchosin home.

He was found hanging from a belt slung over the bar of a clothes closet. At his feet was a bouquet of shamrocks.

While authorities refused comment, a source who asked not to be identified said suicide was suspected. A family friend said the teenager was distraught over his mother's recent death. Vivian Winsloe (née Brownlee) died March 17 of an apparent suicide.

"Suicide is a learned behaviour," said Clare Mully of the Greater Victoria Suicide Prevention Unit.

Nathan is survived by his father and two sisters. The investigation continues.

The Victoria Observer, March 22, 1978

ACT ONE

Behold, I shew you a mystery;
We shall not all sleep,
But we shall all be changed
—1 CORINTHIANS, 15:51

Act One synopsis, *Rigoletto*, an Italian opera by
Giuseppe Verdi, 1851

In a sixteenth-century ducal palace, a female guest
attracts the philandering duke's attention. Count
Monterone storms in, denouncing the duke for seduc-
ing his daughter. When mocked by Rigoletto, a hunchbacked court jester, Monterone thunders a father's
curse upon him. A widower with only one child,
Rigoletto is appalled.

Later at his home, Rigoletto is accosted by a professional assassin who offers to kill the young man seen
spying on the jester's cherished daughter, Gilda.
Rigoletto dismisses him, then embraces his daughter.
He cautions her about leaving the house and orders
her chaperone to guard her. Gilda denies being followed from church and Rigoletto departs. Gilda is
stricken with remorse, having concealed her love for

the man who has been following her. The duke steps from his hiding place, pays off the chaperone, and, pretending to be a poor student, declares his passion for Gilda. Upon hearing footsteps, he is forced to flee. Gilda, singing *Caro nome*, slowly retires upstairs.

That evening, Rigoletto is tricked by courtiers into assisting in the kidnapping of his daughter. When he realizes she is gone, the jester laments that Monterone's curse has begun.

ONE

Tremble, old man, at your ruler's wrath
That you provoked, there is no remedy.
This outburst was fatal for you.
—COUNT MONTERONE & CHORUS, ACT ONE

The child was not schooled in the hangman's knot. It certainly wasn't the sort of instruction covered in Sister Benedict's grade five class. The Sisters of the Perpetual Soul taught their fifty-six charges to live in peace with God and offered what the Mother Superior called a diamond education: reading, writing, arithmetic and religion. More's the pity, for it took her a long time to die. Gasping, kicking and scratching at the smooth leather belt that, in the end, was just tight enough.

THE CASKET DISAPPEARED INTO THE GRAVE, SUNLIGHT stubbornly streaking off its small brass nameplate. *Sweet Jesus, no!* Constable Patrick Painter's stomach lurched and he gulped for air. He tasted salt water, seaweed and cedar. For an instant, he fled Holy Trinity's graveyard by the sea and gratefully felt the nearby Pacific Ocean's cool, wet touch on his face. Memories of beach-bumming and cove-hopping sliced his consciousness as the red Coast Guard vessels winked at him from Patricia Bay. As a child, he'd been terrified of losing his mother. Every night he'd say, "See you in the morning, Mom," a childish command, he now realized. A desperate effort to receive a promise of not being left alone...with him. He'd wait as long as possible to shut his eyes, rubbing the soft sheets, to avoid the risk of sleeping and her dying. Each morning, he would awake with a start. Then he'd leap out of bed, dash into the hall and listen for her soft voice. Only when he heard it could he relax. Sometimes he thought his bladder would burst, but finally he'd hear her, then he would race into the bathroom.

The beeping of the pager startled the small clutch of mourners just as his father reached down to grab a handful of freshly-dug dirt. *Goddammit! What the fuck?* Flushed, Constable Painter peered up under dark bangs and caught the priest's critical glance. A disapproving clucking of tongues slipped its way round the circle of onlookers. Cursing inwardly again, he instinctively slapped his side and the short, nasal bursts stopped. Patrick looked away, eyes skittering from the moss-pocked tombstones, to the round earth mound, to the grave pit—*Oh my God, Mom!*—finally, up into his father's black and staring eyes. The younger Painter knew, with the last sudden, sublime finality that strikes a driver careering off a bridge, that the horror was true. He was alone with the man he loathed.

Leonard P. Painter opened a large hand and a clump of Vancouver Island soil plopped onto his wife's coffin. A long, ragged scar gleamed on his left cheek, contrasting sharply with his ruddy complexion. The recently retired staff sergeant of the Victoria Police Department turned carefully on his heel and tramped away. Several mourners struggled to follow, shoulders hunched with grief. Breathing deeply, Patrick waited while the others followed suit. A small, well-dressed man arrived breathless and late, offered condolences and an envelope, which Patrick shoved unthinkingly into his suit pocket.

Finally, only he and the priest remained. Patrick knew he'd deliberately left the beeper on. What was he hoping for? That he'd have to leave and so avoid the nightmare? *My God, Pat, you'd run from your own mother's funeral? You'd use the damn job excuse on her one last time?* Despite himself, he snorted.

"Patrick?" A hand touched his shoulder. "Son, you all right?"

Painter blinked into the sun. "What? Oh, yeah. My mother's dead and if I were any better, I'd be twins."

"What?" The priest's sunken eyes stared. "Patrick, maybe we should—"

Marching off to his car phone, Constable Painter didn't hear the rest.

SHE STRUGGLED BUT COULDN'T GRASP AIR. VOICES of unattainable beauty rose round her like a shimmering fountain: lyric and mezzo sopranos rushed skyward, chased by a single clear treble. An astonishingly brilliant light enveloped her. Glowing faces and flowing robes darted across her path. Tempest Ivory inhaled profoundly, right from her toes; still no sound escaped her lips. She had to sing. She must!

The voices scaled atmospherically, forcing Tempest's hands over her ears. Ugly and sharp now, the bizarre harmonies jarred her. With a crackling *whoosh*, the light swallowed all the air. The unknown choir rushed at her like sheets of rain, their piercing shrieks pummelled her and she collapsed, trembling and gasping. Her soul shrivelled and she sobbed for her loss. A ringing crammed her skull and she woke with a gasping, heaving shudder.

Sunlight caressed her as she slowly began reattaching herself to her cool satin sheets, her cannon-ball bed, her tiny cottage in pastoral North Saanich, British Columbia. The phone rang again. Her heart still thudded, though her breath returned in frayed whispers. A ragged clank raised the coppery hair on her freckled arms. She wasn't alone. Tempest bolted up, started screaming, "Get outta my house!" and stumbled out of and around her bed into her living room.

A dark, hooded figure streaked from the galley kitchen into the narrow hall. Two strides to the front door. Too tortoise-like to follow, Tempest unhinged her jaw, dug back into her spine and unleashed her only weapon. Her voice rose, effortlessly vaulting high C, saturating the tiny space, slamming the intruder's senses. The figure stubbed its toe near the front door. With a surprised bellow, the prowler reached down, clutched the offending box and hobbled out into the dappled light. Chest heaving in her lace nightgown, Tempest thumped barefoot onto her wooden porch. Just as her motorbike was thrown to the ground, she saluted the interloper with an angry, raised fist as he faded into the surrounding second-growth coniferous forest. Though incapable of physically describing her uninvited guest, Tempest could mentally replay the baritone's startled curse.

TWO

*Oh, such pain! What can wring
Such bitter tears from you?*
          —GILDA, ACT 1

Patrick Painter gaped at the long, slim shadow cast by the horror dangling in the closet and pondered the irony of life. This prickling in his soul, this stinking hot terror rippling up his spine, was the only emotion Patrick shared with his father: an abject incapacity for enduring a child's violent death. Fully trained and hardened by countless pulpy masses of human roadkill on British Columbia highways, Patrick felt his testicles shrink as he collapsed inward from the strain. Forcing a quick, wild-eyed stare, he glimpsed tousled cinnamon hair, bulging eyes, a sagging, blackened tongue and a blue jumper. Holding his breath as if it would explode on release, he backed out of the dormitory.

"For the love of...can we not...?" Patrick whirled to see a small, gray woman peering up at him. At least, she seemed completely gray, with her hair curled in silver waves, an oversized charcoal button-up sweater around her shoulders, and an ash-coloured skirt around her waist. "Patrick!"

Constable Painter hesitated, then reached down and gave her an awkward hug. "Hello, Aunt Winifred," he started then stopped, tongue foolishly large in his mouth.

"Dear boy, thank heavens it's you!" Her small body hummed with energy. "Now we have a modicum of chance for some control." Winifred coughed slightly. Patrick knew she would try to control him so he steeled himself, as he always did when faced with the tiny punch of Catholic fury that was his great-aunt.

"This whole thing's so unfortunate. I was worried, you see, what with the school..." She stopped, noticing his reaction. A faint blush rose on her hollow cheeks. "Oh....dear, please forgive me." She tugged her sweater closed, then lightly touched his shoulder as though afraid it was on fire. "You know I wanted to be there for your father, but..." she hesitated, eyes suddenly dark. "This is such a disaster. First your mother, now this. Your poor father, he must be devastated. I should, must, go to him. He'll be so despon–"

"He's fine," Patrick replied too harshly. *I've just come from my Mom's funeral on my damn birthday and you ask about him!* He swallowed, put on his best officious voice and tried again. "I'm here–".

"It's obvious why you're here, dear boy," she said, her nasal tone mocking his. "The Lord seems to have forsaken us on this day of Saint Patrick's. Now, this is what I want you–"

Patrick tried again, fighting against the internal barrage of inadequacies that his great-aunt commonly evoked. "Sorry, Sister. I'm here to investigate–"

"Investigate?" Her nostrils flared. "Nonsense! The poor child had an accident. Simple as that." She

clapped her hands for effect. "No need for more dra-
matics." She took a short step toward the dormitory.
"Now, tell that hulking two-by-four of a man to get her
down, then follow me!" The aforementioned hulk shifted across the doorway and rolled his eyes at Painter.
Sister Winifred silently marched down the empty hall.

"Can't do that, I'm afraid." Realizing she was gone,
he raised his voice. "Aunt Winifred? Uh, Sister?" He
cursed and nodded curtly to his colleague. The other
cop looked away, hiding a grin.

Patrick hurried after her and found his great-aunt
waiting at the top of a curved staircase. "Snap to it,
Patrick. We've got lots to do."

She nipped down the stairs. Patrick clumsily followed. "Like I said, we can't touch her."

The nun stopped, leaned on a huge newel post and
turned slate eyes up at him. "Can't touch her? You
mean you're going to just let..." Her eyes swept up and
down the stairs and she lowered her voice. "Come
along. We'll discuss it in my office."

Feeling like an altar boy again, Patrick followed her
along another echoing corridor into a small room
painted avocado green.

"Sit!" He did so, on a high, straight-backed chair.
Winifred moved around a large wooden desk, perched
neatly on a swivel chair and began straightening the
few papers on the otherwise spotless desk. "Now,
what's this foolishness about waiting? We can't let the
poor child hang there, surely?"

"Sorry, but it's procedure. Coroner's got to come,
certify death."

"Certify..." the nasal voice hesitated. "But that's
ridiculous."

Finally, he had the upper hand. Checkmate for officialdom.

It had only taken him ten minutes to drive south along the winding West Saanich Road but in that short time, Patrick had been fully briefed by his boss, Staff Sergeant Lalande. "Miserable day for you, ain't it, da Vinci? And Wilma says it's your birthday. Sucks rocks, don't it?" Painter swerved to avoid a tractor and heard the wheeze on the line as Lalande took another nicotine drag. "Sorry to call you out, but Williams is having a root canal–serves him right, the crap he eats–" This commentary was punctuated by a fit of coughing. "–and Evanovich is doing radar on Mount Newton. I'll be there soon's I can get out of the council meeting. Now, watch your mouth, my boy. The school seems a bit out of the twilight zone, if you know what I mean– uniforms, prayers, that sort of nonsense–but the nuns're first class." Little do you know, thought Patrick. Another long, hissing breath and Patrick jumped in. "What's happened?"

"Wilma didn't tell ya?" Without waiting for an answer, he continued, "Some kinda accident. Got a 911 call from Sister Winifred, the Mother Superior. A kid's dead at the Old Soul. She wouldn't say more. Now listen, Painter, this's gonna be a stinker. Don't matter if it's an orphan or rich kid who bought it. The press'll eat it up. Your job is damage control. Get in there and nail it down. Coroner's on her way. I'll get there soon's I can."

"Thanks," Patrick said as he wheeled the cruiser, a Taurus sedan, up the long, forested drive.

"And da Vinci?" his boss's husky voice boomed. "Watch your back. Those nuns answer to a higher calling, and I don't mean our local mayoral might."

You're not kiddin', Patrick thought as he stepped out, adjusted his hat and looked heavenward.

The Academy of the Sisters of the Perpetual Soul, built circa 1896, rose three storeys, capped by a copper-roofed bell tower and gold cross which ascended like a gleaming pulpit into the North Saanich sky. Built in red brick and highlighted by rows of domed windows and neo-classical details like pilasters and a pedimented gable roof, the academy sat on fifteen rolling and forested acres. The Perpetual Soul was founded by early Quebec missionaries dedicated to the education of rural children, and grew to become the institution of choice for many of Victoria's elite Catholic families. In keeping with its charitable founding ethic, however, the academy provided free education to a limited number of deserving girls. At the academy and other Catholic schools, education was paramount, personal comfort secondary. Cold and austere from the outside, the Old Soul's interior remained crypt-like, with gleaming oak floors, dove-gray walls and endless, senseless echoes.

"Her full name?" Patrick asked, shifting in the small chair.

"What? Oh, Amelia, uh, Angeline I believe, Penderghast." She reached down. Patrick heard a drawer open and shut. Winifred carefully placed a small gold chalice directly in front of her. "Now, I've got quite a lot to do," she said, lifting the lid. She reached in, took something small and popped it in her mouth. She chewed for a moment, swallowed and sighed. Winifred dipped the cup toward him. It was filled with jujubes, mostly green. Patrick almost laughed. He'd forgotten his great-aunt's fancy. "Have one, a green one," she directed. He reached in, deliberately fingered a red one, then did as ordered. Her eyes darted sharply to the cup and she ate two yellow jujubes in quick succession. She began to scribble. "Now, we've got to do damage control." Patrick choked, swallowed the whole candy. "First, alert the archdiocese—heaven knows what they're going to say—next, head off the press. You know the kind of trash they'd write if given half a—"

Patrick finally regained his breath. "Could you spell the last name?"

"Pardon?" she said in mid-chew.

He swallowed hard, the jujube burning deep in his throat. "The girl's last name."

"The girl? Oh, of course." She did.

"Age?"

"Eleven, I think." Winifred slid the lid back on the chalice and slipped the cup into the drawer. "Right," she said. "If you'll just..." Painter didn't move. "Well?" she asked finally. "What else do you want?"

"Have you informed her parents?"

Sister Winifred's slate-coloured eyes widened. "Of course not! I, I wanted to prepare. You don't just call someone up out of the blue and..." Sister Winifred leaned back into her chair and stared at Painter. Stroking the silver cross around her neck, she continued, "I don't really know what to do. The archdiocese, well, we've never had..." She paused, then leaned forward. "You see, this is my school. At least it was this morning. Heaven only knows what the bishop's been told now." Her brow furrowed at the thought. Patrick was relieved that there was someone his great-aunt feared. "Here we do things a certain way. My way. Have done for almost fifteen years. For us, religion is essential. We believe that the basics can be nourished and built in at an early age. We teach the girls to respect the person, the environment and our value system. It must have been an accident. How else...?" Winifred blew her cheeks in and out, like paper sails turning in the wind. "First I've got to deal with the bishop."

"That's fine. We'll contact the parents. You have an address?"

"Of course," she replied and pulled a black address book from another drawer. "Her mother's name is Alice, she lives on Finnerty. Here it is."

Patrick jotted down the name, address and phone number. "You seem to know her pretty well."

"I know all my girls, Constable Painter, and their parents and often their siblings. We don't just teach religion in the classroom. It's a way of life, and needs the work of the whole family unit. When these girls leave the Perpetual Soul, they're trained to be proficient individuals, good Christians and independent citizens. Take an interest is what we do here at the Perpetual Soul."

Is that what you do? Patrick thought. What about your own family? But he merely asked, "No Mister Penderghast?"

She shook her head. "Amelia's father abandoned her and her mother years ago."

"What does Mrs. Penderghast do? Must be something pretty special to afford the Old, pardon me, the Perpetual Soul."

The gray eyes hardened. "Amelia is, was, one of our special scholars."

"Oh, yeah, some of 'em get a good Catholic education for free. What did she or her mom have to do to deserve that?"

His great-aunt glared at him. "Nothing! Each year, the archdiocese chooses two worthy girls from the local community. Their education is completely paid for, provided, of course, they suit."

"Suit?"

The Mother Superior's answer was interrupted by a knock. A young nun padded softly into the room. "Yes, Sister Gabriel?"

The young Sister nodded toward Painter. He turned. For a second, she hesitated, then Patrick felt her withdraw. She quickly crossed herself. He was so struck by her brilliant green eyes that he almost missed her soft words. "The coroner has descended upon us, Mother."

"DEATH BY STRANGULATION, NOT THE SLIGHTEST DOUBT."

"Any idea when?" asked Patrick, carefully averting his eyes from the tiny figure being zipped into the body bag.

"At a guess, sometime early this morning," replied Dr. Edwina Harwicke. "I'll know more after the autopsy.

"Right," she said to her assistant, "off you go."

"Was it–?"

"Suicide? You can say the word, Constable. Most likely. Very unusual in children but not unheard of. No note found, but that's not uncommon, contrary to popular belief." Edwina sighed and rubbed her eyes. "Not a very good knot. She struggled, poor dear, but no sign of another person. All I can tell you is how," she said, zipping up her small bag. "You have to find out why." Dr. Harwicke gave the cracked leather an affectionate pat. "At least she won't drown."

"Excuse me?"

"Oh, sorry. Just an expression." In answer to his blank look, Edwina continued, "If you're born to be hanged, then you'll never be drowned."

PATRICK WAS GETTING TIRED. WHERE IN GOD'S name–*now that's appropriate*–was Lalande? With the assistance of the school's counsellor, Dr. Tempest Ivory, who, despite her unusually loud voice, he decided could counsel him anytime, he'd interviewed most of the staff and students. From the jumble of distracted voices and continuous comings and goings of distraught parents, he managed to cobble together a day in the life of Amelia Angeline Penderghast, or Pendy, as her sobbing, red-headed friend, Vita, called her. Early for bloody everything, was how he'd put it in the report. Up at six for mass (why did the Lord always expect such early devotion?), breakfast from seven till seven-thirty, followed by a half hour of chores–poor Pendy would never finish polishing the altar votive candles–and then an hour of free play time until classes began at nine.

"Nine sharp!" little Vita Bell had intoned. "Mustn't be late or Sister Dick–" She grinned nervously and tugged at her blue jumper. "Sister *Bene*dict made you go up to the front of the class and read the daily missive out loud." She spoke with such reverence that Patrick's nape hairs jumped to attention. Vita raced pudgy fingers through her bronze ringlets. "I never had to, but–" whereupon she'd burst into tears again and Dr. Ivory tossed him another disgusted look.

Despite the situation, Constable Painter had to force his eyes off Dr. Ivory–*that's exactly the colour of her skin*–and onto Vita Bell. Dr. Ivory handed her a tissue.

"There, there," he heard himself saying ridiculously, "we're here to help. Who had to read the uh, missive? Aloud?"

"Pendy," she whispered after a sniffle.

"And when was this?"

Vita blew her nose. "Why aren't you in uniform? You're not a real cop."

"I'm plain clothes today. Now, tell me when Pendy, I mean Amelia, read the message aloud."

"Plainclothes? Like on Law and Order?" Patrick nodded and was secretly pleased to see a fleeting smile tease Tempest's lips. *What gorgeous hair.* "It's missive. Sister Benedict must say missive, missive, missive, a hundred thousand times. D'you know it means a message from God?" Patrick nodded again, happy to discover the meaning, encouraging her on. "Yesterday. Pendy was late. She pushed me away, wouldn't play. I got mad and left. Then she was late. Do you have a horse? No? How 'bout a dog? Benton Fraser has one."

"What was the...missive?" Dr. Ivory spoke for the first time. Patrick let the strong music of her voice roll around in his head.

"Never had it before." She stood up, in proper homage to the task: "Old Sins Cast Long Shadows." The child plopped back down. "Don't get it." She chewed her thumb. "What's cast?"

THREE

She was snatched from me!
Who would have dared such a deed?
—THE DUKE OF MANTUA, ACT 2

Patrick Painter couldn't believe his luck. The red-headed vision that was Dr. Tempest Ivory sat stiffly beside him, suffusing the leftover-lunch smells in the sedan with a soft perfume. She'd almost refused to get in when he opened the door and she saw inside. Cursing softly, Patrick hurriedly scooped up the brown bags and styrofoam cups and gave the seat a rapid brushing. She opened the window completely, then carefully edged inside. Though a large woman, she perched delicately, reminding Patrick of some elegant bird on a nest.

The child psychologist wasn't the talkative type. Patrick learned that within the first five minutes when, in response to a weather remark, an inanity he would regret for some time, Dr. Ivory informed him with a cool politeness that she wished to think. Well, excuse me, Painter thought. No need for air conditioning, that's for sure.

While Patrick knew little about women's scents,

even his rather large nose recognized quality. So, as he waited his turn at a four-way stop, he idly ran through the possibilities. He'd heard of–and maybe smelled once or twice on Liz Simmons, or was it Heather Leonard–Chanel Nº 5. He sniffed surreptitiously. No, this was finer, less sweet.

Ages later, she leaned over and carefully picked up a piece of paper wedged between her seat and the belt. Patrick checked an instinct to pull it from her hand.

"What's this?" she asked, unfolding it cautiously.

For crying out loud, he thought as heat fanned his cheeks, it's not gonna bite you. "Uh, nothing. Should've thrown it out with the rest of the trash." He grabbed for it. "Here, I'll toss it in the back."

"Why, it's a drawing!" she said, ignoring his hand. "Some sort of house design?"

Burning eyes staring straight ahead so she couldn't see his reddening face, he shrugged.

"You do this?"

He admitted he did.

"Why?"

Nobody had ever asked him before. The guys at the office used to tease him about his hobby, but a fierce stare generally shut them up. They had never bothered to ask why, though.

"I, uh, no real reason." *God, you sound like an idiot!*

Tempest looked at him, amused. He felt the flame light his cheeks again. "Come on, Constable. Everyone's got a reason. Why house plans?"

"Dunno," he croaked. Patrick swallowed and tried again. "Guess I just like drawing."

She nodded. A single, loose bronze curl waved

across her forehead. "Often a sign of release. Do you find it beneficial, the drawing?"

Release? Beneficial? Christ, she's analyzing me! He switched lanes too sharply and she lurched toward him. Patrick neatly snatched the drawing from her hand and shoved it in his pocket. He caught a whiff of her scent and felt like a greater fool.

"Look, I'm...they're really...I shouldn't have..."

"No problem," she replied coldly, hitching herself up nearer the passenger door. "We all have our little secrets."

"It's not a...oh, never mind."

They drove the rest of the way in an unsettled silence, Patrick obsessively rerunning the incident in his mind, feeling angrier at himself and coming up with a variety of smoother responses. Finally, to break the endless pattern, he concentrated on her perfume. By the time the sedan rolled into Alice Penderghast's cluttered drive, Patrick decided he would call it Eau de Ivory. He liked the sound of that. Very exotic.

SYDNEY MAYNE ADORED SECRETS. SHE SLID HER small hand along the leather book, fingered the raised gold writing and tingled with delight. It hadn't been easy to sneak into the nuns' wing—Sister Dick had nearly walked in on her—but Sydney was slim and quick. She'd hidden behind one of the heavy wooden doors and waited until the clacking of Sister Dick's rosary faded. With the morning's excitement, the students were momentarily forgotten and Sydney had grabbed her chance.

A quick look confirmed the coast was clear, then Sydney blew a raspberry at the statue of the Mother

Mary and scampered along the corridor. The smell of wax tickled her nostrils and she avoided the shiny gaze from the graduating class photos that guarded the walls. She paused at the foot of the narrow stairs leading to the bell tower and felt a chill across her neck. She moved swiftly through the serene nuns' wing, her sneakered footsteps silent on the oak floor. Sydney ducked through another doorway and into what the Mother Superior called her inner sanctum. Sydney had seen it all before, a couple of times at least, but there was never time to look, to find. She was always primed to scuttle away at the slightest sound.

Until this morning. She'd thought about setting another fire until she realized, during the hastily arranged assembly on the front lawn, that everyone was outside. Even old Sister Agnes had been dragged from her beloved library. And the sisters were all upset, talking heatedly among themselves, giving no thought to their charges. Mother Superior was lecturing a stocky, big-nosed policeman and nice Dr. Ivory. The school counselor's presence made Sydney hesitate. She'd had her first private session, as her mother called it, with the doctor and had found it hard to hate her. Still, she didn't owe the young woman anything. And this chance was too good to miss.

Sydney smelled the secrets in the book's leather spine. Full of 'em, just as she'd thought. It must be, for Sydney had watched Mother Superior write in it when she thought she was alone. Sydney thought this the best secret of all: that anyone would think they could be alone at the Old Soul. Smiling inwardly, she shoved the diary in her pillowcase and skipped off to lunch.

"WHY WOULD SHE DO IT? WHY, WHY?"

Tempest Ivory watched Alice Penderghast and marvelled at her pain, her loss, and at how freely she expressed these to all and sundry. For a moment, she felt a stirring of memory, like the wings of a moth. *No, no, NO.* With an effort, she quashed the insect and continued her quiet, persistent questioning of Amelia's mom and her boyfriend, Terry Brethour.

"Did something happen to her recently?"

"What?" the tousle-haired woman asked, blowing her nose.

"Had her mood changed? Was she having trouble at school? At home?" Tempest glanced up into Terry Brethour's narrow face. Alice Penderghast's latest was a scrawny, short guy, with barely enough moustache fuzz for a peach. He had very red lips, which glistened when he licked them. Tempest didn't like the way he avoided her gaze. Almost immediately upon her arrival, her antennae had been tuned to the man who fidgeted beside Alice. She'd seen too many other "latests": weak, demanding men with no emotional attachment to their lover's children. Poverty, ignorance, insecurity, barely-suppressed anger: not a loving family kind of environment. Watching just a couple of National Geographic specials taught that nature was filled with errant males disposing of offspring other than their own.

"No!" Alice cried. "There was nothin' wrong with 'er! Can't you see? Me and Terry loved her. She's all I...Oh, God, Terry, nooo..." Alice Penderghast broke down again. Brethour fidgeted beside her, dirty fingers drumming a tattoo on the cigarette-stained coffee table. Tempest felt nothing for the woman, nothing for the child, nothing for herself. The townhouse, with its unkempt yard, cluttered living room and beer cases lining the hall, depressed the hell out of her. Why do these women do it? The thought popped into her head and immediately she was ashamed.

"Why the fuck're you doing this?" Terry Brethour asked, putting an arm around his girlfriend.

"Hey," Painter piped in from his spot near the door, "watch your language."

Brethour shrugged. "Can't you see she's upset?"

"What about you, Terry?" Tempest asked, deliberately using his Christian name.

"Whaddya mean, me?" His pink tongue snaked out to touch a fat upper lip. "Got nothin' to do with it."

"I didn't say you had. Did you notice any changes in Amelia?"

"You always shout?"

Patrick flushed slightly but Tempest ignored the remark and waited.

"Changes?" Brethour glanced down at his girlfriend. "Course not. She's Ali's kid, y'know. Didn't have much to do with 'er."

I'll bet you didn't. "No? Didn't take her to school, pick her up, give her a bath?"

Brethour scowled. "A bath!? You fuckin' crazy? I never touch—"

"What're ya doing?" Alice wailed. "Terry's got nothin' to do with it. He loved her, didn't you, Ter?" She leaned against him.

"Course I did," he replied coldly. Tempest knew he loved no one but his scrawny, teensy-balled self. He jerked a cigarette pack from his T-shirt pocket and tugged one free. "Anyway, why these stupid questions?" He lit the cigarette and blew smoke into

Tempest's face. "Christ, the kid's killed herself. You gonna blame that on me?"

At this, Alice bellowed and fought against her lover's hold. Brethour snapped. "Why don't you just get the fuck—"

In two quick strides, Painter crossed the room. He grabbed Brethour by the shirt and jerked him to his feet. The cigarette dropped to the floor. "I warned you. Watch your goddamned mouth!" Patrick shoved him back on the couch. Brethour stared up at the policeman, lips quivering like a newly cut worm. As though realizing the ridiculousness of his statement, Patrick stepped back, breathing hard.

Tempest walked over, brushed Painter aside and delicately ground out the cigarette in the overflowing ashtray. After waiting five beats, she spoke calmly. "Okay, Terry, we know this is a bad time, but we need to talk."

"Talk! Ha! You call that—" a dirty finger jabbed at Painter "—talking?" He stood up. Patrick stiffened. "Get outta my house before I sue the shit outta ya!"

Alice sniffled, blew her nose. Painter and Brethour stared at one another like two old fighters. Finally, Patrick shot Dr. Ivory a look. "Okay," she said. "I'll be back." They both mumbled their condolences again, and left.

"Jeez, Doc. Where'd you get your tact? From a cereal box?"

Tempest stared at him. "Trying to be funny?"

"Uh, no." Patrick felt blood rushing to his scalp. "You went at that guy like a pit bull and, well, you coulda been a bit more considerate."

"So you're the psychologist now! Where'd you get your licence? From a matchbook cover? And what would you call that display back there? Policing in the nineties?" She wrenched open the cruiser's door.

"Don't lecture me on my job and don't ever refer to me as Doc."

She wedged herself in. Patrick held his tongue and gently shut the door. He grinned as he walked around the rear.

"WHY DO KIDS KILL THEMSELVES?"

"Pardon?" Tempest blinked and pulled herself back from another hanging long ago.

"Kids. Why do they commit suicide?" Patrick was cruising down the Patricia Bay Highway, wishing he'd taken the slower route through Central Saanich, the most rural of the peninsula communities taking their name from the Salish Indian word for fertile soil.

"Oh, hundreds of reasons. Psychological problems, depression, trouble at school, somebody abusing them." Tempest began to relax. This was safe, her work territory. "That's why I was pushing back there. Something or someone—and I'd bet my right arm it's that bastard, Brethour—hurt Amelia so badly, something in front of her was unsolvable. Death seemed preferable."

"Why d'you think it's him? Bit of a puke, maybe, but I saw no reason to suspect him."

"There you go again—" she snapped. She hesitated, breathed deeply several times. Patrick watched control envelop her like a shawl. When Tempest spoke again, her voice was restrained and soft; the tone that stroked his heart. "Give me a little credit, will you? I've seen his kind too often before. He needs the woman, but the kid's a major inconvenience."

Painter changed lanes to get around an old Volvo. Just as he suspected: an old guy, grey hair partially covered by a cap, was at the wheel, cautiously rolling along as if en route to the dentist. "Does an eleven-year-old understand death?"

Tempest flicked a glance at Patrick. Was he really interested? His nose was rather big, but she liked his solid, open face. "That's a real hornet's nest, that one. Many schools of thought. Some believe that children perceive death as temporary, pleasant. Others have come up with three stages of understanding death." Tempest paused, waiting for a sign to continue.

Patrick was drumming his fingers on the steering wheel. "So, what are they?"

While collecting her thoughts, Tempest adjusted her seatbelt and tugged her skirt over her knees. "In stage one, the child is aware of death, but observes it as a lack of movement. In stage two the child understands all features of death, but only in physical terms; and lastly, the child comprehends everything in the abstract."

"Gimme the Coles notes version, Doc—er, I mean, Doctor. Would Amelia really know that dying is permanent?"

Tempest nodded. "An eleven-year-old would. Most of the literature agrees with Gessel and Ilg. Children from eleven to thirteen have a pretty good idea of what it means. Course, you have to understand that suicidal children view the world and death a little differently."

"How so?" Patrick asked, inwardly delighted with Tempest's sudden animation.

"Well, a child who's depressed enough, driven to hopelessness, sees death as more agreeable and less final than others."

"But you just said—"

"I know. Kane's stages are for average children. Suicidal kids aren't average, nothing about them is typical or normal." She paused, for a moment years away, then blinked. "They are, in their own eyes, under intolerable pressure. Often they're an impulsive or aggressive personality, usually inflexible, can't see things from different perspectives. They have an essential need which can only be met, from their limited viewpoint, through death. They're faced with two options: accept death and all its finality, or continue to live in unspeakable pain. So they do something quite unique, yet very human: they create a third option. It's called a defensive distortion, allowing them to see death as easy, acceptable, and not final."

Constable Painter rolled to a stop at the gates of the Perpetual Soul. "You really think they believe it? That death's not final?"

"Oh, yes," replied Tempest. "I know they do."

FOUR

What thought now agitates him?
How his mood has changed!
—CHORUS, ACT 2

The wind drummed, the bike roared and Tempest Ivory slowly began to relax. She felt, as Tom Cruise would say, the need for speed. Tempest flicked a glance in her side mirrors, popped the clutch and kicked the Kawasaki 600 Ninja into fourth gear. She loved this stretch of West Saanich Road. Whistling wind in her ears, dappled light overhead, smooth pavement and curves. Lovely, tight bends. Curves she'd put the Pig into, as deeply as if she were bowing, only to pull up at the right split second. Nape hairs on end, blood thumping through her head, knuckles feeling bruised. Grinning. Only thing better was singing Mozart's *Queen of the Night.*

We're burying him in a white turtle-neck so you won't be able to see the bruises.

She tried humming, but the rage broke through. It always did, seeping inexorably through her carefully constructed facade of Doctor Tempest Ivory, child psychologist specializing in suicide. She kicked the Pig into a higher gear. The bike began to rattle, her teeth to jar. Still she pushed the throttle.

The child was dead. Why did she kill herself? Who or what had driven her ceaselessly toward shame, to hemorrhage inside?

The room was brilliantly lit, blinding her. She couldn't see the others. No, she wouldn't look. She knew they were there. Her sister mewling, brother hyperventilating. His satisfied grunts. This was what fear smelled like, bitter, rank and sharp. She began scratching, gouging her arms, the power of bringing her own blood wondrous and soothing. He slapped her. So hard that she bit her tongue and tasted blood. Her brother struggled, his gagged mouth tried to speak. A punch, swift, to his thin belly. Then nothing. Nothing but the taste of blood, of rage. Lights, flashes, clicking. No, no, please...please don't, don't...pleeease!

Tempest's hands began to ache, yet she pressured the throttle. A man, she was certain. A fucking bastard piece of shit had abused Amelia Penderghast. Tempest knew. She always did. She had sensed the child's fury, just watching her small body bag being wheeled away.

SHE SAT ALONE IN THE SMALL, DOMED CHAPEL AND marvelled at the coloured light thrown across the altar by the stained-glass windows. *Such a lucky girl!* Amelia Angeline Penderghast had graduated, burst through that mysterious portal into the next stage of existence. She was still waiting for God's portent. He was, as always, absent. Why was it so painful, so confusing, to strive toward the transcendent?

She pondered the significance of Saint Patrick's Day. Surely that meant something. The tunnel nagged her, its intense light seductive, her speed dizzying. She leaned into the hard wooden pew, stared into the kaleidoscope of light and felt, once again, at peace. Warm. Calm. Birth was so traumatic, slapped into hell, but death, death was a blissful experience. A joyous release, panoramic freedom, unspeakable glory. The most interesting event of her life; the ultimate opportunity to face her own truths. She had to have it, had to give it. Just like her novitiate vows: all that I am; all that I have; all that I do. All that was needed was an omen.

"BELLY IN! BELLY IN! HOW MANY TIMES DO I HAVE to tell you? Sustain!"

Tempest tried again. She breathed deeply, contracted her stomach muscles, opened her mouth and released air. The sound rose as her vocal cords vibrated and her spirit soared.

"No, no, NO!" Cyrus Everard slammed a nicotine-stained hand on the baby grand. "You're not concentrating! Remember how it feels in your natural register?" Tempest nodded, jaw shut tight. "That's what I want. You know the physiology—contraction of the abdominals, pushing the diaphragm upward—you must concentrate on breath control. You know, from day one, it's training the breath. It all starts with the breath." *Ohmygod! Not the breath lecture.* "It's not about the sound or the production or the technique, the first thing is the breath..." As he took a step toward her, she could smell the smoke perfumed by whiskey. "It's always the breath. The breath is what gives you complete control over the voice."

Tempest moved slightly back. "Don't lecture me on breath control. Been there, done that, bought the libretto. When can I sing?"

But Cyrus Everard, once into a lecture, could not be stopped. He continued, deep-set brown eyes peering at her through round spectacles. "You have to master the breath in terms of the emission, supporting the voice on the breath. I want a well-rounded sound, vocal freshness, elasticity to phrase over a wide breath arch. One does not sing with vocal cords, Tempest, one sings with the diaphragm." He played a C major scale on the piano. She noticed his hands shook very slightly. *Needs a bloody drink.* "That's the irony and it takes years to figure it out, wrap your mind around it as you'd say. I want Mon–"

"Montserrat bloody Caballé control. I know, I know." Tempest shook her head, the rage building.

"You've said it a thousand times. 'Such vocal technique, such pianissimo.' I've tried." She swallowed, tasted the anger. "We've been working for months. I've done your bloody exercises, forty minutes a day, then scales–five tones, working in halves–to expand my range, till I thought my tongue would explode. I've done the workshops, the classes, we've worked on a repertoire–" *Listen, you asshole! The only time I feel whole and good and alive is when I'm singing. I'm free. No one sees me, my weight, my hair, my shame. They see nothing! They only hear purity and grace; glorious sounds coming from me.* The rage bubbled free, mocking her failed attempts at self-control. "I've had it!" She trembled, astounded by her fury. *Control, breathe, get control.* "Look Cyrus," she said, regaining her calm. "I want to sing. If, if you're not..." She stopped, voice wavering, unable to continue.

"Well, well, well," Everard chuckled and pulled a

wrapped cigar out of his stained shirt pocket. "A
Tempest in a teapot. I wondered when you'd crack."
He smiled through his grey beard, yellow teeth glowing, and sniffed the cigar. For a moment, he seemed
lost, inhaling its scent, a god's elixir. "Most of my students would've blown up at me ages ago. But you, I
didn't know." The long fingers carefully laid the cigar
on the piano, then he cracked his knuckles. "Now," he
said, playing Chopin's *Revolutionary Etude* with a flourish. "Have I got news for you." He paused as the piano
began to shake. "What the hell is that?!"

SHE BREATHED QUICKLY—IN, OUT, IN, OUT—AS FAST
as she could. *Jesus is love, Jesus is love, Jesusis love,
Jesusislove.* Flat on her back, spine straight. Left hand
over her heart, right outstretched, she felt herself lift,
her mind expand, her muscles relax. Silence and solitude, alone with the Lord. Or was she? The Lord ful-
fils us in a way that nothing, no one, ever will. Isn't that
what she was taught? She strained, her breathing fal-
tering. Why was it so hard? She'd tried and failed so
long, so often that the mere thought of another attempt
filled her with exhaustion and weariness. *Jesus is love,
Jesus is...Where is He?* She must know. She inhaled
again, faster, opening herself to Him. One must act in
a peculiar way to experience the divine.

The earth shook and her ears rumbled. In a flash of
awe, wonder and ecstatic vision, she knew. The balance of stillness and involvement. A life of prayer, a
poverty of spirit, God's will. The prodigal deity had
returned. *Jesus is love.* She dropped both arms to her
sides, trembling. He'd given her the sign, now it was
her turn to act.

THE JOURNAL OF SECRETS STARED AT HER, MOCKING her, its powers still unknown. Sydney whipped it open and again tried to read. The writing was small and crushed together like the stuff Sister Clare showed them in ancient history class. What'd she call them? Egyptian herographics or something like that. She ran a grubby fingernail along the ink lines, mouth moving soundlessly. Was that a "the"? And that "Sister T"? No. "Sister F"? With a sigh of despair, Sydney Mayne slammed the book shut. What good was her prize if she couldn't read it?

Another thought edged into her mind: Mother Superior would be looking for it, on the warpath. Old Windy could blow pretty hard. Sydney had seen it, even felt the tongue-lashing. She shivered, eyeing her prize. The only thing Sydney Mayne feared more than *Goosebumps* was the thought of expulsion. That meant going home, or worse, to another school. One where she wasn't in control. She had to return it. But how?

THE GRAVEYARD WAS EMPTY SAVE FOR THE STONE cross sentinels and gnarled Garry oaks. Now, as he walked among the stones, Patrick was in no hurry to see the slight mound covering his mother's grave.

What a birthday. St. Patrick's Day had often seemed traumatic in the Painter family. He remembered his sixteenth, the last he'd spent with his parents. He'd been so excited. Turning sixteen's such a big deal—getting your licence, cruising for chicks. His mother had made his favourite meal: pork tenderloin shish kebabs with baked potatoes, Caesar salad and mile-high lemon meringue pie. There was even green beer, in honour of St. Paddy, and it was the first time he wouldn't have to drink green milk. One tiny thing to thank the bastard for. "He's a man now, Vivian," the old man had commanded. "Let 'im drink like one." Patrick couldn't wait.

That night, the bastard didn't show. Patrick and his mother had waited all evening. Patrick had known that it would happen, began steaming in the afternoon though she kept saying, "He'll be here, hon. He knows how important it is. He'll be here." Somehow, Patrick knew his father wouldn't. The inevitable call had come through in the early afternoon. Initially, his father had said not to worry, he'd give it to another cop. But then Patrick saw his face whiten. His father asked the dispatcher to repeat the address. His dark eyes narrowed and he stopped breathing for a moment. When he hung up, he was gruff, pushing by, saying he had to go. Patrick wouldn't swear to it, 'cause the old man would've beaten him, but he thought his father was about to cry. He never told his mother. Something in the old man's slack expression and slumped shoulders startled him. He couldn't see telling her.

Patrick stopped to read a black marble plaque. "This tree from Kew Gardens was planted to commemorate the coronation of King George VI, May 12, 1937." He looked up at the tree. Tall, spiky white pine, but no big deal. Nothing like a Douglas fir. Wondering where Kew Gardens was, he passed a similar plaque then hesitated, noticing a small white sign. "The Kiss of the Sun for Pardon, The Song of the Birds for Mirth, One is Nearer God's Heart in a Garden, Than Anywhere Else on Earth." He read it twice, then finally with an embarrassed glance around, out loud. The last words echoed in the churchyard, sliding to and fro like the nearby tides.

Patrick surveyed the grounds. A brown wooden-plank Anglican church–consecrated in 1885, the oldest on the Saanich Peninsula–flanked Mills Road. Its three white crosses perched high above the rolling grounds. The scattering of headstones basked in the sun reflected off Patricia Bay. A beautiful spot. His gardener's eye relished the variety of trees and shrubs dotting the immaculately kept land.

On their occasional visit to the family plot, his dad would say the site was much better appreciated by visitors than by the residents. The bastard would smirk then, pleased with his own stupid joke. His mom always smiled. But Patrick knew she was smiling for herself, not for him, freed perhaps by the moist salt air. "Course it is," she'd say, caressing a granite cross. "Graveyards are for the living, not the dead." She'd stroll to the covered bench near the bay, while his father marched to the car to grumble. This garden of souls was the only place where his father was unsure. God and death were stronger than Leonard P. Painter. Patrick would sit quietly with his mother while the sun disappeared from the sky, dashing brilliant colours off the glittering waves. Sometimes they'd spot seals lolling on the wharf or a hovering merlin shimmering in the winds, waiting to plunge.

He was at the mound looking down. *Christ, I don't believe it.* His mother was dead, he'd seen her lifeless body. Been the one to identify it after she'd fallen unconscious in the drugstore aisle. Yet faced with the mound, the surrounding tombstones, the graveyard, he couldn't quite accept it. No chance to make it up. *Oh God, Mom. I'm so sorry. I'm so sorry.* He knelt and gently laid the bouquet of daffodils, carefully picked from his garden, across the black earth. He was momentarily bolstered by the cheerful yellow and white blossoms.

With an effort, Patrick Painter left his mother and walked to the arched bench. The ground vibrated, the waves licked the horizon. Patrick tensed, waiting for the earth tremors to end. *A small one, thank God.* He glanced up, and a nearby tombstone gave him a start. *Great. She's going out with a bang.* Tears running down his cheeks, he waited and watched the sun set for her for the last time.

"AN AUDITION?" TEMPEST WHISPERED.

God frigging almighty!! "An audition for *Rigoletto*? Gilda?"

Everard nodded curtly. "As long as we're not swallowed up by the quake and sent straight to hell this very minute, yes. In two days."

"Two!? How can I poss—"

"Short notice, of course. I only heard about it a couple of hours ago. Vic Opera's in a bitch of a bind. And who else would they turn to?" He dropped onto the piano stool and began *Caro nome.* The rising sounds of Gilda's famous aria chilled her. "Seems their Gilda, Carlotta Camus, broke her leg in some silly motorcycle accident." Tempest froze. The Pig was parked near St. Ann's, too far away even for Everard's eye.

Cyrus Everard looked up sharply. "It's a damn good thing you don't ride that beast anymore. This is the chance of a lifetime. And, dear girl, you may fall on your knees and thank me." *That'll be the day.* "I've been chatting up Jeff all along."

"You have?"

The long, yellowed fingers hesitated, then began *La*

donna è mobile. "Of course, you little fool. Do you think I want to hear you sing scales forever?" He coughed, the once-famous voice hoarse, as though the notes were squeezed through a cheese grater. "He wanted you for Zerlina this fall but I laughed at him."

"Zerlina? I had a chance—"

"You'd rather a few lousy lines than sing Gilda?" Everard snorted. "My God, child, I'm obviously wasting my precious time. I thought you wanted to be a prima donna."

"I'm not your child, nor am I a fool." Everard's eyes flashed and he slammed the piano keys. The ugly sound reverberated in the small room. *Come on, get a grip.* She took two measured breaths. "Course I do. It's just that...you never told—"

"I tell you what you need to know," he bellowed. "I'm managing the career, right? I'm the one with the experience, the contacts, the plan. Because I refused, refused to waste my time and your talent on bit parts like Zerlina, you have the chance to play Gilda. A chance any soprano would kill for."

"Okay, okay. I'm glad. Christ! I'm thrilled." She paused, a thought suddenly terrifying her. "What'll I sing?"

"Ah!" Everard said, fondling the cigar. "This is where the fun begins." He jumped up and began to pace the small room.

"As you know, standard fare for coloraturas like yourself varies." He sniffed the cigar. "Often an aria from *Lucia di Lammermoor* or from *Il Barbiere di Siviglia,* perhaps Leila in *Les Pêcheurs* or Olympia in *Hoffman.* We want to show your range, better than average—it still needs work so don't get all high and mighty on me—and brilliant colour, but not expose our little weakness in technique. Nothing too obscure or the judges will tend to listen to the piece and not to you. I think, to begin, Susanna in *Figaro.*"

Tempest smiled. She loved Mozart. His tessitura, her coloratura soprano, truly a marriage in music heaven.

"Of course, *Caro nome*, but that'll be last." Tempest's stomach fluttered. Everard began humming *Carmen.* The flutter winged throughout her body. "Yes, yes. Micaela's aria, perhaps even the recitative for warmup." He strode back to the piano bench and pounded out the first phrase of *Caro nome.* "Begin!"

FIVE

With children and madmen
It often pays to pretend;
—CHORUS, ACT 2

"Children commit suicide for many reasons," Tempest explained to her audience. "Fundamentally, they have what they view as an unsolvable problem. For the most part, the reasons fall into four categories: extreme rejection from their mother or parents, physical and/or psychological abuse, a massive attack on their identity, or an estrangement from their family."

The morning after the incident, as the Mother Superior called it, found the faculty sitting around a large oval table in a wood-paneled room off the chapel. Tempest had earlier offered to counsel both faculty and students and, after a long pause, Sister Winifred agreed. Tempest had arrived early, escorted by Sister Benedict, who worried her beads as they walked up the hall and muttered, "Oh, dear, oh dear, nothing like this has ever happened here." The endless anxiety and rhyming repetition irritated Tempest and she was relieved when the elderly nun left, promising to return shortly. *Don't hurry on my account.* Her clacking beads and mumblings faded out as Tempest looked around. Framed paintings of the stations of the cross lined the walls with chairs at the table seemingly positioned for each visitor. Perhaps it was Sister Benedict's behaviour, but Tempest wondered if you were supposed to sit and gaze upon each one in succession, like some religious Mad Hatter's tea party. She dropped into a chair below *Christ's Condemnation by Pilate*.

First, she'd given them a brief background on suicide, including the statistical rates which showed its dramatic increase, especially in young people, since the early fifties, its frightening prevalence among teenagers—the most common cause of death, after car accidents—and its relative rarity in children Amelia's age. She explained that many suicides were mistaken for accidents, as distressed children often jumped into oncoming traffic or down stairs. That more girls attempted it but failed, and that boys were more successful because they chose more lethal methods, such as hanging and guns. And that depression, long known as a cause of suicide in adults, was beginning to be diagnosed in children. Ninety percent of adolescent females attempting suicide were first-born girls, unusually close to their mothers. Tempest added the same information about age and children's stages of awareness of death that she'd given to Constable Painter.

"You're certain that Amelia committed suicide?"

"Yes, Aunt, I mean Sister Winifred," Patrick jumped in. "Dr. Harwicke, the coroner, is sure of it. She examined the knot and the...uh, well, she's certain."

"Oh dear, oh dear. Why would poor Amelia do it?" Sister Benedict paused and looked around the table. Tempest noticed that, appropriately, she was sitting beneath *Christ's First Fall.* "She seemed happy enough. Did you see anything wrong, Sister Eileen?"

Sister Eileen, rigid under *Christ's Receiving of the Cross,* shot upright in her chair. "Me?" she squeaked. She swallowed and began again in clipped, English tones. "No! I had nothing to do with it. Nothing!" She turned to the Mother Superior. "That's exactly what I'll be telling the bishop. He's very interested in what I have to say."

"I've spoken to the bishop," Winifred snapped. "He's very supportive, as always. He's not to be bothered again."

"Bothered? So my calls to him are a bother? Is that what he said, Sister?"

"Oh, dear," muttered Sister Benedict.

Winifred gritted her teeth. "Of course not, Sister." She tensed and Tempest felt she might leap across the table at Eileen. "It's just that he's a busy man. I've fully briefed him. He's left it to me, as the Mother Superior, to handle the situation. Proper procedure, right, Sister Eileen?"

Eileen flushed slightly and mumbled something.

"Yes, Sister?" Winifred asked.

Sister Eileen played with a pencil. "The girl was always a bit flighty."

"Flighty?" asked Tempest, a bit sorry the heavenly dust-up was over. "What aspects of her behaviour were flighty?"

Eileen flushed further. "Oh, I don't know. She was...a little scatterbrained now and then. Nothing too unusual. Many of the gels are." *Gels? Where are we, Suffolk?*

"Any particular time she was flighty?"

"I don't think so..." Sister Eileen gazed at her with wide, deep-blue eyes. Tempest returned the stare, feeling that she was looking into two empty wells. "Perhaps after the weekend. You have her Monday mornings, Sister Gabriel. Have you noticed anything?"

Gabriel smiled slightly. "Mondays are always a new journey. The girls are all a little excited, Amelia no more than the rest, I think." Her green eyes focused on *Christ's Death*. "Weekends of wonder. It's awkward for any of us to return to the concrete and logical. We have so far to—"

"Is this some sort of post-mortem?" Sister Eileen interrupted. "Where we're to accept blame?"

"Oh dear, oh dear," Benedict whispered.

Tempest heard the old nun's beads clacking in earnest. "No one's assigning blame," she replied calmly. "Sister Winifred asked me, in my capacity as school counsellor, to speak to you and to the students. A suicide is always a very distressing event—"

"Dear, dear."

"—and it helps to talk about it. Because you're dealing with the children, I hope that this will assist you in helping them cope, too."

"So Dr. Ivory," asked the Mother Superior, "what *do* we tell them?"

"That Amelia was upset, that something was wrong. Encourage them to talk about her. Provide an outlet for their emotions, encourage activities like creating sympathy cards or drawings. Listen, and look for body language clues to coping difficulties. The girls must be made to feel comfortable to talk, if they want to." Tempest looked each nun in the eye. When she came to Sister Gabriel, the emerald eyes pulled her in.

Tempest blinked and turned away. "If you listen, pay attention, you might see or hear something that troubles you. If that happens, please call me."

"You mean we failed Amelia?" Sister Eileen asked in an offensive tone.

"No, I didn't say that." Tempest noticed Constable Painter stir at the back.

The nun's eyes narrowed and Tempest realized she'd been wrong. There was something down in those blue depths. Something quite nasty. "You as much as did, telling us to listen, to pay attention. As though I didn't before. This wouldn't have happened if I..." She hesitated then glanced quickly around. "Well, I'm not going to sit here—"

"Sister, please!" The Mother Superior's voice snapped; Benedict's beads suddenly stopped. "No one's here to place blame. Dr. Ivory's doing her job, just as we've all done." She turned to Tempest. "If that's all, Dr. Ivory? Good, give us a few minutes to organize the girls. Sisters?" In response to this last demand, the Sisters of The Perpetual Soul rose in silent unison and quietly padded down the hall.

"Great," said Patrick when he and the psychologist were alone again. "I thought that went really well, don't you?"

SYDNEY MAYNE CRAWLED OUT FROM UNDER HER bed. Her knees were stiff. With a shiver, she brushed a cobweb from her hair and adjusted the weight of the diary tucked into her underwear. The dormitory was empty, finally. Sydney had held her breath while all but one of her roommates pounded out the door, late for the hastily called assembly. She had thought Rosie

Buntic would never get her hair right. While Rosie hummed and primped, Sydney began planning her route. It was the only way to ignore the ache in her back.

Some of the Sisters might not be needed at the assembly and might be in the nuns' wing instead. That meant she'd have to duck out the back and re-enter at the library. With a bit of luck, Sister Eileen would either be on hall duty or immersed as usual in the Book of Revelations. Sydney had often thought of putting something really revealing between those pages but she steered clear of bugging Sister Eileen. She'd seen the heavyset nun go to town on Doris Hillaby for chewing gum in the library. Sydney had almost choked on her own Juicy Fruit. Sydney could sneak by the library and use the old kitchen route into the back of the nuns' wing. If approached, she would have to talk her way out of it. Sydney smirked. No big deal for her. A bit of a headache, perhaps? *Oh, Sister, I'm sooo glad you're here. My head hurts. Have you any aspirin?*

Her pigtails properly twisted and ribboned, Rosie had gone, her footsteps echoing rapidly down the curved staircase. Sydney moved quietly into the hall. She hesitated, then cocked her head. Someone was singing. She crept along until she stood below a narrow, dark entrance. The voice stopped. Sydney shivered. She had heard from an older student that beyond was a steep ladder up to the bell tower. Some girls said the tower was haunted.

Sydney shook her head slowly, certain she had been mistaken. No one was allowed past the small, locked door. She slipped back to the staircase. The diary must be returned, its secrets unrevealed. Keeping it was too risky. As she peeked round a corner, she wondered briefly why Mother Inferior hadn't said anything about missing it.

"SO, YOU'RE A FRIEND OF AMELIA'S?" PATRICK ASKED the small, red-headed girl.

The girl blinked huge grey eyes. The Mother Superior prompted gently. "Give the police officer a proper answer."

"Yes," she whispered.

Patrick shot a disapproving glance at his great-aunt, hoping she wasn't going to coach the girl throughout the interview. She had insisted on accompanying him while he spoke with Amelia's classmates. Officially, the police were allowed to talk to the girls alone, if they were only seeking information. Nevertheless, some of the parents had attended the little kiddie chats, as Staff Sergeant Lalande called them, with their offspring. It seemed that Vita Bell's parents didn't think it necessary to interrupt their routine and race along the Peninsula to protect their child. Patrick was relieved. He'd spoken to seven "kiddies" and assorted parents and found it harder and harder to force a smile. Getting info out of junkies was a breeze compared to this polite crap.

How could anyone stand being a parent? Especially to a girl? That small tumble of alien energy, unendingly demanding and noisy. The thought gave Patrick the heebie-jeebies. An only child, Patrick had occasionally wondered about girls but never really knew any. They seemed very strange with their dolls and cliques. He'd once asked his best friend, Kevin Higgins, about his older sister. "She's a pain," Kevin had replied. "Always in the bathroom, making herself up. Don't know why, 'cause she's as ugly as a pig's ass." They'd both laughed at Kevin's daring use of ass and ended up shouting: pig's ass, pig's ass, *pigsass!* at the cars along McTavish Road. He never asked Kevin again but he continued to wonder. He'd always felt as if the girls at his school were laughing at him, probably at his nose. In high school, he'd dated a couple but, other than a backseat grope or two, never got much closer. Women. Patrick sighed. Any more like *Mrs.* Annette Benjamin, the overly protective cow who practically draped her chunky self atop her daughter, and he'd pray for the riot squad.

"D'you really have to question Jade?" Mrs. Benjamin had demanded before he introduced himself. "She's such a sensitive child," she said, moving her large, floral-patterned bosom across his path. "I don't want her disturbed. Besides, she didn't even know the girl, did you, sweetie?"

Sweetie, who'd eaten a dozen too many by Patrick's account, sucked at her index finger.

Patrick took a deep breath, introduced himself and explained that he wanted to chat with the girls in Amelia's class. He smiled down at Jade. "Now, Jade, just tell me about Amelia."

"I've already told you! She didn't know the child."

"Please, Mrs. Benjamin! It'll only take a few minutes, if you'd just let me talk to the girl."

So it went. After much hullabaloo, and just moments before he was set to rip out her index finger, he managed to pull a sentence out of Jade's mouth. "She was friends with Vita."

Now, it was little Vita who stared up at him. He glanced warily at Sister Winifred and flipped to a new page in his narrow notepad.

"I'm very sorry, is it Vita?" The nun nodded. "Vita, that's a nice name." The lashes blinked faster. "I'm sorry about your friend."

"She died."

Startled by her bluntness, Patrick paused. "You see, Vita, we're trying to find out why Amelia was so upset. That's why I'm talking to you. Did she seem upset to you?"

Again the blinking eyes. *Christ! This's like interviewing a baby owl.* "It means life."

"What?" Patrick looked at Sister Winifred. She raised her eyebrows.

Vita rubbed her eyes. *Maybe the kid needs glasses.* "My name, it means life."

"Does it? That's interesting," Patrick replied, thinking the exact opposite. "Well then, little Miss Life–" Vita smiled faintly. "–tell me about Amelia. On Wednesday, before she, uh, well, on Wednesday last week, did she seem upset to you?"

"Upset?"

"Good heavens, child, you know the meaning of the word," Winifred jumped in.

Vita's eyes widened.

Patrick scowled at his great-aunt. "It's okay, Vita. You know, was she worried or anxious, even crying? Anything like that?"

The twelve-year-old paused, then slowly shook her head. "D'you have a horse?"

"No."

Sister Winifred swallowed, then began tapping her

fingers together. He shot her an angry glance.

"Oh. Well, Benton has one." Vita peered up at him. "You're a Mountie, aren't you?"

That bloody TV show. "Yes, but—"

"You should have a horse, then. Why don't you get one?"

Winifred chewed a fingernail.

Yeah, right. That'd go over well with the Staff. Patrick tried following her tack, hoping to gain her trust. "Maybe I will. You like horses, then, Vita?"

"Not really. They scare me."

Sister Winifred hiccuped, then excused herself.

Oh, to hell with it! "About Amelia, are you sure you didn't notice anything? Anything at all. Did she say anything, do anything strange?"

"Well," the blinking started again, "after she stopped crying, she said something 'bout pictures."

S YDNEY CAREFULLY RIPPED THE MATCH FREE FROM ITS book. *Learn how to be a mechanic,* the inside cover read. She smiled. More like a firefighter. A short pause to ensure silence, then she made a move to strike. She hesitated, pondering the probable results. If caught, she would be suspended, most likely expelled. Sydney stared at the match head.

She needed a diversion and fast. There were too many nuns fluttering about their wing. She'd almost been stepped on by Sister Dick and when she'd managed to escape without notice, Sydney had collided with a threesome arriving from the assembly. Her time was up. She quickly explained that she'd been asked to find the Mother Superior, having just seen the nun walk into the admin office along with the police jerk and

Jade Benjamin. Sister Dick joined them and told
Sydney that Sister Winifred was busy. Before Sister
Dick could ask another question, Sydney walked hastily down the echoing hall—*girls are not allowed to run*—
tossing a quick "thank you" over her shoulder.

She had to get the diary back. She knew she'd be an
obvious suspect for the fire—the third one she'd set—but
since she'd only been caught once, Sydney felt she had
an even chance to escape. Better than if she were
found with the diary. Sydney struck the match and
held it to the bunched-up toilet paper. Immediately, the
paper flickered and the flame spread. She backed off
quickly as the fire rippled across Rosie Buntic's bed.
That'll teach her to primp around. Sydney quietly slipped
downstairs and into the auditorium.

DR. IVORY WAS ON THE SMALL STAGE, FLANKED BY
Sisters Eileen and Louise and a rectangular table. To
Ivory's left, a large-screen television flickered, credits
rolled, then static. One student started to clap, felt the
terror of being alone and stopped, head suddenly
down. There were a few nervous giggles. The psychologist walked over, shut off the TV and faced the students. She wore baggy jeans and an oversized T-shirt.
Her dark red hair hung in a swirling ponytail.

From his vantage point off stage, Constable Painter
could see Tempest's breasts rise and fall. He could also
see the young faces staring up at her. Entranced.
Patrick Painter was amazed. Somehow the ice queen
had melted into a different season and the kids knew
it. Patrick was captivated all over again.

Dr. Ivory smiled broadly and began clapping.
"Come on," she said. "Everyone!" Slowly the hands

came together and soon the auditorium rocked with the rippling sound. Tempest put her hands above her head, swaying like a rock star. Patrick's loins ached. The girls laughed and shrieked, letting off the tension built up by watching the short, powerful suicide-prevention video.

"Great," she shouted and the noise slowly died down. "Hey, we're pretty good! D'you think they'd let us on Letterman?" Again the kids laughed. Patrick grinned as he watched the confused zip-zap eye contact between the Sisters, neither of whom applauded.

"Okay, okay, enough joking around," Ivory said with a smile. "Not only was that fun, it was healthy. Yep. Don't ya feel loose?" Several heads nodded. "That's because of the release. We just sent a ton of tension packing. We let it loose. And it was fun. You can use this in your lives. Any time you feel overwhelmed, do something crazy: yell, jump up and down, punch a pillow. Anything."

"What do you do?" a voice asked.

"Me?" Tempest paused, slightly off guard. "I, well, I sing." She moved a step closer. "Like this." She opened her throat and released into the air the most beautiful sounds Patrick Painter had ever heard. Fifty-five mouths gaped, fifty-five butts froze to their seats. Abruptly, Tempest stopped. "So," she spoke softly into the stunned silence, "as you just saw in the video, talking about suicide's important, getting it out in the open. Keeping it all inside is bad news, really bad news."

She headed to the table and opened a large box. She pulled out an egg and put it in the middle of the table. "This," she said with a sweeping glance of the students, "is you. And no, I'm not calling you eggheads or local yokels." She paused, waiting for the joke to hit home. "It's just here for demonstration.

"Now, let's recap. Thinking about suicide is not weird or unusual." She reached into the box and removed a piece of wood the size of a paperback novel. "About half of the girls your age think about it. Yes, half of you. Look around, one of the girls sitting right beside you has thought of committing suicide. So, don't think you're the only one. Remember, you're not alone. We all feel overwhelmed sometimes, too much home-work–" She balanced the block carefully on the egg "–too many hassles with parents–" she placed a second block on top "–or you hate your hair, or the guy you like asks your best friend out."

Dr. Ivory went on listing young girls' stresses and piling on blocks. "All this crap adds up and up and up until you feel you can't take it, until you just want the pain to end." The egg cracked and a couple of pieces of wood clattered to the floor. Several girls giggled ner-vously. The yolk streaked down the table leg. Sister Eileen rubbed her hands.

"So, thinking about suicide is no big deal, right?" She paused, eyes sweeping over the young faces. "Wrong. Big-time wrong. In my business, they call sui-cide a permanent solution to a temporary problem. Anybody understand?" No one spoke. "Thought not," she replied in a mesmerizing voice. "That's a bunch of psycho gobbledegook for making a big mistake. One that you'll never correct. Why?" her voice snapped. Startled, the girls retreated in their seats. "Because death is The End, The Big One, the trip no one returns from."

Ivory dropped her voice to a whisper. "And all because someone just like you felt alone, left out. Without a friend. Just like Amelia Penderghast."

Patrick was surprised that Tempest mentioned the dead girl's name but the students' reaction convinced him she was right. A couple of girls gasped. Others started to cry. Dr. Ivory had brought the unknown home. Sister Louise started to rise from her chair but Ivory ignored her. She sat down.

"Amelia was hurting. She felt she was alone. And she's not coming back. Not ever. This does not have to happen to you. Just like Joanne–" she pointed to the TV "–you can talk to someone. Get some help. Just like our clapping gave us a break from the video, talking to a friend can help. If you're worried about a friend, now you know you can ask them straight out about suicide. It won't make them do it. It will make them think that, maybe, they're not alone. Maybe that's all Amelia–" An alarm began, clanging loudly in the auditorium.

It's about time, thought Sydney, as she scrambled out with the others.

"Fire!" shouted Sister Louise.

SIX

He who trusts her
And foolishly gives her his heart
Is always wretched!
—THE DUKE OF MANTUA, ACT 3

Sydney dodged the last of the firefighters, feeling both triumphant and defeated. The confusion had been fantastic! Within seconds of the alarm, all of the students, visitors and faculty of the Perpetual Soul had streamed out onto the broad front lawn. She couldn't resist waiting for the fire engines and was delighted when two red trucks from the Sidney and North Saanich volunteer fire departments wailed up the long drive. That's when she made her mistake. As the crew started pulling out the hoses and pushing the crowd behind a protective barrier, Sydney made her move to slip around the back. Just as she ducked free of the yellow caution tape, a large hand grabbed the neck of her jumper.

"Where d'ya think you're goin', Missy?" asked a giant dressed in beige overalls.

Sydney struggled against his grip. "Bathroom."

The grip lessened and the hand patted her head.

Sydney squirmed. "Sorry, kiddo. No can do. Place's closed up tighter than a duck's ass. You'll just hafta wait or—" The giant peered down at her below a broad-beaked helmet emblazoned with the word Chief. He dropped his voice. "—or mebbe you'll just hafta whiz behind a tree." With that, he pulled up the tape, gently pushed her under it and dropped it back down. "Sister!" he shouted. Eileen turned. "Keep an eye on the kids, will ya? Don't let 'em through." Sister Eileen threw an impatient look at Sydney and edged toward her. Sydney tucked one hand under the diary and slipped into the crowd of girls.

Now, hidden around the back of a giant Douglas fir, Sydney eavesdropped as Patrick talked to the fire chief.

"No substantial damage," the chief was saying. "Smoked badly. Course the bed's ruined, but that's about it."

"Any idea how it started, Jack?"

The chief pulled off his helmet and ran smudgy fingers through his grey hair. "Guess it coulda been kids playing, but..."

"It's happened before," Patrick said.

"Yup. Bout time we found out who did it, don't you think?"

"Sure, but how?"

"Funniest thing," Jack replied, reaching into his shirt pocket. "Young Al found a book of matches with one missin', near the doorway." He handed Patrick a plastic bag containing a yellow matchbook. "Don't worry, he had gloves on."

Sydney's hand shot to her pocket. Nothing! She dug around frantically, then checked the other pocket. Empty.

"Untouched by fire or water. Maybe has a print?"

Sydney curled up at the base of the tree. *Oh, oh.*

"Great," Patrick replied. "I'll get it off to the lab." He paused, a new thought taking over. "Shit! That means printing all these nuns and girls."

Jack giggled. Patrick almost laughed in spite of himself, because the chief's laugh was more suited to his petite wife. Of course, no one would ever tell him that.

"Not funny, all right? Oh, go on, get outta here. Hey, and tell Harriet I said hi."

Jack struck his leg with his helmet. "Almost forgot! She wants you to come over next week. Barbecue some salmon, maybe. Crack a coupla cold ones, how's that grab ya?"

"I'd like that." Patrick said, salivating at the thought of Harriet's cooking. He hesitated. "Anyone else coming?"

The volunteer fire chief had turned and started to walk toward his beloved truck. He glanced back and grinned. "Course! Harri wants ya to meet someone."

Patrick groaned.

Jack slammed the heavy door and leaned out the window. "Don't sweat it, man! Eat the food and drink, no one's asking you ta sleep with 'er." The truck gurgled to life. "I'll be in touch." With a toot of the siren, Jack rolled down the lane. Painter went to call his boss.

SISTER WINIFRED WAS TROUBLED. THE OLD SOUL was already under review. Administration and upkeep costs were soaring. Tuition had increased by thirty percent over the past three years. While raffles, donations, and even sales of school T-shirts contributed, it still wasn't enough. The bishop wanted amalgamation with

the other Catholic schools. Winifred had fought him
with every cell in her body. The academy, her academy, was known throughout British Columbia for its
scholastic and social standards. Its unique size and
location, the carefully chosen, dedicated staff and her
obsessive husbandry combined to produce fine, edu-
cated Christian women. Had done so for years. The
Perpetual Soul wasn't just a school, it was her sole
child, her only family. No one would take that away.

So, it wasn't enough to have ongoing threats of cut-
backs and closure, of Sister Eileen sneaking to the bishop
behind her back, vying for the role of Mother
Superior. A child had committed suicide in her school,
then there was another suspicious fire, and now, her
diary was missing. With all the anxiety and demands
of the past few days, she hadn't noticed. But, as she
replaced the telephone receiver after attempting to
soothe yet another panicked parent, she realized it
wasn't in the drawer. She shuffled through various
papers and newsletters. No diary. With the meticu-
lousness of a professional cleaner, she searched her
small apartment. The book was nowhere to be found.
Of course, nothing in the nuns' wing was ever locked.
The mere suggestion was an insult to the religious.

Winifred sat at her desk, very still. The diary rarely
left her apartment, never her sight. She thought of all
the notations scribbled within, dating back over a
decade. It wasn't a diary by conventional standards,
not much angst or personal musings. Instead, she used
it to note significant academy events. One day, she
hoped to write the history of her religious order in
British Columbia and of her greatest accomplishment,
the Perpetual Soul. She fingered the silver cross

around her neck, contemplating. There were a number of incidents several years back when she was battling the local diocese for complete control of the academy. The local bishop had proved prickly, uncertain that she, a mere woman, should have ultimate authority. Sister Winifred had always found the rampant sexism and sexist language of the church distasteful and added more than her usual dose of personal comment. The new bishop, though less sexist, was weak, taking counsel from any who flattered him. Eileen was a sycophant from way, way back.

A nagging disquiet settled upon her. She began to wish she'd broken house rules and locked the darn thing up. There were many things in the diary that could prove, at the very least, embarrassing and, at the worst, disastrous.

THE FINGERPRINTING WAS A NIGHTMARE FILLED WITH snickering girls, affronted parents and slighted nuns. The RCMP couldn't demand the children's prints, but using the old saw about cooperation and the need to eliminate suspects, Staff Sergeant Lalande had finally convinced the parents to go along with the procedure. Patrick couldn't wait to see Tempest's reaction, but wait he would, as she was unavailable until the next morning. Didn't matter. He and his fellow officers had their hands full. They'd set up two tables in the entrance hall and the lines stretched into the side corridors. No one, except for a couple of Nancy Drew wannabes, was happy. It had taken just under an hour to get set up and create two master lists of all students, faculty and recent visitors to the Old Soul.

None of the slap-dash-roll-of-a-finger crap you saw

on television: fingerprinting was an art. Hand and paper position, constant pressure and rotation all contributed to its complexity. Patrick had twice failed the fingerprinting technique course, struggling to manipulate his spade-like hands. Only after considerable practice and effort did he finally pass, as his instructor told him, by the merest of a whorl. And that was on adults, mostly male!

Patrick took one look at the chubby palm Jade Benjamin offered and sighed. He looked up into her mother's indignant eyes and barely held back a moan. "Okay, then, Jade. This isn't going to hurt." He carefully took the child's hand and rolled each finger through the moist black pad.

"This is outrageous!" Mrs. Benjamin snapped. "Fingerprinting a ten-year-old. I won't have it."

"Sorry, Mrs. Benjamin. It's just routine."

"Routine? Ha! That's what you always call it."

"Call what?" Patrick asked, Jade's thumb poised to print.

"The overpowering police presence in our society." *Oh, not that one again.* "It's got to stop. It's bad enough you're never there when we need you, but now with this terrible photo radar, you don't even have to be there and still we get fined."

Struggling to complete the printing of Jade's left fingers, Patrick didn't stop to question her bizarre logic. When finally finished, he handed Jade a cleaning towel. "Not sure how photo radar ties into fingerprinting, ma'am."

"Don't use that tone with me, Officer. I'm telling you, I don't like it. Not one bit. Why, my Jade wouldn't light our fireplace, much less another child's bed."

"I'm sure you're right, ma'am. That's all and thank you." Patrick urged the next child forward. So it went for over half an hour. One kid, an innocent-looking tyke about nine, stepped on his toe, while smiling brilliantly for her worried mother. Patrick muffled a yelp. When he turned to thank her mother, he touched the brat's button nose with his inked finger, just playfully enough to get away with it. The kid walked off, rubbing it until dark smudges spread across her cheeks.

Finally, his line ended with Vita Bell. Patrick was glad of the coincidence, as he wanted to complete the earlier interview.

This time he wasn't fazed by the blinking. "So," he started, pushing Vita's fingers into the pad, "what did you mean back there about Amelia saying something about pictures?"

"Pictures?" Vita pondered her blackened fingertips. "Will this wash off? The Sisters don't like it when you get your clothes dirty."

"No sweat," Patrick lied, taking her right hand again. The ink hung around like last year's cold. "I'll give you a cloth to clean it when we're finished. Bet your mom would get upset, too."

Vita pulled her hand free; her grey eyes blinked faster.

"I'm sorry. What'd I say?"

Vita closed her eyes. "Don't have a mom."

Patrick touched her hand gently and she let him roll her thumb and index fingers. The prints were perfect. "Aw, I'm sorry, kid. How 'bout your dad?"

She waited until he'd finished the hand, then shook her head.

Shit! An orphan, and she's only twelve. So that was why

only Sister Winifred had accompanied her in the interview. He'd ask his great-aunt later. Patrick didn't know what to say to those big, sad eyes and finally settled on something trite. "Gee, that's tough," he said, wincing at his lameness. She didn't seem to notice.

"Now, about those pictures. Did Amelia say what kind?"

"Kind?"

"You know, some kind of painting? Art, maybe?"

"Art? You mean like that?" she asked, pointing to an old oil portrait of the Virgin Mary over the entrance arch.

He shrugged.

She thrust him her clean hand. "Don't think so," she replied with a knitted brow. Patrick inked her other hand and quickly rolled the prints. All but the baby finger were good. He looked at the slight smudge and thought, What the hell.

"Amelia was worried that he was gonna take some kinda pictures of her."

"Take some pictures?" he asked, handing her a cloth.

Vita nodded, red curls bouncing.

"You're sure she said take some kind of pictures of her?"

"Uh huh," she said, scrubbing her finger tips. "You sure this's comin' off?"

TEMPEST SAT ON HER BACK DECK, RIFFLING THROUGH the libretto for *The Trials of Rigoletto*. A masterpiece by nineteenth-century Italian composer Giuseppe Verdi, many cognoscenti have called *Rigoletto* nearly perfect, containing all the essential elements of opera: wonderful, stirring music; a powerful story; terrific roles for voices from soprano to baritone and chorus; arias, duets, trios and, arguably the most celebrated quartet in all of opera. And all fitting neatly into a three-act, less than three-hour structure.

The libretto, from the 1971 London/Decca version conducted by Richard Bonynge, provided a cast list (Joan Sutherland as Gilda, Luciano Pavarotti as the Duke of Mantua, and Sherrill Milnes in the title role), details about the recording, an essay by William Weaver and a detailed synopsis. A shame that she only had it in CD format, which tended to cut out the blue and higher overtones. Tapes or old records were much better.

Like many opera students, Tempest knew a note or two about *Rigoletto*, mostly as it concerned her vocal abilities. Thank heaven it was in Italian—its five basic vowels much easier to sing. French, with its fourteen basic vowels, was a much more difficult language to master. With her first performance only days away, she knew there was no better way to get the background scoop on an opera than to read the libretto.

She found Weaver's essay, to her delight, interesting and informative. Verdi wrote *Rigoletto* in forty days. Quite impressive, thought Tempest, who knew it often took longer than that to understand some operas. Verdi snatched his creative spark from Victor Hugo's disastrous play, *Le Roi s'amuse*, which survived only one performance. Poor Victor hadn't foreseen the resulting scandal created by his "immoral" play; the authorities in late 1832 were appalled by Hugo's depiction of a licentious and unrepentant king. The play suffered a series of censor-induced changes and wasn't seen again for fifty years.

Plain old Joe Green (Giuseppe Verdi to the Italians)

knew how to play the game, thought Tempest. Though hounded by censors, he benefited from Hugo's modifications and only made minor changes. As a result, *Rigoletto* the opera enjoyed immediate popularity and, just to pillory poor Hugo more, triumphed for thirty years before Hugo's play re-opened.

Inspired, Tempest stood, stretched and began her daily regimen. First, twenty minutes dedicated to expanding her range. As always, as she began to sing the rising and falling woo, wooooo, woooing sound, she was grateful for her quiet half-acre lot, nestled into larger chunks of provincially protected farmland. It was physically draining enough just to open your mouth and sing without having to worry about who was listening on the other side of the door. Often she sang ditties or Italian art songs to maintain singing posture. Nothing too challenging, the key was to retain suppleness. The horses never seemed to notice; a cow or two would often join in, especially when she moved into the second twenty minutes, a baaa-like nasal ditty that was pretty ugly. But hey, art isn't always beautiful, let's end that myth right here, she thought.

At eighteen, Tempest Ivory had received her mother's bequest. The generous sum was as much a surprise as her mother's explicit instructions that not a penny go to her father. That suited Tempest, who desperately wanted to escape the stifling life of Vancouver Island. Dutifully, she put half aside for her older sister, though she hadn't heard from her in over seven years. The rest she plunked into a bank account and treated herself to university in Vancouver.

She started in psychology, fascinated by the odd twists of the human mind. Tempest was content, though not happy. Happiness had deserted her long ago. That first year she kept to herself, studied religiously to ensure her position at the top of the class, and began to explore the second-growth forest that sheltered the University of British Columbia like a thick, dark shawl. It was on an early fog-shrouded trek that she began to hear the sounds. She thought it was one of the music students.

Burdened by a difficult second-year course load, Tempest's sleep patterns shifted, haunted by towering vocals. Unable to rest and taxed by distressing experiences in a local psychiatric facility, she began hallucinating, missing classes, failing for the first time in her life.

It happened while she was interviewing a young manic-depressive. She'd spent an afternoon a week with him for over four months. He never said a word, sometimes unwilling even to make eye contact. After their first meeting, where she stupidly tried to shake his hand, she never approached him. His look of terror and invasion numbed her to the soul. His file was sketchy but he'd apparently suffered substantial physical and emotional abuse. Now, at age fourteen, he was interned, a danger both to himself and society. Tempest had only seen an uncommunicative boy and, one sunny day, was shocked to find him leaping about the tiny room, mouth and limbs on overdrive.

The youth couldn't stop talking, brushing long greasy strands of hair aside as the words, if that's what they were, poured out. Tempest tried to look relaxed, safe, in on the conversation, but the boy's erratic behaviour disturbed her. What was he saying? Sick from lack of sleep, she tried to settle him, to communicate, to be part of this energized world. It only made her head ache more. With so much said after so long, there must be meaning. But the gibberish, errant movements and amazing stare proved too much. Shaken, Tempest left early and fretted about her career choice as the city bus wound its way back to the campus.

After a while, she realized nearby passengers were staring at her. Startled, she heard herself humming a tune she couldn't place. Her head and stomach-aches were gone, and she felt light-headed. With a joyous laugh, she yanked the stop cord. To the passengers' astonishment and her elderly seat mate's applause, she marched off the bus singing at the top of her lungs. She was deliciously happy. A modification of her course load to include music and languages guaranteed her successful graduation.

Tempest inhaled the fresh country air in her backyard and began to sing softly, concentrating on technique and control. Singing was now second nature, the words and notes arriving subconsciously, and she felt like an instrument being played by someone much greater than herself. As it was much harder to sing *piano* than *forte*, she continued the soft rising and falling phrases. Only when she relaxed, fully addressing foundation and musculature, did she allow the volume to rise to crescendo, moving from *mezzo forte* to *forte*, and finally, with a sweeping flourish, *fortissimo*.

I cannot bear the end, the last note. The quiet breaths as I regain my thick body and reattach to my heavy surroundings. The pain is so acute, I pray for death. The cruelty of returning refuels my anger.

A cow bellowed in unison and she collapsed, sobbing, on her wooden deck chair.

SEVEN

Betrayed, desperate heart,
Do not break with grief!
—GILDA, ACT 3

"Need any help?"

"Not from the likes of you." Leonard Painter smiled, but his eyes were as hard as the sunlight glittering off the ruffled marina waters. He wore stained jeans, deck shoes and a ripped white T-shirt covered by a thick flannel and down vest. A small knit cap topped his grey crew cut. The wind had burned his face to a brick red, leaving the jagged cheek scar aglow.

Too damn happy by half. Patrick felt his hands clench and worked to relax them. Why the hell did I come? he thought. No matter what Mom wanted, this is never gonna work. He deeply inhaled the thick sea air.

"Can I come aboard?"

His father shrugged and returned to scraping the wooden deck. Feeling as welcome as an ice-cream truck at a health spa, Patrick zipped his rain jacket and clambered onto *The Paintbox*. He grabbed sandpaper and a block and began scrubbing.

They worked quietly for a quarter of an hour, their

scratchy silence interrupted by shouts from other boaters, piercing shrieks from hungry seagulls, and a blast from a nearby ferry. Though he preferred the tranquillity of putzing around in his garden, Patrick enjoyed manual work of any kind.

The Capital City Marina was fairly quiet on this raw March day and he felt at ease on the stationary boat. Going out to sea was a whole other matter. His mother told him that he'd been born with a caul and would never drown. A safe bet, he'd always felt, because the merest whiff of side-to-side motion enraged his stomach. He couldn't read on a bus, much less ply the Georgia Strait on his father's precious twenty-eight-foot cabin cruiser.

Another nail in the coffin that smothered his relationship with his father. "What's wrong with you?" his father had bellowed, not bothering to hide his disgust as Patrick puked unrelentingly over the side. "Every West Coast boy loves the sea." Patrick cherished the ocean, needed the salve of its salty bite, shifting colours and remarkable reflections, but from shore. After his tenth birthday, he never went out with his father again. Patrick and the shimmering, drifting leviathan called a wary truce; he wished for the same with his father.

Patrick stroked and niggled at a spot and felt the anger slip away with every movement. A quiet sense of relief edged in, as it always did when he disappeared in his garden, and his thoughts tugged and wriggled, finally floating as freely as the Bonaparte gulls hovering and chuckling overhead. In a few minutes, he was sweating. He stopped to remove his jacket.

"That's it, then?"

Patrick hesitated, hand on the zipper. "What?"

"That's all you're gonna do? Ha!" Leonard snorted and stroked the Scar of Bravery, the long gash riding his cheekbone. Picked up years ago while wrestling some prickhead junkie with a bigger knife than brain, Leonard Painter wore it proudly, like his badge, and caressed it constantly. Patrick thought his father would paint it red if he could get away with it, anything to make sure it was noticed. Staff Sergeant Painter thought the mark proved he was a cop and a man, but Patrick always felt it proved nothing more than his dad's sluggishness. Course, he never said that to the old man.

"Never could stick to anything, could ya? Why, I could sand this entire boat in the time it takes you to do one fuckin' foot."

Patrick froze, knew he was being baited, so he removed his coat slowly, fumbling a little from tingling fingers. He wrestled an irresistible urge to dive across at the old man and pound his thickened flesh until it was raw and bleeding. At five-nine, Patrick was half a foot shorter than his old man. The size difference was something his father had lorded over him since he was able to walk. Stockily built, like his mom, he lacked only twenty-five pounds on the bastard, but years of catching a fist or two, sometimes a boot, had left him cautious. And humiliated.

"Chicken, ain't ya?" His father had risen and now stood squarely across from him, dark eyes blazing. "Come on, punk," he whispered, dirty hands climbing into fists. "Mama's not here to protect you anymore. Come on! You've always wanted a piece of the old man, well, here's your chance."

Leonard stepped in, swung quickly with a nasty right hook. Patrick ducked, side-stepped, stumbled over a paint can and tried to regain his footing. Painter Senior roared, dropped his head and charged.

Patrick lunged and slid on a wet sponge. His father's head thumped his side and he crumpled. Gasping, he saw the toe too late and threw up an arm in defence. The deck shoe glanced off his right temple. Patrick scrambled up, dodged another blow, then lunged low at his father. He lifted the retired cop off balance. With a yelp of surprise, the old man plunged into the oil-slicked waters.

Chest heaving and head pounding, Patrick stared at his father's bobbing slick head.

"Get me outta here, ya bloody bastard!"

Patrick turned, slumped down against the gunwale and caught his breath. The boat rocked from his father's fists, droplets of salt water shimmered against the weak spring light.

"Gimme a hand," he snarled. The splashing continued. "Patrick! For Christ's sake—"

Patrick grabbed a life preserver and tied the rope end to a side clamp. "I came here for Mom. God knows why, but she wanted us to patch things up."

"Just drop the bloo—"

"Climb in by yourself," he said throwing the doughnut just out of his father's flailing reach. "I'm not sure I'm up to it."

Ignoring his father's cursing, Patrick jumped off the boat. He waved to an incoming catamaran and strolled down the wooden dock, grinning at the splashing sounds behind him.

"TOLD YOU TA FUCK OFF."

Tempest nudged a boot into Terry Brethour's doorway. "I'd like to see Alice."

Brethour scratched his groin. "Who gives a horse's ass what you want? Now, piss off." Brethour shoved, Tempest felt the door slam against her toe. Gritting her teeth, she leaned into it.

"I'm a psychologist. She needs my help."

His pale eyes bored into hers. "The last thing she needs, fat lady, is your headshrinking shit." The eyes flickered over her head to the green motorcycle parked on the cracked driveway. "That your bike?" he asked, his voice rising in astonishment.

"Uh huh," Tempest replied. *Great! Something in common!* "You ride?"

Brethour hesitated, then ran a grimy palm along his mouth. "Not that piece of girl shit!"

Girl shit? Tempest thought. Let's see you on it, prickhead.

He started to push the door. "Now, I'm warnin' ya, get ou–"

"Terry? Who's there?" It was Alice. An uncombed mop of tea-coloured hair popped into the doorway. "Oh, it's you, Dr. Ivory." Tempest had received warmer greetings while canvassing for the Canadian Psychological Association.

"Hello, Alice," Tempest said, saddened by the young woman's haggard look. "Just came by to see how you're doing. I–"

"How d'ya think she's doing?" Terry snapped. "Fuckin' awful. The place's a mess and she hasn't cooked since it happened."

Poor little slimeball, Tempest thought, marvelling at

his selfishness. "Could I come in, Alice?" she spoke directly to the grieving woman. "Just to make sure you're all right."

Alice hesitated, running a hand through her greasy hair. Tempest's nose flickered at the sour smell of sweat, dirty socks and something else. More a sense than a physical smell. A cool bristling along her neck reminded her suddenly of Albert Singleton, a former patient. A small, nervous man, cowed by his culpability, Albert was brilliantly deceptive. He'd chatter on endlessly in his soft, high-pitched whine, confessing to a cornucopia of piddle-ass sins. All the while veiling, protecting, shielding the truth. It took Tempest a few sessions to twig to his duplicity, a couple more to zero in on her own disquiet. That was the hair-trigger sense. She knew then that Albert, devastated by track-trodden Catholic guilt, carried a weight so heinous it permeated his skin, personality and soul. He was compelled to confess, but desperate to survive.

He was the first patient for her vocal counselling technique. Singing released her soul and focused her mind and body, so why not add it to the already accepted methods of music therapy? Albert, at first shy to reach down and vocalize, eventually began mumbling, then howling and finally feverishly singing somewhat on pitch. When months later, he collapsed in her office, blood staining the back of his shirt, and whispered in the softest *pianissimo* that he'd kidnapped, raped and tortured three babies, Tempest was horrified but not surprised. She hoped that his stunning internal confrontation resulted more from her skill at psychology than at his self-flagellation. Ruefully, she doubted it. Nothing wounds a Catholic like guilt.

"No blood—"

Tempest was still struggling to concentrate on her inner alarm when Alice cut him off with an exasperated moan. "She's here ta see me, Ter." She raked both hands through her hair. "God knows I could use a little sympathy."

"Sympathy! Jesus H. Christ, what more can I...hey!" Tempest shoved her way through the door and brushed Brethour aside as though he were a cobweb. "Make us a cup of tea, would you, Ter?" she said, leading Alice Penderghast into the jumbled living room.

"THE PERP BROKE IN JUST BEFORE SIX. I WAS IN THE milkin' barn and the wife was collectin' eggs." Richard Naylor grimaced, flashing an irregular set of stained teeth. "Made a godawful mess."

"Perp?" Patrick smiled at the old man.

"Heard it on the TV. Ain't it whatchya call 'em?"

"Did he take anything?" Patrick asked, ignoring the question. Am I the only person on the Peninsula who doesn't own a TV? he thought, jotting down Naylor's tombstone information.

Naylor made an awful noise like a hork in his throat, pushed Patrick aside and let rip a stream of black spit over the young officer's shoulder. Patrick held back a groan but still shrank at the sound. Shuffling awkwardly to the side, he repeated his question.

"Heard ya the first time," Naylor said, as a drop of black oozed down his chin. "Mebbe old but I ain't deaf. Clara is, but that's another kettle o' fish." He horked again. Patrick stiffened but the old jaws just swallowed. "Jus' our egg money from the stall." He pointed over Patrick's shoulder toward the long drive.

Patrick glanced back and nodded. Like many residents, the Naylors sold home-grown produce from unstaffed stalls by the roadside. Patrick bought free-range eggs and whole-wheat sunflower and molasses bread from ones just like it, twice a week. He'd often thought of setting one up at home to sell the masses of flowers from his garden. Most had steel boxes locked and bolted to the table top. They weren't burglar proof but certainly staved off the amateurs.

"Mind if I come inside?"

The old man shrugged and held open the door. Patrick squeezed into the small entranceway and followed Naylor as he shuffled down a narrow, hardwood-floored hall into the kitchen. Patrick wondered how old he was but felt it impolite to ask. When he saw the ancient cupboards, massive black woodstove and simple lighting fixtures, he figured the old dude was the original owner. Naylor admitted as much as he reached for the kettle. It was a stove-top version and Patrick found himself anticipating the shrill steam whistle. "How much d'you think's gone?" he asked.

The old man pulled a colourful jar from the spotless counter, opened it and took out one tea bag. "Hard to say, usually the wife empties it each night but last night she wasn't feeling good and I forgot." He removed his ageing ballcap and winked. "See the game last night?"

Patrick shook his head. As one of the few Canadian males to eschew the national sport of ice hockey, he knew better than to admit it. "Did they win?"

He hadn't the foggiest how the Vancouver Canucks were faring but from the mini-pools at the Sidney/North Saanich Detachment, he knew playoffs were in full flight. He'd even thrown a couple of toonies into the betting pot, rather than suffer the inevitable hassle from his fellow members. That way, they shut up and didn't bother him.

Naylor chewed for a moment. The kettle shrieked. Still he chewed. Patrick calmed the urge to jump up and rip the kettle from the glowing element. "Nope," the farmer said after a large swallow, "more useless than tits on a bull." Patrick's ears were ringing and the small window overlooking a large pasture began to fog over. "Should be boiling 'bout now," Naylor drawled and slowly walked to the kettle.

"So," Patrick asked a couple of minutes later, gingerly sipping his tea. It was hotter than volcanic steam and weaker than a wet noodle. "How much did you lose?"

Naylor poured a teaspoon of sugar into his chipped cup and stirred. Patrick waited, nursing a burnt tongue. The farmer scooped another teaspoon and whirled the spoon again. After the fourth teaspoon, Patrick's teeth began to ache and he remembered the dental appointment he'd arranged for next week. Naylor took a long sip then smacked his wrinkled lips. "Mebbe fifteen bucks."

"Fifteen!" Patrick tried to reduce his astonishment at the tiny sum. "Izzat...uh...anything else taken?"

"Nope. He must of heard me comin' from the barn 'cause alls I saw was his ass, running down the lane t'ward Dr. Ivory's."

"Dr. Ivory?"

"Lives next door." Naylor leaned forward and Patrick caught a whiff of tobacco-laced tea. "Good lookin', if ya like 'em with a li'l meat."

You old goat, Patrick thought, embarrassed by his

warming cheeks. He asked the rest of his questions, getting nothing of import. A female voice shouted cheerfully from the front door.

"In here," bellowed Naylor. "The missus," he whispered as a big-breasted woman trundled in. He grinned and made a squeezing movement with his hands. Patrick reddened and stood up.

"Tea's ready," Naylor shouted and winked at the Constable.

"SHE WAS ACTING A LITTLE WEIRD, I GUESS."

Ah ha! Tempest thought. The truth comes out. "In what way?"

"I don't know." Alice Penderghast sniffled, pondering the question. "She...she seemed far away."

Tempest nodded. Emotional distancing was often one of the first signs of trouble. "You notice anything else, like inability to sleep or loss of appetite?"

Alice ruffled her hair, which grew greasier with every touch, then examined her hands. She found a single unevenly-coloured strand and immediately began pulling it through her uneven teeth. Tempest smothered a shiver and leaned closer.

"So she wasn't sleeping?"

Alice nodded slightly and snapped the strand in her teeth.

"It helps to talk about it," she said softly. "Children don't commit suicide because of stress or their parents. It's a very complex event stemming from many factors. You mustn't blame yourself."

"Blame!" Alice's watery eyes snapped onto Tempest's. "It wasn't my fault!" Her voice rose hysterically. "Not my fault, not my fault! Noooo." The denials echoed in the littered room. Alice's hands attacked her head again, slashing across her skull so violently that Tempest feared she'd rip chunks of hair free. "Oh, 'Melia," she wailed, "why'd you do it?"

Tempest reached across and grabbed the wind-milling hands. "It's okay," she said, struggling to hold Alice's arms still. "Okay, shhhh, now. Okay." Alice Penderghast relaxed suddenly, slumping against the young psychologist's shoulder. Tempest stiffened and patted her clumsily. "No one's saying it's your fault."

EIGHT

Who can attack me? I do not fear them;
No one touches a man protected by the duke.

—RIGOLETTO, ACT 1

Patrick Painter knocked on the yellow door for the third time. Still no answer. Disappointed, he pulled out his notepad and quickly scrawled a message asking Dr. Ivory to meet with him to discuss the recent break-in next door. He glanced at his messy writing, swore softly then crumpled the paper and began again, writing carefully but boldly, he hoped. Shoving the paper into the door jamb, he dropped down the steps and walked around the tiny house to the unfenced back yard. Not much for gardening, he thought, pitying the plain lawn. Hoping she would arrive any minute, he wandered about, planning shrubs and flowers for the level half-acre lot.

The cottage itself was lovely, a small square bungalow painted a creamy yellow with bone-white trim. Landscaping, such as it was, was natural. A smattering of firs beckoned you up the curved drive and two large Western red cedars stood guard in the back.

Patrick padded about whistling cheerfully, checking

exposure and eyeing the views. He'd have pyracantha along the front, north facing bow-window, accompanied by holly and rhododendron. Near the narrow entry, he'd mound a huge garden bed and fill it with foxglove, hollyhock and a variety of poppies, topped off by a bird bath. With the spectacular southern exposure at the back, he'd dig a small water garden, add a sundial and surround it with mallow, lupin and more poppies. You can never have too many poppies, Patrick thought happily, knowing he had envelopes full of seed to offer. And maybe a harlequin maple over to the right.

A disembodied crackle yanked him from his earthy musings. With a shock, he realized he'd let an hour slip by in Tempest's yard. He grabbed at his shirt mike while sprinting to his squad car.

THE KITTEN WHIMPERED AND WRIGGLED FREE. Arching his back slightly, he bounced under a nearby shrub. Vita moaned and dropped to her hands and knees. "Here, Blackie, Blackie," she whispered. "Come on, kitty. Come on."

The small black body slipped further into the bush.

"Come on, Blackie. Ple-ease, come back." She was half under the bush now, panic rising. Animals were strictly a no-no at the Perpetual Soul. She wasn't sure how she was going to care for Blackie, but from the moment the tiny feline bounded up to her earlier that day, she was hooked on his small, white-splotched face.

She'd heard faint mewing during her morning stroll in the apple orchard. The other girls were rushing about near the school, chasing a soccer ball or huddled together whispering, waiting for the early bell. Since Pendy had gone, Vita had been alone. No one had liked her when she played with the loud-mouthed Amelia but she didn't care. Pendy was fun and she liked Vita, she'd said so. Ever since, the other girls had taunted and teased her, whispering that Pendy was better off dead. Vita Bell had felt lost and lonely until Blackie's arrival.

The kitten had devoured the crumbling baby cookies she'd taken from breakfast. She knew he needed milk but how to bring it without attracting attention? She had been pondering this dilemma when Blackie broke free.

Abandoning her attempt to crash her way through the hedge, Vita scrambled back and dashed around the outside, eyes earthward, searching for the tiny black feline. She spotted Blackie leaping onto a nearby tree and almost cried out, when the sight of a dangling foot silenced her. Crushing herself into the hedge, she peered up. *Oh no, Sydney.*

Intently reading a small book, Sydney Mayne didn't see her. At least until Blackie jumped playfully at her stockinged leg.

"Oooh!" cried Sydney and the book thudded to the grass. Blackie trailed from her left shin. She took a swipe, caught the kitten by the side of the head, and he twisted, then plummeted toward the grass. At the last second, he righted himself and touched down lightly on all four white paws. With a haughty arch of his back and a tiny hiss, Blackie darted into Vita's open arms.

"Don't touch that book!" Sydney commanded, skidding down the tree. "Lookit my stocking! The little beast ripped it." She hobbled to the book and grabbed it to her chest. "You've gotta get rid of it, y'know."

Cradling Blackie, Vita just shook her head. "Whatchya reading?" she asked, changing the subject. It wasn't a book, she decided, staring intently at the leather cover. It looked vaguely familiar.

Sydney shoved the book behind her back. "None of your beeswax. You're in a lotta trouble, you know. No pets."

"It's not a book," Vita cried, remembering. "That's Sister Winifred's journal!"

In a flash, Sydney was on top of her, grabbing for the kitten with her free hand. Vita shied free, and the cat scratched wildly. Sydney dropped the journal and yanked Blackie from the red-haired girl's bleeding arms. With a savage twist, Sydney snapped the kitten's neck and dropped it to the grass.

"Oh noooo," wailed Vita, dropping, clutching the lifeless body. "How could you! You, you're a–"

Journal in hand, Sydney leaned over the sobbing girl. "Tell anyone and you're next."

She kicked Vita. The girl yelped.

"Got it?"

SHE INHALED, CONSTRICTED HER STOMACH MUSCLES. Tempest Ivory was an aria away from her lifelong dream. To her astonishment, not a breath could she draw nor note produce. For the first time since she left home, Tempest was terrified.

The quiet of the rehearsal hall pounded in her ears. One of the judges coughed gently. Her accompanist turned nervously toward her. Tempest began to panic, belly muscles tightening, throat raw, until she feared her voice–her instrument of life, her inner soul–had abandoned her. Just like her mother.

The thought of her mom triggered a blinding memory and she snapped shut her eyes: an opera stage, a hauntingly glorious voice, her mother smiling, curtsying low, a rolling clap of applause. The crowd's roar overwhelmed Tempest, moving through her like a tidal wave. She took a breath, down from the backs of her knees, and opened her eyes.

"May I have a moment?" she asked, projecting a wavering voice well beyond the brilliantly lit floor lights.

"Of course," replied a deep voice she recognized as Jeffrey Winterbottom, the director of Vic Opera. "Take as long as you need."

Though she had to coax them, her legs finally moved and took her into the safety of the wings. A stage hand hurried over but she waved him away. Leaning against a partial set, Tempest began breathing slowly, deeply, rediscovering her posture, regaining control. Everard's words echoed in her head. "Don't panic, child. Nerves are your foundation, the musical strings for your vocal bow. Touch them, play them lightly, as though they were glass. Use them to lift your voice, to express your emotional range."

The first part of the audition had gone so well. She'd followed her coach's instructions to the letter, drinking tons of water, smiling, even introducing herself by saying, "I am" and not, "My name is". The song from *Figaro* came across beautifully. She knew from her balance, from the sound rolling from her throat, that the colour was brilliant, that she was in character and her pronunciation–always a bit of a stretch–was bang on.

Everard had covered the marking criteria—illustrated by endless examples from his past—in copious detail.

Upon successfully attacking *Figaro*, Tempest was certain she'd proven her quality of voice, breath control, evenness of register and control of coloratura. Musicality, intonation, phrasing and style were evident.

So why the freeze-up, you idiot?

The ascending succession of trills necessary to vault into the bloody high E finish of *Caro nome* loomed ahead like a brick wall. Music lovers were known to boo vociferously if Gilda's signature song ended in anything less than an E-flat.

Caro nome was originally written for lyric sopranos, whose voices rarely attained the dizzying musical heights of the coloraturas. But over time, higher notes were added and it became customary for coloraturas to sing the demanding female lead in *Rigoletto*. Many singers used their own variations, adding cadenzas or solo passages, allowing a display of virtuosity and providing an individual imprint for Gilda. Tempest was confident in her command of the showpiece's high notes but dreaded expressing the dreamy, starstruck emotion of the young girl singing about her first romantic kiss. Cyrus had tried, unsuccessfully, to show her how to find the emotional centre—a technique taken from acting—or essence of a song. As he continually reminded her, being emotional just wasn't her bag. Sometimes he'd soften that blow by reminding her that the great soprano, Renata Tebaldi, wasn't the actress Maria Callas was, either. Yet her glorious singing and vocal purity bewitched millions.

"In bocca al lupo," she whispered to herself. Into the wolf's mouth. A traditional opera backstage sendoff.

She reached into her bag and pulled out a spritzer bottle of water. Quickly dousing a handkerchief, she inhaled the humidity deeply. If the Met can mist the stage for several minutes before a singer's entrance, why not?

Crepi lupo, she thought, giving herself the proper "Let him choke" reply. Stuffing the tissue into her bag, Tempest strode back on stage, Everard's last words ringing in her head. "Opera's an open and shut case: open your throat and shut your mouth."

SHE GUNNED THE MOTORBIKE AND BLASTED PAST A young woman on a tall, grey horse. The *Rigoletto* curse was upon her. Her throat felt singed and tears rippled down her cheeks as she battled the panic and anguish. It was her chance, the big one, and she'd blown it as surely as she knew the thoroughbred would shy, buck and bolt at the sound of the bike's shrieking engine. The rider barely had time to raise her crop in alarm as her steed side-stepped and reared. Through her side mirror, Tempest caught a flash of white, rolling eyes and painted hooves as the horse plummeted to earth. She fought off a base fear to rev the engine into streaking speed and flee. Tempest cut the power, rolled to a stop and turned.

The horse pounded the shoulder toward her, the woman struggling for balance, yanking on the reins. The roiling hooves trampled the roadside brush. Tempest saw the blood-red flaring nostrils and clambered off her bike. With a grunt, she managed to move the Pig just as the big animal rumbled by. Dirt showered her, mixed with a rich scent of manure, and she leaned heavily on her bike.

About a hundred yards further, the woman gained control and pulled the steed up sharply. A car rolled by, slowing to peer at Tempest and then the panting horse. Tempest ripped off her helmet and hung her head, red curls dangling limply, breathing in ragged sobs.

"You bloody idiot!" a woman's voice shouted.

Tempest looked up to see the grey horse picking its way to her, nostrils and sides quivering.

"You coulda killed us!" The woman wasn't as young as Tempest had first thought. Deep lines stood out sharply in the reddened, shocked face.

"Look, I'm really sorry."

"Sorry!" The horse stood over her now, breathing heavily; Tempest could have touched the silver mane. The woman raised the crop and Tempest thought she might strike. "Sorry doesn't cut it," the woman said, lowering the crop when she realized the rider was a woman. "I should report you for dangerous driving."

You wouldn't be the first, Tempest thought. "Look, I said I was sorry. Your horse isn't used to traffic, it shouldn't be on the highway." She straddled the Pig.

"Not used t—"

The roar of the bike cut her off. Tempest shoved down her helmet and flipped the visor. "No harm done," she shouted and slowly rolled onto the road. "Maybe you should consider something with wheels."

Tempest chuckled. Though she felt idiotic and ashamed by her sudden stupidity, the dizzying rush of the bike's speed and her sucking fear as the horse flew by was intoxicating. She might have to try riding. To feel those live muscles reaching and straining must be something else. Gearing up, she poured on the speed and danced with the swirling curves of West Saanich Road.

The memory of her audition, her *Rigoletto*'s curse, matched her every move. Just her luck, her first opera would revolve around a malediction, one where a father's evil ravages his daughter, to boot. Since she first heard about the tryout, she'd spent a lot of time reviewing the opera and its history and listening to its music and other sopranos' interpretations, sometimes swearing loudly at Sutherland's or Caballé's vocal dexterity. Much of the info was boring, but she was intrigued by the use of a recurring musical theme to represent a person or idea in an opera. Applied in the very first opera, *Orfeo* in 1607, it had embellished many other works over the centuries, including Wagner's famous four operas of *The Ring*. Victor Hugo, in developing *Le Roi s'amuse*, centred the story on a father's worst nightmare: the damnation of his innocent and beloved daughter.

Giuseppe Verdi had created a unique, recurring musical phrase for the curse in *Rigoletto*. Lasting about forty-five seconds, this phrase formed the prelude to the opening scene, highlighting the curse that would be cast upon Rigoletto. Its rising, ominous brass rumbles were repeated in variations throughout, forming the opera's musical heart. The opera was almost called *La maledizione* or The Curse, but was changed at the demand of the Italian censors. Verdi instructed his librettist, Francesco Maria Piave, to remember that "the whole subject lies in that curse".

Tempest streaked along the quiet road, reliving her audition note by note in her mind, easily achieving both emotional release and superior voice quality. If only she hadn't frozen, hadn't left the stage.

She was mentally reaching *Caro nome*'s difficult final trills when it happened. With a shudder, then a sideways squirt, the Pig fell from under her, slewing across the road. Tempest tried to roll free from the motorbike but her left foot caught, pinning and dragging her as it raked to a stuttering stop in a wet, weed-choked ditch.

NINE

That thought, why does it still
Trouble my mind?
Will misfortune strike me?
Ah, no, that is folly!
—RIGOLETTO, ACT 1

"Dr. Ivory?" Patrick asked the receptionist in a small, brightly lit booth. He noticed that the next digit on the first-come-first-served numbering system was two. He swallowed a smile. He must have seen that bright red tape dispenser a thousand times and the next number was never greater than three. Life on the Peninsula. The last time he'd brought in his mother, crumpled with pain and terror, the number had been one.

The woman glanced up from a computer screen and nodded over her left shoulder. Patrick walked gently, trying not to let his police boots echo on the polished floor, and followed the signs to Emergency.

The Saanich Peninsula Hospital, or San Pen, served the roughly forty thousand inhabitants of the Peninsula from several sprawling, low buildings nestled behind the hamlet of Saanichton. Patrick had visited often, following up on accident victims or catching a word with the coroner.

Patrick had never been spooked by the bright corridors and antiseptic scent of the hospital, until nine days earlier, when his mother was wheeled in, whimpering but alive. Two days later, she was wheeled out, cooling and dead. Now, the glare was harsh, casting heavy shadows and the air was thick and rumbling with whispers of death.

"Constable Painter?"

The voice startled him. Tempest Ivory, her full face shiny with the effort of hiding pain, rolled round the corner. She was in a wheelchair pushed by a skinny orderly, her left foot bandaged and outstretched.

"I'll do that," he said, elbowing the young man aside.

"What're you doing here?"

"You okay?"

She nodded, wincing. "Few scratches, turned ankle. Bike's much worse."

"Will they let you go?"

Tempest glanced around the empty corridor. "Seems so. Guy was just wheeling me out."

"Allow me," Patrick said, propelling the chair through the automatic doors. They closed with a hiss; Patrick immediately relaxed in the cool evening air. "Wanna lift?"

She was quiet as they drove north through Central Saanich in his black pickup. He'd given her his fleece pullover, pleased at its hugging fit, which she wore beneath her leather jacket, gaping tears along the back and left arm. Usually Patrick would admire the long, sloping view of the Cordova and Sidney channels, intrigued by the tiny spots of light.

Tonight the sprawling farmlands, ocean and looming Gulf Islands might as well have been invisible. His eyes should have been on the road but were mostly cast sidelong at Tempest. Her profile in the dimming light stirred him; he wondered if he'd ever touch those soft cheeks.

"You in pain?"

She shrugged, winced, and then tried to laugh. It was the first time he'd heard it and the crinkling noise delighted him. "A little bruised. I'll live."

"What happened?"

"Do y'know where my bike is?"

"Nope," he replied, ticked that she ignored his question, didn't take him or his job seriously. He jammed his right foot down and with a squeal, the pickup lunged forward, devouring the narrow road. He flicked a glance her way; Tempest remained calm but he thought he noticed a tightening in her fingers. Patrick slammed the brakes. The truck spun toward the daffodil fields; he thought he'd lost control, but it righted itself, shuddering to a stop.

Neither spoke for a long time.

"Like speed, eh?"

She slammed her hand against the dash, then quickly inhaled from pain. "What's that supposed to mean, you idiot?" she shouted when she'd found her breath. "You coulda killed us. Who gave you the right—wait just a damn minute! What d'you mean, 'Like speed?'"

Patrick kept his eyes on the furrows of flowers, watching their yellow faces pale in the darkening light. He'd expected a reaction but not of this magnitude. Perhaps it wasn't such a sharp idea to look her up on the police computer. It'd seemed so natural when he'd heard of the accident.

"You checked up on me, didn't you?" She was leaning into him, her perfume combining with the fresh night air. "You had no right, that's an invasion of privacy!"

Patrick tried backtracking. "Heard about your accident on the radio. When they said it was you, well I, I..." His voice trailed off. What could he say? That he wanted to know everything about her and was willing to bend more than a few rules to find out? He'd never reveal that, no way. So, like many on the defensive, he pulled up short and kicked back.

"One more tickie, no more bikie," he said, regretting the childish rhyme the second it escaped his lips.

"Tickie?! Bikie?!"

He flushed at the heavy sarcasm. *Christ! Now I've really blown it!*

"Cut the crappy poetry, Constable. My driving record's none of your business. Now start this piece of shit and take me home!"

Patrick wanted to apologize, to hear that laugh–like someone crushing crêpe paper–again. Instead, he started the truck and they drove without speaking. As they reached her laneway, he was desperate to reinitiate contact. He couldn't bear to leave her like this.

"Did you skid on something or catch some gravel?" He pulled up her drive. She opened her door before he could and twisted to get out.

She moaned as her left foot hit the dewy grass, and fell back. He trotted around the front and offered his hand. She stared at him for a while, cool green eyes watchful, then shook her head slightly–Patrick felt it as a blow—and reluctantly took his hand. He wrapped his arm, lifting her slightly. Her light perfume licked at him. Though she stiffened, she said nothing and they slowly edged into her cottage. The heat from her body electrified Patrick and he battled a desire to squeeze. What would that old coot Naylor say? he thought, deliberately relaxing his grip.

The living room was stark, neater than the San Pen. A large piano owned two of the four coved corners. He gently dropped her onto a rose-coloured leather couch. "Want some water?" he asked, moving into the kitchen before she could answer. Tiny didn't describe it. He found himself wondering how she manoeuvred between the appliances then flushed, ashamed.

"How 'bout a cuppa tea or coffee?"

"Since you're so damn comfortable, tea would be great. Bags are in the cupboard beside the stove."

He grinned, found the tea and plugged in the kettle. Step number one in basic police training: insinuate yourself with the accused.

"Did ya see my note?"

No answer. He repeated the question when he brought in a couple of steaming mugs.

Tempest took a sip and yawned heartily. Patrick laughed, reminded of a terrier he'd had once, named Brodie, who yawned just as loudly. He'd hear him in the night, wriggling into position at his feet. Brodie's yawn was so noisy, so satisfying, that Patrick often laughed out loud and reached down to tickle the dog's soft, white ears.

Taken aback, Tempest tried to muffle another yawn.

"Sorry," he said, face burning. He stood up, began pacing the small room. "You gonna tell me what happened or should I just wait to read the full accident report tomorrow?"

"Wouldn't you rather look it up, get the info behind my back?" Patrick kept moving. "Not sure," she said softly, blowing on her tea. "Happened fast, tire blew, maybe."

Patrick glanced over the colourful artwork lining the pale walls, the images familiar, but he couldn't name the artists. He was about to put his cup down on the piano when he caught her concerned movement. Casually, he took a sip and placed the cup gently on a nearby coaster.

The piano was decorated with a vase of dried flowers and one photograph. He picked up the photo. Three fair-haired children laughed out at him. He glanced at Tempest but she looked away, taking another drink. He ran his fingers along the heavy silver frame, admiring its unusual shape.

"Were you robbed recently?"

The question surprised her but she quickly recovered. "Why do you ask?"

"Your neighbour, Richard Naylor, was robbed. He said the guy came your way. That's why I left the note." He replaced the photo and turned to her. "The one you never answered."

"Okay, okay, so I didn't answer the bloody note!" Tempest ran a hand over her face. Patrick noticed the bruised knuckles and wanted to kiss them better. "Look, I really appreciate the ride home, but I'm exhausted. Can we talk about this some other time?"

He drained his cup of tea as noisily as he could. "Sure, come on down to the station tomorrow, we can talk all you want."

Immediately, he regretted his officiousness. Why did she make him so edgy? Her silence beat at his ears; he felt like throwing himself at her damaged feet and pleading for another chance. Instead, he stood at the piano and stared at the photo of the little kids, wondering which girl she was, the one with ringlets or braids?

"Don't think he took anything," she said in a cold voice.

"Why didn't you call us?"

"I just said, nothing was taken. I saw no reason to involve the police. Now," she added with another blatant yawn, "can I go to bed?"

"If you'll fill out a statement with me...at your convenience."

She tried to stand. He moved nearer and flashed an open palm.

"I'll let myself out. You gonna be all right?"

"Sure. Lock it when you leave, will you?"

He stood in her minuscule entrance, reluctant to depart. "Uh, good night, then, Dr. Ivory."

"Night," he heard her soft reply.

As he shut the door, something fluttered to the porch. Reaching down, he picked up a small brochure. *Vic Opera, 1997-98 Season*, it read. Patrick raised his hand to knock and saw the light disappear in the living room. He played the brochure under his nose and walked to the truck, inhaling her lingering scent.

THE SUN'S RAYS FILTERED THROUGH THE SMALL chapel's stained glass, throwing pale colours across the wooden pews. Sister Winifred strode up and down the narrow aisle, oblivious to the filtered rainbow. Several days had gone by and no sign of the journal. She thought she'd find comfort and direction in this hallowed recess with the Virgin Mary gazing solemnly down from above the simple altar. Instead, she grew angrier and more frustrated, her strides shortening, speed increasing.

She knelt, crossed herself and prayed. Or tried to pray. God seemed to have abandoned her, as he had poor Amelia. She worked harder, striving for that precious moment of purity. Sweat dripped from her brow, reflecting the increasing sunlight, and still nothing. Nothing but an abiding sense of despair and inadequacy.

Where had the Lord gone?

It was so easy, twenty-five years ago, as a novitiate. Before the sweeping changes of Vatican II, nuns suffered, akin to the labours of Hercules, in order to obliterate their egos and wills. To erase any shred of identity; to forego human love for something more powerful, more absolute. Total conviction, embracing the Lord Our God, His only son, Jesus, and the Holy Spirit within.

Nothing like a pretence of self-sacrifice, even martyrdom, to release a rush of selfish piety.

Such utter nonsense! Abandoning oneself in an egotistical attempt at redemption and forsaking one's responsibilities to hide behind walls veiled with mystery and divinity. Sister Winifred bolted up, energized by her yearning. There was nothing in this holy place for her. What she sought could not be found cached in the pillars of western religious doctrine.

The academy was quiet, still early for all but Sister Benedict. No doubt prostrate across her narrow bed, beads flashing as she entered God's solitude. Immediately, Winifred felt ashamed at her un-Christian thoughts. Poor old Dick. One of the last of the contemplative spiritualists. Perhaps she soared into divinity. If so, Winifred should genuflect and adore, not scorn and belittle.

A slight creak caught her attention. The main hall-way was empty, still dim. A closet door near the far end was ajar. Admonishing herself for denigrating Sister Benedict, she didn't pay attention. Until she came abreast of the open door and witnessed the horror within.

Vita Bell, her tongue blackened and lolling, swung from the bar, a bouquet of shamrocks at her feet.

ACT TWO

Shall we continue in sin,
That grace may abound?
—ROMANS, 6:1

Act Two synopsis, *Rigoletto*

In the palace drawing room, the duke is alone and disconsolate because his beloved Gilda has disappeared. The courtiers arrive and tell him how they kidnapped Gilda. Overjoyed that she is in his palace, he rushes to the conquest. Rigoletto appears and becomes angered when the duke refuses to be disturbed, suspecting the young man is with his daughter.

Gilda bursts in, tells of meeting the young man and of her abduction. Rigoletto comforts his daughter, swearing that they will leave this awful place. Monterone is then paraded by, en route to prison, broken by the failure of his curse. Rigoletto vows to avenge his daughter and the old count, while Gilda pleads with him to forgive the man she loves.

TEN

You are my life! Without you,
What joy would I have on earth?
Oh, my daughter!

—RIGOLETTO, ACT 1

Upon seeing another small, trailing silhouette, Patrick Painter fought disbelief and disorientation. Floating in déjà vu, he had an eerie repeat of his conversation with Dr. Edwina Harwicke about Amelia's suicide.

"You're sure?"

"About suicide?" Harwicke asked as she completed her examination of Vita's bruised neck. Patrick couldn't watch. One glimpse at the swollen face and protruding eyes was enough. Though the kid's blinking had irritated him, he'd give anything to see those huge grey eyes blink again.

"Nothing that smacks of foul play." The coroner nodded to her assistants and they began the awkward task of bringing her down.

"Mind you," she added, scribbling in a small pad, "don't know if I'd want my daughter going to school here." She chuckled. "Course that's pretty academic."

"Sorry?"

"Have neither daughter nor the money to send one here if I had." Harwicke bent for a moment, then straightened and gently placed the shamrocks in a plastic bag. "You know, Constable, someone brighter than I said the moment you're born, you're old enough to die." She looked at Vita's small body. "Can't say as I agree." She shook her head slowly. "Something's rotten in the state of Denmark, Constable, or," Dr. Harwicke added, zipping up the bag, "should I say Ireland?"

"HANDS UP...THAT'S IT...OVER YOUR HEAD. GOOD. Feel more open?"

"No. This is stupid."

Tempest sighed. Nothing like an uncooperative singer. She wasn't sure that her idea of music therapy would work on Sydney but Sister Winifred had pressed her to try. "The child's a menace," Winifred had said. "She bullies the other girls and I'm certain she's our arsonist. Here's a chance to prove your worth. Get that girl to talk."

For a moment, Tempest regretted having told the Mother Superior about her fledgling youth behaviour program at all. Though healing with music was a long-standing therapy for mentally and physically disabled individuals, traditionally it focused more on playing instruments, active listening skills and rhythmic movement.

Tempest felt that singing, with its innate improvements to speech, language skills, vocalization, breath control and articulation, suited a variety of emotional or behavioural difficulties. Besides, nothing gave you greater freedom, vision, self-esteem and total-body toning than unhinging your jaw and creating your own personal fanfare.

"Keep 'em up," she repeated to Sydney. "What we're trying to do is open up your diaphragm. You know what that is?"

With her thin arms drooping half-heartedly over her bowed head, Sydney Mayne looked like Charlie Brown's Christmas tree. Tempest stifled a laugh.

She rose from her piano and reached across to gently touch the girl's stomach. Sydney flinched and dropped her arms.

Tempest pulled back sharply. "It's okay, sorry. I just wanted to show you where the diaphragm is."

"Here?" Sydney poked her small chest.

Tempest nodded, sat back down. "It's a muscle that separates your body into two. When you lift your arms, that's right, you open your rib cage and diaphragm. Gives you a more expansive, bigger feeling. Now normally we don't sing with our arms aiming for the sky, but for now, I just want you to experience feeling big. We're never allowed to be big in real life, especially females. This's the place to let go. Remember what I said at the beginning?"

The girl's eyes darkened.

"This's a place to have fun, not to behave politely or correctly like at the academy." She pointed to the small music stand in front of Sydney. "The floor, as they say, is yours. So..." she began playing the piano, "...let's try again, okay? Arms up, knees bent."

"*Come and take a walk with me*...sing, Sydney, sing with me."

The child opened her mouth and mumbled. Tempest stopped playing.

"My arms hurt," the girl whined, dropping them heavily to her sides. "This sucks."

Tempest started singing and playing scales, working her way up the piano. After a few minutes, Sydney's face grew darker. Finally, she pounded the music stand. "Thought this was my lesson."

Tempest played a few more bars. "It is, but only if you want." She leaned back. "What do you do for fun? Play games, go swimming, read?"

Sydney chewed her lip. "You married?"

Tempest ignored the question. "Well, I sing. It's so much fun to just let yourself go. Like shouting. D'you ever get to shout?"

The girl's eyes were puzzled. She shook her head.

"Want to?"

A slight nod.

Tempest played with a flourish. "Great! Let's begin there, shall we? Why don't you shout 'Hey?'"

The girl hesitated. Tempest nodded.

"Hey," she spoke in a voice not much louder than when speaking.

"Heeeeeyyyyy!" Tempest's voice boomed in her small living room. Sydney put her hands to her ears.

Tempest shouted again. This time, a slight smile danced on Sydney's lips.

"Go on, give it a shot."

"Heeyy!"

Tempest pounded out a couple of chords. "That's it. Louder!"

"Heeeyyy!" The girl grinned and lifted her arms. "Heeeyy, heeeyyy, heeeyyy!"

"That's it! How'd you feel?"

Sydney's eyes shone. "Loud....strong."

"Great, isn't it? Now, sing along with me. *Come and take a walk with me.*"

Sydney chirped along. Tempest watched her carefully, touched by the child's fragility. You might just as well strip naked as sing in front of another human being, you felt so exposed and vulnerable, she thought. Like turning your back on a stranger and hoping they'll catch you if you fall. Trust in another human being was a priceless gift, one that was stolen from Tempest at an early age. She was certain Sydney had also been deprived of this blessing, if not wholly denied. Perhaps it wasn't too late for this little girl. It would take time, she knew her therapeutic approach had to be cautious.

"That's it. Now, make me wanna come with you....Yes! Good, very good."

The girl kept singing, struggling slightly to move higher as Tempest worked her slowly up a semi-tone at a time. Soon, the child was flushed and breathing heavily.

Tempest raised her fingers from the piano and smiled. "Good, excellent! You've got a lovely voice." Sydney beamed. "Take a little break." She handed her a glass of water. The girl drank greedily.

"That's a gas!" Sydney said wiping her mouth. "I thought you were just a boring shrink."

"I am."

Sydney paused, uncertain if Tempest was joking.

Tempest smiled. "But I'm also a singer."

"I didn't know singing was such fun! Can I come every day?"

"Sure, that's just the beginning, little one. We're going to have lots of fun but we're after much more."

"More?"

Tempest nodded. "No hiding, no half-hearted efforts, you gotta trust and let go. Singing's about instinct and projection, but mostly it's about speaking the truth. Think you can promise that?"

Sydney lied. "Uh huh."

"NOT SURE WHAT YOU WANT ME TO DO, WINNIE. Always glad to help, y'know that. A shock, of course, that another girl's died but why in God's name—pardon my French—why call me?"

Why indeed, thought Sister Winifred. I must be really losing it. The shock of seeing Vita Bell hanging in the main foyer closet rattled her to the bone. What could possibly be going on? Two deaths, two suicides— she could barely think the word—in her school. She had to uncover the answer, for as God, or whoever was up there, was her witness, the bishop would want an explanation. PDQ. One that would appease him, the diocese, probably the whole blessed Holy See and calm the parents' and students' fears.

"As you know, Leo, my name is Sister Winifred. I'm calling you because she's the one."

Leo ignored the dig. "What one?"

Winifred's nasal voice dropped further. The door to her office was closed. That in itself would command attention. She'd searched her office more often than she'd done the rosary but still no sign of the journal. She didn't have much time. She hated involving her braggart of a cousin, but she felt ambushed. "The one you brought," she whispered.

"The what? I brought?" His voice halted. A prolonged pause. Then she heard him inhale sharply as an old memory, long submerged, shot to the surface. "Long time ago, that. You swore it'd never come out. I trusted you, woman—"

"She's dead, you self-serving idiot!" She struggled to lower her voice again, shocked at how quickly she fell into a baser level of communication with Leonard. Just like when they were kids. "Now, we've got a problem."

"We? Ha, that's a good one, Sister. I don't see any we's over at that school. Nobody knows anything about this, 'cept you 'n me. I've done my part, kept my mouth shut for yea—"

Winifred's blood pounded in her ears. Her religious decorum evaporated during confrontations with Leonard P. Painter. When they were children, Leo had tormented her, mocking her nasal voice and thin body. "Hey there, Skinny, Whiny, Winnie," he used to shout, following her to high school. "Who's gonna wanna date a bag o' bones like you?" No one, Winifred recalled sadly, but that was beside the point. The man was a jerk. His macho conceit had always astonished her. Such cheek! His large nose and piggy eyes were nothing to write home about, but amazingly, many girls did. Leo had been a very popular young man, a quick-tempered braggart with a real-estate developer's charisma.

"Listen to me, Leonard P-is-for-puny Painter, someone else might know. Now, we may have to act fast if anything's found out. So, start using that pea brain of yours to come up with another explanation. Make it good, make it fast."

"Or?"

"Kiss your precious pension goodbye," she said, choking off a wail of exasperation.

"IT'S OKAY TO ASK YOUR CHILD IF THEY'RE THINKING about suicide."

An audible gasp rose from the small auditorium. The staff of the academy, lining the outside aisle, turned shocked faces to Dr. Ivory. Patrick stood quietly near the main entrance, his face expressionless. The parents of the children attending the Perpetual Soul filled the room, many shifting uncomfortably in the small seats. Though of diverse backgrounds, income brackets and social status, their minds were remarkably focused on one issue: what was happening at the Old Soul?

"It can be a tremendous relief to know someone understands how they feel."

"What if my questions...you know, push...?" the young woman near the front hesitated. A couple of people nodded.

Tempest gently shook her head and stood up from her chair at the front of the stage. "It's a tough question to ask. Each circumstance is different, may demand a different approach. At the back," she gestured to a long, low table near the door, "I've got some brochures from the local crisis centre. Please take one with you, read it carefully. Call me if you have any questions."

"Forget the bloody brochure!" a man near the back shouted. He stood up, almost upsetting his chair. "Two girls have died already. I need to know now."

The sound of clapping rippled through the room. Mother Superior called for quiet. Like an unruly class, the parents responded slowly.

Tempest waited until they were settled. All but the man sat down. "I understand your fears, sir. First thing to do is calm down. Please."

A woman sitting beside the man pulled on his arm. He dropped heavily into his tight seat.

"Okay," Tempest started, leaning against the back of her chair. "If you think your child is having trouble coping—perhaps they're not sleeping, not eating, acting odd, the warning signs are outlined in the booklet—trust yourself. We all know how hard it is to get a child, especially a teenager, to talk."

Several parents nodded, a couple almost smiled.

"So, be ready to persist. Don't just say 'what's wrong?' and give up when they shrug and mutter 'nothing.' Ask again. Show the child you care. Say something like 'I'm worried about you. You seem very down lately. What's going on?' Then wait and listen!" She paused and looked down at the crowd. "I hear this from kids all the time. 'My parents don't listen!' This, folks, is really important. Don't lecture, don't offer solutions or worse, tell them how much better off they are than the kids in Bosnia. No, no, no! Just listen! If your child actually feels you're listening, they'll understand that you're taking their problems seriously—you'd be amazed what stuff kids internalize—and that you care and want to help."

"What if my kid says," the speaker, a man in the front blinked, "she...she wants to die?"

The auditorium was silent. It seemed to Tempest that the parents stopped breathing.

"That's good," Tempest replied. The crowd inhaled quickly. "It'll be a shock, that's for sure, but it means you've gotten through. At this point, don't hesitate, don't euphemize, go straight at it. Take a deep breath and ask some terrible questions: have you thought about how to do it? When do you think you'll do it?"

"Won't that just give 'em ideas?"

Tempest shook her head. "The best way is the direct way. Don't let your fears or society's stigma stop you. This is your child's life we're talking about here. Be honest. It'll allow them licence to admit their feelings, their own fears."

An elderly, bespectacled woman in the middle put up her hand. Tempest pointed to her and nodded. The woman hesitated, then stood up very slowly. Her voice was low but carried. Tempest thought she may have been a singer. "I heard they sometimes happen in waves, that one suicide can lead to others."

"Yes," Tempest replied, "it's felt that suicide, especially in young adults, is a learned behaviour."

"D'you think that's what happened here? That the second child, what's her name?"

"Vita," a nearby voice said.

"That poor Vita mimicked the first?"

At the church, he looked so small, so white that even the brand new turtle-neck seemed dirty. She wanted to touch his reddish hair, push down the stubborn widow's peak. Would God take him to heaven? As she returned to the first pew, she heard whispers from two women sitting close behind. The older murmured, "Such a shame. The dear boy, so young!" "Terribly sad," the other spoke in a hushed voice, "that he'd copy her." She shook her tight grey curls. "Something's terribly wrong."

As a practising psychologist, Tempest Ivory had never been faced with two suicides before, much less those of young girls. The literature clearly stated that often a child who killed herself got the idea from someone else. Tempest knew copycat suicides happened. But in this instance? What about the shamrocks?

She shook the thoughts from her mind and focused on the elderly lady. "Yes, it's true that many children who commit suicide are copying someone else. That's why it's so important to talk to them and get them professional help. Don't think that just because you've discussed suicide, the risk is over. Youth suicides are usually impulsive. If you can restrict the idea, even for a couple of hours, often you save them. But remember, they need professional help, and they need it immediately."

ELEVEN

An errand of mischief brought us here;
—MARULLO, ACT 1

Singing had never left her so drained, as barren as a prairie sky. The last parent shuffled down the main steps. When it came to emotional outpouring, Tempest was in a league with the Royal Family. Revealing personal pain was too brutal, commiserating with others exhausting. Tempest watched the parents move carefully, as though stepping on a brittle surface. Embers of rage glowed in the depths of Tempest's soul. She put her hands over her face and drooped forward in the hard, wooden chair. And tried to forget.

She heard a soft, sharp sound and looked up, startled, into Patrick Painter's dark eyes.

"Sorry," he said, flushing, "thought you might like a cup of tea." He drew a large hand away from the cup, accidentally brushing against it. The milky water slopped onto the table. Patrick cursed and glanced around wildly for something to soak it up.

Sister Gabriel appeared, though Tempest didn't see her approach. The young nun smiled and gently wiped the table dry. Tempest stared at the smile, the green eyes and thought: I'd trade my voice for an hour of such serenity.

"Thanks, Sister."

"My life's a service to others, Constable," Gabriel replied. "As is yours, I expect." She peered intensely up at him. Patrick mumbled something inaudible and began inspecting his nails.

Sister Gabriel's acute examination also disturbed Tempest. A memory flickered: early childhood...a family outing...Beacon Hill Park? The Gorge? No, a museum of some sort. She sipped the tea and concentrated. Not the Royal, no stuffed animals or dinosaur bones, more people...famous and...infamous! The Victoria Wax Museum! Another face, another pair of glittering green eyes, minutely examined the statues, especially those of notorious criminals, her small body leaning over the red cord in disbelief. "They're so alive," she had whispered.

"Do you pray, Constable?"

Patrick rubbed his nose violently. Tempest avoided his eyes. "Uh, guess so, Sister."

"You, Dr. Ivory?" Gabriel asked Tempest.

"No," she replied, more harshly than she meant. "I, I mean, I don't go to church or anything." Why were those eyes so haunting? "Guess it's the scientist in me. You know, doubting Thomas."

"Ah, Thomas, yes. Very interesting case." Gabriel shot a glance at Tempest. "You know of course, he regretted his doubt." She stroked her rosary and returned her stare to Patrick. "It's the spirit within that one must seek. Prayer opens you, allows you to feel. It's crying out, you know. Calling you to pray. A life beyond this. Perhaps you're just not listening."

"I don't know," Tempest replied, surprised at her conversational engagement. "Somehow a belief in God, in particular in the afterlife, has always seemed to me to be a silly societal concept designed to keep us in line, like a bunch of ignorant baboons."

She paused and Patrick shuffled his feet. Expressionless, Gabriel's eyes watched her. She felt impelled to talk.

"You know, if you're good, you get the carrot—which is heaven. If you're not, you get the stick—hell." Patrick was furiously cleaning his nails. "Religion seems to me to give a few folks an astonishing, undeserved power. Being good just makes survival sense. Act criminally, eventually, you'll get yours."

Tempest stopped. *What are you saying? Shut up!* She shook her head slightly, feeling a flush rise in her cheeks.

No one spoke for a full minute.

"Sometimes I think it'd be lovely not to wake up one morning," Gabriel finally whispered.

Patrick began coughing and Tempest's memory vanished.

"I can think of nothing nicer, can you?"

Patrick just stared at the thin woman. Tempest gripped the cup tighter.

"Such a relief to be gathered unto God, don't you think, Leonardo?" Gabriel said and slowly slipped away.

Patrick dropped into the chair next to Tempest. "What the hell was that all about?" He glanced at her, grabbed the cup out of her hand and downed the remains in one gulp. "And who's Leonardo?"

"Huh? Oh, no idea," Tempest replied, trying to visualize Gabriel's stare.

"WHAT WOULD A CHILD DO WITH 'LA MALEDIZIONE' or the curse theme in *Rigoletto*?"

Tempest rubbed her eyes for the twentieth time. *How the hell should I know?* She stood and stretched. Sometimes Everard's ideas were total wingnuts, just like him. *Why the hell should I care?*

Tempest was bushed. She'd been reviewing *Rigoletto*'s orchestral score for hours, studying the parts for all the instruments. It really helped if you knew you were to sing with the jagged thrill of a dozen violins or against the resounding blast of an eighty-piece orchestra.

Next she would have to master the music, carefully dissect each song into manageable four-bar sections. Studying their internal structure, singing them until they flowed from her like an aura.

Learning an opera in a couple of weeks was like entering a miniature donkey and a blind rider in the Grand National Steeplechase. It could be accomplished, but only by those cursed with tenacity, self-loathing and delusions of virtuosity. Given a three-legged ass and tight blindfold, Tempest Ivory would vault the National's last obstacle in the lead.

At least, under normal circumstances. Two children dead, at their own hands...even as a psychologist, this was nearer the madding crowd. Her concentration wavered as it had all evening. The earlier phone call from the motorcycle shop hadn't helped.

The ringing had interrupted her practice. "You gettin' a new roof?" the mechanic had asked. She said no and asked him why.

"Kinda odd, is all," he said in a muffled voice. It took Tempest a couple of seconds to realize he was chomping gum. "Bike's in pretty good shape, overall, just a few dents but..." he chewed some more.

"Yes?"

The mechanic swallowed. "Well, ma'am, not sure if this's gonna worry you but both tires blew. You were damned, excuse me, very lucky not to be dead. I asked all the guys, never seen the likes of it. If you'd been on the highway, well, I don't wanna think about it."

"The tires were brand new!" Tempest protested. "You installed them last month."

"I know."

Frustrated at the man's pace, Tempest struggled to hold her temper. "Well, they've got to be under warranty or something. Obviously, they were fault–"

"Dr. Ivory? Uh, warranty's not an issue here. You see, each tire had five roofing nails shoved in deep." He chewed loudly. "Now, we've seen one or two, mebbe even three if I dream a little, but never five. And never in both tires."

"Five?" Tempest tried unsuccessfully to visualize a roofing nail. Whatever they were, where in God's name would she have run over ten?

"Yup. You didn't run over a box of 'em, did ya?"

"Of course not!"

It sounded like he blew a bubble. The pop snapped in Tempest's ear. "Sorry ma'am, just a little grease-monkey humour. Anyways, the bike's all set."

"Fine. I'll pick it up tomorrow."

"Okee dokee." The chewing grew louder. Tempest started to put the phone down. "Dr. Ivory?"

"Yes," she replied, grabbing the phone back to her ear.

"You don't have any enemies, do ya?"

It took her a while to settle after the call. What on

earth did the gum boy mean? Enemies? Ridiculous! There must be some simple explanation, some construction zone she'd crossed.

The music sheets stared at her, the notes a pockmarked jumble. Standing, she tried a few diaphragm and butt exercises, loosening, tightening, loosening, trying to focus...still her mind wandered. She shoved the roofing nails from its forefront; up popped Amelia's suicide—something amiss at home, she was certain. The first child's fury still gnawed her; she would harass Terry Brethour for the truth. Then Vita's death. Curiously, she sensed no rage. The shamrocks troubled her but she refused to go down that memory lane.

She pulled up the arms of her baggy sweatshirt. Puckered scars, some red and recent, but most white with age, marred both wrists. Tempest bit her lower lip and ran a finger along the freshest. The soft stinging raised the hair on her arms. The wounds were a blessing, proof that she, Tempest Ivory, had a soul, had emotions and most importantly, felt. If she'd seen the same in a client, Dr. Ivory would be concerned. Self-mutilation, especially fancied by young women, was a classic symptom of those who are dissociated from pain and abuse and are emotionally numb. Fuck that! she thought, reluctantly yanking down the sleeves. Who knows? Maybe Gilda's dress has short sleeves. That didn't bear thinking about.

She pushed beyond, driving her thoughts to a nagging notion. Was there something else, something missing? She began wandering about her dark cottage, working her facial muscles, looking for a sign. The movement and concentration refreshed her. She

padded onto her deck. The patchy white skin of a couple of young Holsteins, seemingly chatting near her
back fence, glowed in the moonlight.

"Come and take a walk with me," she sang, her voice
rising over her head and billowing toward the cows.
Four black ears twitched and the whites of the cows'
eyes rolled her way. One of the heifers stamped and
belched.

Tough audience. She stepped back in, down the short
hallway and yanked open the front door. The smell of
burning cedar and wet grass greeted her as she
plopped into the shadows on the front steps. The door
shut behind her with a sharp click.

It came to her a few seconds later as the sound reg-
istered. The door!? She pulled herself up and turned.
It was closed. The box. Tempest shoved open the door
and looked inside the entrance. The box that acted as
a doorstop was gone. And so were her family secrets.

THE SPRAY GENTLY SOAKED THE MINIATURE SEED
pots. Patrick twisted the shut-off valve and bent for a
closer look. The palm-like leaves of the hollyhocks
were very apparent and he gently plucked a couple of
weak ones and tossed them aside. The rows of poppies were germinating on schedule but he knew he
had a lot of culling and transplanting ahead. Now,
when he saw the tiny masses bunched in each pot, he
wished he'd been more careful to independently sow
the minuscule seeds. The lupins were late but upon
careful examination, he noted a slight ridge in the soil
where the developing seed would soon break
through.

As a police officer and a single man, Patrick Painter's

life was one endless shift on call. Though his schedule was set on a weekly basis, the limited number of staff at the Sidney/North Saanich Detachment necessitated huge chunks of overtime. The money nestled in the bank quick enough, but he often railed against the relentless demands of protecting society.

Gardening gave him unspeakable joy: he delighted in triggering growth, fussing over the vagaries of pruning and struggling organically with insect incursions. Most gratifying was his green thumber's insight into the earth's natural order and common sense. Satisfied with the future of his garden, he rewound the hose, switched off the water tap and headed inside.

His house was almost insignificant. Patrick lived in Sidney, a small town near the end of the Peninsula. He envied Dr. Ivory. Would that he could afford North Saanich's larger lot prices! His small, square yard was peppered by clumps of blooming daffodils, fading crocuses and emerging tulips. Not a blade of grass to be seen, soon the yard would become his unique and colourful canvas, brimming with a parade of pigments from mid-May to mid-October.

As he removed his jacket, he noticed a letter in his pocket. He paused, puzzling for a moment over where it had come from. Then he remembered the small man at his mother's grave site. Throwing the jacket on his bruised couch, he ripped open the envelope and unfolded a sheet of thick yellow stock. A smaller, white sheet fell free. He reached down, grabbed it and began reading as he padded to the fridge. Patrick choked on his first gulp of light beer.

Anxiously, he fumbled to open the yellow paper. A brief message was typed on the letterhead of a local law firm, Higgins, Tully, Hilliar & Mason. He started reading.

Dear Mr. Leonard P. Painter,

*I am acting on behalf of your wife. She engaged me
shortly before her demise. Her request was simple:
deliver the enclosed to you after her death.*

*Should you have any questions, please do not
hesitate to call me.*

Sincerely,

Kim Hilliar

He finished the beer in two long swallows. He
glanced back at the envelope. An easy mistake. It was
addressed to Mr. L. P. Painter, initials Patrick shared
with his father. He examined the white sheet carefully. The paper was old, yellowing slightly at the corners. It was deeply creased, having been folded several times. There was no salutation, just a couple of sen-
tences, written in broad, round strokes. The note was
signed V.W.

A woman's hand? No way to tell. He'd always
laughed when, reading the English mysteries his mother loved and bought for his birthday, the bloody-mar-
vellous detective was able to correctly deduce gender
from handwriting. He'd never found it so obvious.

He went to the refrigerator for another beer. Guzzled
it quickly. Who was V.W? Was she writing to his
father? If so, how did it come into his mother's hands?
If not, why would his mother send the letter? Patrick

sat on his lumpy couch, mentally rolling through the questions.

One thing was certain. He'd find out before the other L. P. Painter. He reread the note, whistling quietly under his breath.

TWELVE

A guardian angel watches.
—GILDA, ACT 1

Twenty violin bows slashed, their quivering strings hopscotching ever higher. The shivery sound of a single trumpet towered above them. The bows stopped, the trumpet's last notes trailed for a few seconds, then faded. The chorus inhaled as one and opened their mouths.

No voices were heard. The concert hall was strangely quiet. Tempest, her mouth agape, lungs bursting, stared wildly at the ghostly figures beside her. Though she strived, she too was mute.

Slowly a voice entered her head. Initially she wasn't aware of it but suddenly it was deafening. She cowered and the voice receded. The chorus vanished. She stood alone on the stage and recognized the voice. A single boy soprano effortlessly singing the shockingly high notes of *Pie Jesu.* Not just any boy soprano. The vocal purity, the tremendous line, the chilling interpretation could only belong to one singer. Her brother. Summoning her, tugging her.

The song changed, deepened into the throbbing yet

thrilling music of the curse in *Rigoletto*. Underlying it
was another tune, a ragged rhythm that gasped and
clicked. The boy was singing *Ch'io gli parli*, Count
Monterone casting a scourge upon the hunchbacked
jester. Still she felt her brother's swelling presence, an
implacable tidal undertow.

Tempest woke with a jerk. She lay dazed, echoes of
her brother's voice caressing her ears, images of his
face haunting her thoughts, the mechanical rhythm
pulsing. Tears flowed, she attempted no control.
You've been gone so goddamn long, she sobbed. What
do you want?

PATRICK PULLED HIS PICKUP TRUCK INTO THE CAPITAL
City Marina yard and squeezed into a parking spot. He
switched the engine off and yanked on the emergency
brake. The marina swelled with boats and crews, many
tackling last-minute repairs before spring fishing.

He watched with growing amusement as a fifty-foot
yacht, christened *The Office*, slid slowly in and out of a
berth, its baby-boomer skipper frantically wheeling
while a pair of teens scampered from stem to stern,
dropping buoys and shouting directions. An old salt—
sou'wester pulled low over his forehead—rowed nearby in a small dingy, nicknamed *The Ol' Fool*. An ageing
Labrador perched on the tiny bow. Patrick wouldn't
swear to it, but he thought both were grinning.

He sighed and reread the document which had
stunned him that morning.

When he had arrived at the detachment a couple of
hours earlier, he'd been dismayed to find a pile of fingerprint information on top of his already cluttered
desk. He knew he should be thankful the computer

check had come through faster than expected but that left him with the boring task of sorting, looking for any matches between the prints found on the matchbook and those from the staff and students of the Perpetual Soul.

A deadbeat where small talk was concerned, Patrick mumbled greetings to the secretary and constable on phone duty, brewed a strong cup of tea and dropped into his ancient chair. Most of the other officers of the detachment had new, ergonomically correct chairs. As the newest member, Patrick was given an old, wooden swivel chair from government surplus until the arrival of next year's equipment. Of course, no one guaranteed him a new seat, the money could be spent on a zillion more urgent articles. He'd watched his fellow officers carefully as the chair was pushed his way, several pairs of eyes hoping for a negative reaction. He grabbed one of the arms, swung into the hard seat, swivelled into place at his tiny cubicle and picked up the phone.

He'd recently asked for and received a move from northern B.C. back to the Island on compassionate grounds, and there had been plenty of evidence of anger and jealousy in the early days of his transfer, cops not being the most subtle of folk. Patrick knew not to sweat the small stuff. He'd made that mistake in Fort St. John. He was thankful and relieved to be able to support his dying mother. If only he'd returned sooner or, better still, had never left. Her death within a month of his return acted as both salve and salt in his wounded relationships within the detachment.

He knew his immediate purchase of a thick seat and back cushion caused great amusement, but the whisperings and challenging glances faded as he began doggedly handling more than his fair workload. His relaxed acceptance of overtime and extra duty curried additional brownie points each day.

The computer had found a match. Patrick looked at the name and tried to visualize the person. He shook his head, unsure...too many fingerprintees. He couldn't remember individual faces. No matter, he'd know soon enough. What to do next? That's where it would get interesting. He was about to leave when he noticed a curious notation beside one name:

Sister Gabriel, born Darcy Winsloe,
Victoria, BC, 19/8/67.

Special remarks:
Pickup Victoria, soliciting 24/6/84;
charges dropped IE;

Officer: L. P. Painter, VPD.

Well, I'll be damned, thought Patrick. The old man arrested one of the nuns for prostitution! He leaned back and whistled lightly. Insufficient evidence, well, well, well. Wonder what that's all about? Bolting upright, he gathered the papers and hurriedly signed out. He had to know.

Or so he had thought. Now, twenty minutes later at the marina with the paper in his hand and his father's boat in view, Patrick was no longer so certain. He hadn't spoken to the old man since the dunking and was uneasy as to his reception. Probably be told to take a long walk off a short pier, he thought. He drummed the steering wheel as *The Office* bashed against the dock for the last time. The teens tied her down and leaped ashore as though the ship were aflame. A glance at the captain made him laugh. The barrel-chested man slumped at the wheel, running a dishevelled handkerchief across his glistening brow. Relief roared out of him like the north wind.

Ah, what the hell! Patrick thought, clambering out of his truck. It's only salt chuck.

TEMPEST GUNNED THE BIKE ALONG WEST SAANICH Road and zig-zagged half a mile of dotted lines to test the new wheels and her swollen ankle. The rubber caught nicely and her muscle shrieks lessened. Satisfied, she geared down and began planning. In eighty minutes, she was expected at the McPherson Playhouse for first rehearsal. Just enough time to rattle Alice Penderghast's dirty cage.

Turning into the cracked driveway, she nudged around the same broken toys to park the Pig. No sign of Brethour's old rattletrap. Thank God for small mercies, she thought, and hobbled up the steps to pound on the cracked front door.

THIRTEEN

The storm draws nearer!
And the night grows darker.
—SPARAFUCILE, ACT 3

"Thinkin' of comin' aboard, are ya?"

"With the Captain's permission," Patrick replied with a respectful salute.

"Seems I got no choice," his father said eyeing the gunwale, "you'll either chuck me overboard or throw me in jail."

Patrick stepped on board and gave his father a professional once-over. The hair was still grey and the eyes dark, but was it a trick of the midday light or did the old man seem slightly stooped?

"Whatchya want, anyway?"

In a bit of bravado, Patrick eased onto the gunwale and tried to look relaxed. *Hope to Christ he doesn't pop me one.* "Jus' thought I'd check up on you, see that you got out all right."

Painter Senior snorted. "No damn thanks to you." He turned his attention to buffing a brass fitting.

That familiar movement—the bend of his back, the sun-burned neck, the gentle caressing—choked the air from Patrick's lungs. He chewed his tongue to quench the tears.

He was five years old, watching his father fondle the old green Plymouth. Even though he didn't understand sexual expression, he was disturbed by the devotion of those huge hands.

"Outta m'way, boy. Can't you see I'm working?"

"But, Dad, can't I–"

The slap was a snap of lightning. Patrick's face collapsed, a red welt emerging, but he staved off the tears by biting his tongue.

"Why d'ya make me do it?" Painter shook his head. "Told ya time and again. But you don't listen."

He yanked Patrick up by his shirt collar. "Don't want ya near 'er. Ya got that?" He raised a fist as big as a loaf. Patrick shrank. "Go to your mother."

How he hated that car! And envied it. It crushed him to see the man he adored bestow more love and affection on a box of metal and chrome than his own flesh and blood. Soon, he hated the man. One day, he would destroy the car.

"Well?" Patrick realized his father was questioning him. He blinked and the marina came back into view. "What're ya really here for, then?"

Patrick shrugged, uncertain how to proceed. His father's reactions were always a toss-up and Patrick had learned long ago the vagaries of tossing a coin: no matter how often you flicked one, your chances of landing heads was less than even. He hurled up a loonie anyway.

"Saw your name as arresting officer today. Popped up on a routine fingerprint check."

Leonard Painter kept on buffing. "Must be on a hundred files."

Patrick nodded. "Just wondered if you might remember, is all. You brought in a young girl for soliciting."

Painter's scar glistened as he smiled. Patrick dreaded that smile, the one that didn't reach the old man's cheeks, much less his eyes. "Nothin' new 'bout that."

Patrick dropped off the gunwale and peered overboard. He was enjoying stringing out the mystery. "Mebbe, mebbe not," he said to the dark waters below.

The hand halted but the head remained bowed. "Whaddya mean?"

Patrick turned and smiled, taking great care not to let it slip past his lips. "How often d'you arrest a nun for being on the game?"

Leonard Painter's head snapped up. "A what?"

"You heard me. A nun, a Sister of the Perpetual Soul."

The old man started to laugh, deep rumbles from his chest struggled for air. Patrick waited, watching as the coin dropped, tails up. When he could catch his breath, Painter swabbed tears with the cleaning cloth, drawing a yellowish stain across his forehead. "That's a good one," he finally whispered, shoulders still jumpy. "Sweet Jesus, a nun."

"Name's Sister Gabriel."

"Gabriel?" His father shook his head and bent again to his task. "Rings no bell."

He watched his father closely. "You knew her as Winsloe, Darcy Winsloe."

Leonard Painter hesitated a titch too long in his rubbing. "Winsloe? Never heard of her."

"Mebbe this'll refresh your memory," Patrick said, thrusting the fingerprint results under his father's nose.

Painter deliberately wiped his hands, then dropped the cloth to the deck. He slowly pulled reading glasses out of his breast pocket, cleaned them carefully—*For Christ's sake! Get on with it!*—and reached for the paper. The yellow stain grew suddenly, magnified by the spectacles. Patrick hopped back aboard the gunwale, eyeing his only parent.

Painter read the notes, shook his head, read them again very slowly. "Says I brought her in, so I must of, but can't say as I remember." He flashed probing eyes at his son. "So, she's a nun now, is she?" He removed the glasses and dropped the paper beside him. "Well, well, well," he mumbled, scooping brass cleaner onto his rag, "musta done somethin' right, eh son?"

"You're sure you don't remember? I mean, how many girls wouldya've arrested for soliciting back in '67? It's Victoria, for Christ's sake."

"You think I'm lying, boy?" The dangerous smile returned. Usually meant a stroke or three of the bottle.

When Patrick was younger, he'd watch for the uneven step and hesitant speech. Arm hairs prickling, he'd back away, unharmed. The times he'd misjudged or been taken by surprise taught him to read his father's arrival more carefully than even the local tide tables. Having to wait out the night on a sand knoll was nothing compared to the beatings.

Before he'd discovered the courage not to sail, he'd stood, one calm June night, in his damaged Laser and watched helplessly as a ferry plowed toward him. The thrum of those powerful engines, the churning white waters, the enveloping blackness were nothing compared to hearing the front door click and the old man's uneven footsteps. And that brittle smirk.

"Or mebbe you think the old man's losin' it."

"No, no, nothing like that," Patrick replied quickly. He dropped to his feet. "I, I just thought you might remember, that's all." He paused and cleaned his left thumbnail. "Heard about the suicides?"

Painter's eyes flashed. "At the academy? Who hasn't? Place's gone crazy, girls hangin' themselves." He eyed his son. "You on it?"

Patrick nodded, expecting his father to demand more details. "Aunt Winifred's in a real mess."

"Yeah?" Painter pursed his lips. "Wouldn't know. Don't talk to her much." He snapped closed the lid on the brass cleaner and started below deck. Patrick stared at his back, wondering how he could be so disinterested. Typically, there was nothing his father enjoyed more than hearing the nitty-gritty of the area's latest case. Except maybe for giving his son professional advice.

"You thinking o' callin' her?" Patrick shouted down to him. "I'm sure she'd appreciate the support."

No reply. Patrick waited another minute, then moved to the hatch.

"That old bitch?" Painter's voice was muffled. His head poked up. Surprised, Patrick stumbled back and flushed.

"Ha! Steer clear of her, boy, she's got more balls 'n Farmer Jones' prize bull."

"YOU'RE ANGRY AT HER, YOU HATE HER!"

Alice Penderghast dropped her head into her hands. Her hands flew through her hair, and it flopped about in greasy strings. The airless room stank of beer, stale cigarettes and angst.

"You've every right," Tempest continued, "look what

she's done to you. She didn't think of you, did she? Or what you might go through." Come on, Alice! she thought. Come on! You want to talk.

Alice started to whimper.

Tempest awkwardly patted the distraught woman's knee. Why was it so hard for her to comfort adults? A distressed child yanked her heart; an anguished parent just irritated. "It's okay. No one's blaming you. These feelings are natural."

Alice blew her nose and peered up under reddened eyes. "People think I didn't try to help," she wailed. "That it musta been my fault."

"No, no, you mustn't say that. Children can have many little problems that just accumulate. It's no one person's responsibility."

Of course, Tempest believed exactly the opposite. She'd seen this pathetic scenario too many times: an incompetent and incapable young mother—after all, Alice was only twenty-five with a nine-year-old daughter—whose early pregnancy and single-parent responsibilities scotched whatever sorry little work opportunities to which she may have aspired. No choice but to accept welfare until the child was in school and then to find, in her twenties, her half-hearted grade ten was worth little more than hunt-and-peck typing skills and considerably less than a young man of similar age with a strong back. Who could blame her for continuing welfare and choosing the young man? And then another young man and another?

Indeed, the gnawing anger, crushing frustration and emotional drain of parenthood were hardly surprising. Even couples who were emotionally and financially secure often despaired at the grinding parental load.

Tempest contemplated Alice Penderghast, the ill-kept body and unexplored mind, the messy household, the less than absolutely bloody useless prick of a boyfriend, and sensed the potent mixture of guilt and grief seeping from the young woman, like sour perfume from her pores. The woman was completely incapable of coping; her abject self-absorption impeded her judgement. No wonder poor Amelia sought an escape from her gloomy legacy. A little push and who knows? She felt Amelia pressing against her chest, like a burden. The child needed to be set free.

She started by covering ground familiar to Alice. "How long have you and Terry been together?"

"The fifteenth of next month, it'll be our first anniversary." Her head came up with a small show of pride.

"A year, that's great," Tempest said wondering how many other one-year anniversaries Alice had celebrated. "How did Amelia feel about him?"

"Oh, they were great friends, right from the start. In fact, they knew each other before we did." She giggled. "Isn't that weird?"

Tempest nodded, alarm bells sounding ever so softly. She prepared to strike.

"Seems Ter saw her at work—he's in construction, you know, real clever with his hands, is my Terry, done all sortsa stuff round here—said hello or some such. 'Melia wasn't at the academy then." She paused as though struck by a thought.

"Yes?"

Alice's face collapsed. Tempest waited. As any police officer, priest, talk-show host or therapist knew, silence was often the best response. Alice's fingers raked her hair. Finally she whispered, "She'd be alive if they hadn't gotten her in that place, don't you think?"

No, I don't think so, Tempest thought, but she just nodded slightly. "You were telling me how Amelia met Terry."

The swollen face brightened. "Oh yes. Some boy was teasing her and Terry ran him off and walked her home. She musta been upset about the boy 'cause she ran straight to her room. When I saw him, well..." She paused, a soft pink spread up her neck and throat. "I had ta thank him, didn't I? So I offered him a cup of coffee and...you know, one thing led to another."

"And Amelia? She was happy?"

Alice nodded her head vigorously. "Oh yeah, they did a lotta stuff t'gether. Sometimes even without me." She eyed Tempest. "That's how hard Ter worked to make her his own."

The alarm bells increased. *You don't know how hard...or do you?* "How'd Amelia respond to these just-the-two-of-them outings?"

"How d'ya think? Course she was tickled pink."

"What sort of things did they do together? Get ice-cream, go skating, that sort of thing?"

"Sure," Alice replied unconvincingly, her face rash now a bright red, "they did all kinds of things."

"Like?"

"I dunno, for Christ's sake! I wasn't there." Her hands returned nervously to the dull hair. Tempest expected clumps the colour of sodden leaves to fall free at any minute. "They just did stuff. What's it matter, anyway?"

"Doesn't really. Just curious, that's all. So Amelia adapted."

"Course she did. Why wouldn't she? A man around the house, someone who cared–" She stopped and fingered her shirt tails. "Don't look at me like that!"

Tempest kept watching, waiting to see if her strategy worked.

"Don't!" she shouted. "What're ya tryin' to make me say? That Ter...that he...well, I won't! Why, he was even showin' her his new hobby. Most guys wouldn't have the time a day for a kid like her."

"No, I don't suppose they would. What's the hobby?"

"Photography," she said proudly. "Ter's an artist. He takes real good pictures–took some of 'Melia–thinks he might sell 'em."

The ringing filled her head. "May I see them?"

"What?"

"The pictures of Amelia."

Alice suddenly withdrew; Tempest could feel her closing ranks, slipping from her control. "No. They...they're the last shots of my baby. I don't want you touchin' 'em." She stood, one hand scratching her head. "I'd like you to go now."

Tempest wanted to stay, to push further. She knew the woman was troubled, torn between her responsibilities as a mother and her independence as a woman. One look at the set of Alice's jaw told her she'd get no further. At least not today. The steady weight of Amelia remained. She wondered how she would sing.

As she started the bike and tugged on her helmet, Alice stood quietly at the door. Her mouth moved and she pointed skyward but Tempest couldn't quite hear the words. A few seconds later, Tempest glanced in her side mirror. Terry Brethour's truck chirped to a stop on the road. She knew he saw the green bike and edged to the side to watch. The car whirled into the drive and jerked still. Brethour jumped out and stared at her. Even from a distance, Tempest could sense his anger. He stuck a middle finger in the air. She gunned the Pig and shot into traffic.

ALICE SHUT THE DOOR WITH A RAGGED SIGH. WHY did it matter if Dr. Ivory knew Terry was going to do the roof? Anyway, would he? She leaned against the scuffed wood, banging her head. Again, she struggled with those secret thoughts of relief, the ones that leaped into her being whenever she thought of a future with Terry, now cut free from parental responsibility. She wasn't really glad that Amelia was dead. Must be just a phase. She'd miss her soon, she was sure. Still...

She fingered the roll of film in her pocket. She was almost afraid to look at it, much less get it developed. She was thinking of the photos in the magazine—disgusting bits of glossy paper—she'd found along with it in the basement when she stubbed her toe on a carton. She stooped and tried to push it aside. Another bit of Terry's junk. Its weight surprised her so she popped open the lid. The jagged edges and broad round heads of aluminum roofing nails winked at her. She grunted and shoved it against the wall. She'd hoped he'd do the roof as promised, though when she was alone and nicely beyond sober, she conceded that Terry was a bit of a lazy jerk.

An overwhelming feeling of exhaustion knocked her like a fist. The depression, an ever-present burden, kept her low and enervated. She had thought that her listlessness came from coping with Amelia. Now with the girl gone, the weight of living still seemed massive.

She felt the cool plastic of the film case. Musta been more of the same trash from the guys at the site. He'd brought it and the magazine home by accident. No other reason for her Terry to have such filthy pictures of children. She knew what men were like, God knew she'd slept with enough of them. Worse still were those horny pigs in construction. They always wolf-whistled at you as you walked by, calling names, makin' you feel like a piece of dirt. Not her Ter, of course. A freelancer, he only worked on contract. He didn't really belong with the rest of 'em.

Alice heard the tires screech and the car door slam. Instead of opening the door and greeting her man, she shuffled into the living room, cast aside some old newspapers and sweatshirts and plunked down. Alice gripped the roll as tightly as she could. With her free hand, she wrenched her hair.

Still the nagging feeling of knowing nudged to the surface.

FOURTEEN

Not allowed, not able
To do anything but mock!
—RIGOLETTO, ACT 1

"Seven years, imagine! Arms up."

"Excuse me?" Tempest glanced down at the thin woman expertly measuring her hips and waist.

"Up!" Gertie Clement repeated while jotting numbers in a tiny book.

"I meant," Tempest replied, hoisting both arms out from her sides, "what's seven years?" They were in a small dressing room, backstage of the McPherson Playhouse. Tempest felt the familiar rustlings of panic in her gut, tightness in her chest and throat. She was to sing on stage in an hour and she was so excited, she trembled. Deep breaths, she told herself. Deep breaths, deep! Calm down.

She was thrilled to finally be part of an opera. Such a grand event! She knew her music, soon they'd start blocking, staging and musical rehearsals. All in just a few days. Tempest was amazed to find how much longer actors had for rehearsal. In the theatre, the stage director wanted you to arrive as a blank page upon which he would write. In opera, the script and direction were already given by the composer. The interpretation was up to the stage director but the inflexion, phrasing, all came from the singer and composer. Exceptional composers were those who almost wrote the staging in the music. Puccini was famous for this: amazingly you always knew where you were supposed to be and what you were supposed to be doing. There were obvious general written gestures, like "she places the candelabra near the dead body," but in addition you had to listen to the orchestral accompaniment to find out whether you were supposed to stand still or move. Tempest had read somewhere that Maria Callas used to say, whenever you're on stage and don't know what to do with your hands, nine times out of ten, stand still and listen to the music and you'll know. Whether it's to run over to the table or out the door or to the chair to sit quietly, you'll know.

God, I hope so, she prayed. Verdi's staging wasn't as obvious.

Gertie popped a small blue pencil back into her mouth and pulled the tape around Tempest's torso. She muttered numbers under her breath and grabbed the pencil. "You're a big one, aren't you?" She scribbled in the booklet. "Seven years is the wait for *Magic Flute* tickets in Germany."

Her pre-singing exhilaration collapsed. Stinging from the comment on her size, Tempest didn't know what to say. How about: Oh, I've seen bigger? Or maybe the time-worn: It's muscle. You know, the diaphragm? Of course, here she was being fitted by Gertie Clement, with what, thirty years' experience, having tailored dresses for hundreds of singers. Who was she trying to fool? And why? Her extra weight had been a salvation in her youth and a benefit to her voice.

Fuck it! she thought, keenly disappointed in her continued sensitivity to her weight. She'd wasted years of energy on the male-orchestrated beauty myth. With her psychological training and one-on-one analysis sessions, she thought she'd vanquished that beast. One minor comment—possibly completely innocent, seeing how the woman *was* measuring her for costume—and she slipped right back. A chubby teenager again, schoolboy taunts chasing her home.

Tempest clenched her fists and stopped sucking in her gut. *Fuck you!*

"Imagine anything like that in Canada?" Gertie rambled on, unaware of her offence.

Tempest kicked herself for overreacting. "Like what?" she said, arms now overhead.

"A seven-year wait for opera tickets..." Gertie stopped and shoved the measuring strip into her bib pocket. "...aren't you listening?" She peered up at Tempest through huge, thick glasses. Tempest felt as though she were a bug impaled in a case, so close was the scrutiny of the magnified eyes.

It took Tempest a while to remember where she'd seen that colour of green before: silvery with yellowish veining. She had it: the underside of the cabbage leaves she'd often see in late fall along Wallace Drive in Central Saanich.

"Are you...? No, never mind. Ever tried carrot juice?"

Tempest stopped herself from shaking her head. "I'm sorry, carrot juice?"

Gertie reached into a coiled mass of grey-streaked

hair and adjusted a pin. "Real good for concentration. You oughta try some." She patted at her hair, fingers nimbly diving in, securing a pin then swiftly moving on. "I drink a glass a day. Makes the world of difference." She paused. "There's something familiar 'bout you...that hair...sure you haven't sung here before?"

"Positive."

Gertie stroked her bib, shaking her head slightly. "When I heard your voice...I thought...oh, never mind. I've seen so many young singers." She dipped into her bib and popped something orange in her mouth. Chewing she said: "Vitamin C. How old d'you think I am?"

Uh oh. Dangerous territory. Tempest hated when women asked that question. Seemed a loser every way. They always wanted to be younger. Somehow you were supposed to pick an age that complimented but wasn't ridiculously young. Or, God help you, too old. She could never tell. At twenty-eight, anyone over thirty-five was old, over fifty-five simply ancient. She'd put Gertie even farther, in the kissin' the grave category.

"I'm not really—"

"I'm sixty-two. Fit as a fiddle and proud of it!" Gertie shoved a hand again into her bib and pulled out several small pill vials. "These're the ticket. Natural vitamins, minerals, herbs." She dropped the pills back into the pocket. "Heaven knows what's in the stuff they call food today." The pale green eyes stared up at her. "You know they add fish cells to tomatoes?"

Tempest shook her head.

"Let me see your nails."

Before she could respond, Gertie had Tempest's right hand in hers. "Not bad nails, but could use some gelatin. Skin's nice." She held the hand up to the light. "Hmmm...yellowish tinge. Blood's okay? No jaundice or anything?"

"No." She could feel her throat constricting, body tensing, all the relaxation gained from her earlier warmup disappearing. Tempest tried to free her hand, to regain inner poise and repose. Today, she needed all her range, the dark for amplitude and volume, the bright to carry. Contrary to common belief, it wasn't the bass in an orchestra that carried, it was that little freakin' triangle, that PING! that sailed to the farthest corner. "Look," she said, "I'm fine. Thanks."

Gertie held tight, started to turn the arm over, cold fingers pushing at Tempest's shirt sleeve. "Let me see—"

Tempest yanked hard, too hard for a sixty-plus woman to resist. Gertie pitched forward and let go. Tempest threw up her free arm and caught the dresser by the shoulder.

"No need to be violent!" Gertie pushed back and straightened her bib and hair.

"I'm, I'm sorry. I didn't mean..." Tempest faltered. What could she say? How to explain the scars? "Could we just get this over with?" she asked finally, her voice sharper than planned. "Please."

Gertie hitched up her floral dress and smoothed the checked bib. "Whatever you say, Miss," she said, green eyes downcast. "You're the star."

Shit! Tempest thought. I've waited all my career to be called that. Now it just makes me feel like a jerk.

SISTER WINIFRED SLIPPED INTO THE ECHOING SILENCE of the chapel. If ever she needed an answer, it was now. The academy was back into a strict regime, her attempt as Mother Superior—how long would that last?— at re-establishing a routine as a panacea for students, parents and faculty. She had been mildly surprised at how quickly and easily the girls coped—of course with teens you never knew—slightly disappointed at her staff's melodramatic response and more than a touch irritated with the relentless parental pressure.

She dropped into the back pew, comforted by its simplicity and hardness. The past few days had been catastrophic, an affliction cast down by whom? The Lord God Almighty? The bishop? (One and the same, from his manner.) The alignment of the stars? Or perhaps the academy itself?

She shook her head at such ridiculous fancy. None of the above, of course. The girls died at their own hands from grievous circumstances beyond her control. She had to believe that. She leaned forward, palms pressing on the wooden railing.

Exhausted from insomnia, disquiet and apprehension, Winifred stared at her fingers, astonished to find them trembling. The tremor spread octopus-like, tentacles shuddering along her limbs and core. In the past forty-eight hours, Mother Superior had been subjected to endless questioning by the police, by her staff, by the students' parents, by the bishop. In turn, she had conducted her own inquisition, querying students, staff and parents. To no avail. She could find no reason for the suicides. Of course, she didn't interview Vita Bell's parents. How could she?

That was the issue Winifred brought to the holy altar.

She'd been taught that the religious life was lonely and slow. Only in isolation could one realize the staggering need for God. First a gradual renunciation of self—bit by bit, moment by moment—until one was empty and bereft. Followed by muteness of lips and heart to deepen the relationship. Finally, a minute-by-minute waiting for Him to fill you. Slack off and you were lost.

Throughout her religious life, Winifred had sought His grace, struggled to live in His presence. But other than a momentary transcendence once or twice—which, she admitted, could have been more to do with fasting than spiritual awakening—she'd failed in her heavenly pursuit. Nevertheless, she tried praying, deliberating emptying her mind and soul to facilitate reception.

Nothing.

She shook her head and began pacing the narrow aisles. Sometimes movement freed her, opened her to impression.

Still no answer.

The glow of a single votive candle drew her near the raised altar. Perhaps a token payment? How pagan, she thought, fumbling for a coin in her pocket. She lit the candle beside the one already flickering, then concentrated on their yellow flames.

No use, she thought. Whatever heavenly link might have been there, was broken long ago.

She sighed and began to turn away when something glossy caught her eye. Through the slit in the coin box, she could see something.

Paper?

That little blighter, she thought, immediately angered. Several months back, she'd found notes of a disturbing nature stuffed into the box. As the sole key holder, Winifred had told no one. Instead, she kept vigil, using a confessional as a blind—appropriate, she thought at the time, as it was the place to reveal sins— night after night until she nabbed the culprit, note in hand.

At first the delinquent had the audacity to lie, then to cry, and finally to flee. Winifred caught her easily— she'd popped the catch on the chapel door so that it would lock upon contact—and wrenched Sydney Mayne's wiry body around.

Winifred pushed the child into a pew and lectured her on the horrors of the deed. Despite the tirade and threats of religious condemnation, Sydney's brown eyes remained clear and her small jaw steady. Winifred was running out of punishment possibilities when she struck precious blood.

"I'll have to phone your parents," she said, expecting results from the tried-and-true threat.

"Go ahead," the child replied.

Winifred was a little taken aback by Sydney's bravado. "Well, depending on their reaction, this could mean expulsion."

That got the girl's attention. Her back stiffened. "You mean kick me out?" she asked, eyes wide.

Ah ha! thought Winifred. Gotcha, you little beggar. "In a New York minute."

Then came more tears. This time Winifred knew they were real. The child was terrified of being sent home. Not too unusual. In her tenure at the academy, she'd overheard heated shouting a couple of times when parents arrived to pick up an expelled child. Then she felt guilty, worried at the treatment the girls might receive once forsaken by the safety of the Old Soul.

I can't believe she's at it again, she thought, staring at the coin box. Pursing her lips, she unlocked the box and removed the foreign objects.

One look and her heart faltered. The tremble returned. Unable to catch her breath, Sister Winifred slid down beside the votive table. Three black and white photographs fluttered to the altar.

FIFTEEN

Perhaps in the world some fear me,
Perhaps some resent me,
Others curse me.

—RIGOLETTO, ACT 1

"Uh, hello Temp...I mean Dr. Ivory"—God, how he hated talking to answering machines—"Patrick, Constable Painter here. I, uh, was wondering if you'd join me for a drink tonight? I'd like to get your opinion, you know, professional." *Shit! You sound like an idiot.* "Got some info you may be interested in. Guess you're not in...well, you know my number. Oh, by the way, steer clear of Terry Brethour, okay? Got a sheet...mostly petty stuff, B&Es, that sort of thing, but I just found out he works part-time as a roofing assistant. He may—" The machine cut him off.

Damn! Patrick stared at his phone. Should he call back? And say what? Brethour might be after her? That he thought of her continuously? He reached for the switchhook. *She'll think I'm such a fool.*

"Painter!" yelled a deep voice beyond his cubicle.

"Yeah?"

"Call on line one."

"Okay." The warning would have to wait. He punched the number. "Constable Painter."

"Patrick?"

The woman's voice was familiar, but so soft he couldn't nail it. "Speaking."

"I need your help."

He frowned, thinking he should recognize the caller. "Yes, ma'am. What's the problem?"

"It's..." the voice cracked then suddenly boomed, "It's Winifred. I...I've found something you should see."

"What?"

"I can't discuss it on the phone. Come right over," she paused. "Please."

THE RESPIRATOR CHUGGED AND RATTLED IN THE same *draw, catch, draw-draw, gurgle, catch* mechanical rhythm that had haunted her dreams since her father's stroke two winters earlier. Tempest marched across the small room to open the blinds, a futile exercise as they revealed a brick wall paled by the dull afternoon light. She snapped on a nearby lamp—she'd never be alone in the dark with her father again—drew a breath of the stale, acrid air of the long-term care hospital and perched in a nearby chair. Sometimes she envied his slumber, his eternal earthly rest. Her contacts itched but when she scratched her eyes, it felt like raking sandpaper across her pupils. If she could only sleep!

The click of the light switch, darkness folding over her like a shroud. Soft blue glow from the flickering TV. Her father reaching for the tape, sliding it into the VCR. His hand finding her thigh.

"*Wanna tea, Dad?*" she'd ask, jumping up quickly, out of

the room before he could answer. The water boiled too fast, there was only so much clattering she could do before the shouting began.

Carefully carrying the tray, setting it near him but not too close. He'd pull at her, brush her budding breasts, eyes fixed on the naked couple rocking and moaning. Resistance brought a lecture.

"What's wrong with you, girl? You a lezzbo or somethin'? Get over here..."

Sitting, tense as a trapped mouse, barely breathing...waiting.

The machines forcing air into her father's pilotless lungs surrounded his bed, standing guard like attentive, peering aides. They were alone now in their concern. For the first few weeks after his stroke, there'd been visits from staff at the school board where he was chief superintendent. Some even brought flowers, though Tempest wondered if they resulted more from guilt than empathy.

Perhaps they knew a different man. She could only hope so. Soon, the visiting troops dwindled in number, then disappeared completely. She looked down and struggled, as always, to reconcile the slack face and still body with her childhood terrors.

Tempest had cosseted and kindled such enmity toward her father that it, along with the base, traitorous devotion that peeked round its edges, had defined her personality more sharply than genetics.

Now, the man who had sheltered her and fed her hatred was gone, leaving an empty, useless shell. Where was the emotional release in confronting a blob? What sort of intervention techniques blasted through an oxygen-deprived fugue?

His eyes fluttered, then opened. Tempest held her

breath, but there was no sign of recognition in the dark blue irises. Still, their gaze encouraged her to speak.

"I've got my first big role," she said, feeling foolish, then surprised at how much she wanted to say that. Ever since she'd received the news, she had been dying to tell someone. "It's Gilda, you know, *Rigoletto.* They loved my voice!"

What the hell? I have to tell someone!

"It's a great part. Verdi, wonderful melody. I, there's a terrific aria, lovely duet between a father and daughter..." She hesitated. His eyes drooped. "And a spectacular quartet."

She looked away, into the brick beyond the window, talking to herself, to an imaginary father. One who cared, who listened, who was proud.

"It's an enormous task, I got called at the last minute. It opens next week."

She saw her reflection in the glass: a damaged woman alone. Her enthusiasm dimmed, quickly turned harsh. She stood and paced around the bed. "It's kinda ironic, you know, it's a story of a deformed father—sound familiar?—and his daughter..." Tempest felt her throat tighten. "But this guy loved his daughter, loved her. Still..." she added in a choked whisper, "he destroyed her."

SIXTEEN

Angel or demon,
What does it matter to you?
I love you...
—THE DUKE OF MANTUA, ACT 1

"I didn't think you'd come." He leaped to his feet and held her chair.

Neither did I, she thought, sitting down. As he leaned forward to guide her, she caught a whiff of aftershave and a glimpse of dirt under his nails. He looked different in civilian clothes, younger, softer somehow. "Not sure I could refuse," she replied as he sat down across from her.

In response to his puzzled look, she smiled slightly. "You are the police, after all."

"Oh, I never meant—" He saw the smile and grinned.

He's pretty sweet. The thought popped into her mind. She immediately chastised herself. *Stick to the business at hand, Pesty.*

"Nothing official."

"Oh, I thought you called to discuss the suicides."

He nodded. "Course. I, I meant coming here—" He looked around at the small, crowded pub near Port

Sidney. "Thought it would be...uh...nicer than at the station." He paused, heat flaming his cheeks.

The waiter came by. Patrick looked up thankfully.

"Care for anything to drink?"

Patrick leaned toward Tempest. "Would you like a glass of wine, maybe share a bottle?"

Tempest felt herself pulling back. "I don't drink. You have orange juice? That's fine."

"I, uh, I'll have a beer."

"Lite or dark?"

"Doesn't matter. Anything. Make it a lite."

The waiter left and with him went their conversational courage. Tempest glanced round the restaurant, spotting a long-term patient. He quickly looked down. She sighed. Nobody ever wanted to admit knowing her in public. It was as if she were a walking contagion. She stared at the sea, dark grey and choppy. Who could blame him? What would you say? "Oh, dear, I'd like you to meet my shrink, Dr. Ivory." That'd go over well.

"Tempest? Uh, Dr. Ivory?"

"What?" She found Patrick staring at her. "Sorry."

"Loonie for your thoughts?"

"Oh, nothing...did you say loonie?" Patrick grinned. *He is cute.* "Aren't you the big spender!"

They both laughed and began chatting about their histories and life on Vancouver Island, sipping the drinks brought by the waiter.

"You've been off the Island?"

"Yes," Tempest replied. "Went to UBC. How 'bout you?"

"Spent four years in Fort St. John."

She raised her eyebrows. "Pretty chilly. With the police?"

He nodded.

"Like it?"

Patrick paused, remembering the long hours of patrolling, the taste of moist, chewy air, the smell of wet cedar and burning wood wrapping his guilt in an old-growth forest. "It's a great escape. You? Like the Lower Mainland?"

Tempest wrinkled her nose. "Thought so at first. You know how Island life, oh, I don't know, squeezes sometimes?"

He laughed. "Squeezes! That's a great way to describe it."

"That used to bother me, still does, I guess, but after a while at university, I realized I was missing something...something intense that I didn't get from the crowds, from the hustle and bustle. I noticed it coming back on the ferry one Christmas. You know Active Pass? Well, as we wound through it, passing the other ferry, I started to feel..." she paused. *Why'm I telling him this?* Her comfort level fell, as it always did when she went beyond idle chatter. She never felt at ease in the world, especially with men. *Just like one of my patients: damaged goods never heal.*

"Go on. How'd you feel?"

"Light-headed," she replied weakly. *Boy, you sound like such a flake!*

"Relieved, you mean?"

He understood! "Well, yes. Like a weight blew off my shoulders. It sounds crazy, but I felt like I was seeing more keenly."

The waiter arrived, giving her time to regroup, reinforce her facade. After some thought, Tempest ordered chicken fingers and fries. She always stuck to simple-to-eat foods when dining out. Pasta and spinach salad were among her favourites, but since eating either could result in a stained blouse or stuff caught in her teeth, she declined. Patrick, blissfully unaware of such Miss Manners-like concerns, ordered spaghetti.

"So, what d'you think's happening at the academy?"

Tempest sipped her orange juice. "Not a simple question."

"I know the girls must of been terribly upset. But they're so young! Who'd even think they'd know much about suicide, much less how to do it?"

"Amelia was depressed, frightened...I'm sure Terry Brethour abused her." In response to his reaction, she raised her hand. "I know I don't have proof. I don't need it. I know. Sexual abuse is a horrible, soul-destroying thing. It results in a powerful sense of shame, something Jean-Paul Sartre called 'a hemorrhage of the soul.'" Tempest paused, eyes downcast. "That child believed that death was better than living, simple as that."

Patrick had no idea who Jean-Paul Sartre was, but his gut told him Tempest was right.

"And Vita?"

"Don't know."

The meals arrived. They ate in silence, watching vessels chug in and out of the port. In the falling light, they ordered tea and dessert: lemon meringue pie. Patrick couldn't believe it when not only did Tempest order dessert—most women were slaves to some diet—she chose his all-time favourite. He liked her appetite, loved her round, sensual figure.

"What'd you think of the shamrocks?"

She almost choked on meringue. Coughing, she grabbed a glass of water.

"You okay?" Patrick was beside her, hand on her back.

She swallowed and nodded. "Fine," she gasped finally. "Tell me about your job. You like it?"

He shrugged, ran dirty nails through his black hair. "For the most part, yeah. Staff Sergeant's a bit of a pain, you know the greyhound syndrome?" He leaned across the table and winked. "Always has to piss on everything." He gave a short, deep laugh. "Some days, though...it's just S Squared, D Squared."

"Excuse me?"

He flushed. "Oh, cop talk. Means...Same, uh, Shit, Different Day."

She laughed.

Patrick flushed deeper.

"I like that. Sounds like it could fit a lotta jobs."

"Yours?"

She frowned then started to smile. "Could be. Could very well be."

"You like being a shrink, sorry, a psychologist?"

It was a question Tempest often asked herself. So far, the jury was out. "I like working with children, helping them. They're so...exposed, so vulnerable."

"Can you help them?"

She raised her eyebrows. "That's the ten-thousand dollar question." She paused, pushing a small piece of crust around her plate. "I think so. I couldn't keep going if I didn't believe..."

"Don't think I could bear it, hearing kids talk about abuse and stuff like that." Patrick shuddered. "Can't stomach the thought of someone hurting them. Guess you're good at it, eh? You seem..." he hesitated, "...so relaxed, in tune with children." He laughed nervously. "I always feel big and clumsy, afraid I'll harm 'em somehow."

Tempest looked at Patrick for a long time. "You'd never harm a child. That's as clear as your love of gardening."

"Huh?"

She nodded toward his fingernails. He stared at his hands, flushed and just barely stopped himself from hiding them under the table. "My mom used to garden," she said, surprised at the words spilling from her mouth. An image of her mother deadheading pansies, bronze hair tumbling over her eyes, filled her mind. She blinked. "She scrubbed and scrubbed but her nails were always dirty." Her voice trailed off, throat suddenly clogged.

"Hope you don't mind," Patrick said sheepishly, "I thought I cleaned 'em." He caught the waiter's eye, and with Tempest's nod of approval, ordered another pot of tea. "Tell me about your music."

When she didn't reply, he mumbled: "Well, I...I saw the piano, the music sheets...your voice..."

"I sing."

"What, in a choir, folk songs, that sorta thing?"

"Opera."

"Oh." He poured tea, added milk to hers and gently shoved the cup near Tempest's hand. "Don't know dick 'bout opera."

So what else is new? Tempest thought, waiting for the inevitable change of subject. Sports or local gossip?

Patrick sipped from a steaming mug. "What's it like? All's I've ever seen is a fat...uh sorry, large lady screaming with bull horns on 'er head. That what it's like?"

"Anything but."

"You...you really can sing like that?"

Tempest nodded, pleased at his interest, but unwilling to engage. Getting close to the danger zone.

"Wow. Love to hear you sometime. Where do you do this opera stuff, downtown?"

"Sometimes." *Time to move on.*

"Singing anytime soon?"

"Your message said something about Terry Brethour. What'd you mean?"

Surprised by the change of subject, Patrick hesitated. "Oh, yeah. Glad you reminded me. Guy's definitely trouble. Seems he sometimes works as a roofing assistant. I just thought, well, what with the nails in your bike, you oughta be careful."

PATRICK PULLED INTO THE DARK LANE OF THE Perpetual Soul and stared up at the glowing silhouette of the bell tower. A long way up or down, depending on your perspective. He suddenly felt a chill and rubbed his hands rapidly together. Patrick hadn't planned on visiting his great-aunt. What he had planned, he was embarrassed to consider. *Well, what'd ya think, Paddy boy? She'd invite you between the sheets?* He sighed and slowly dragged himself from the truck. *A kiss woulda done the trick.* His thoughts lingered on.

Sister Winifred answered his first soft knock.

"Thought you weren't coming," she said. "Been waiting for hours."

"Sorry. Work," he lied, glancing at the statue of the

Virgin Mary. *Forgive me?* "You had something to show me?"

Winifred was already marching down the hall. Patrick quickly caught up with her and followed her along the poorly lit hallways into her office. She glanced each way down the hall, then closed the door.

She walked round her desk, motioned for him to sit and did the same. Slowly, she pulled open a bottom drawer, riffled around for a moment, then extracted a thick envelope. She held it out to him but did not release it into his outstretched hand. "This must be between us."

Patrick shook his head. "You call me here as a relative or as a cop?"

"Relative."

He touched the envelope. "This 'bout the suicides?"

She nodded, her slate-coloured eyes narrowing.

He dropped his arm and sat back. "No can do. You have evidence, you gotta give it to the police. You know that." He reached again. "Give."

"But..." she sighed. "All right."

Patrick dug the photographs out of the envelope. Years of training steadied his expression but still he whistled slightly under his breath. "Where'd you find them?"

"In the votive candle collection box."

"Any idea who put 'em there?" She hesitated. "Come on. You know something, tell me. Who?"

"I'm not sure."

"You have your suspicions, right?"

Winifred fingered the silver cross around her neck.

He held up one photo. Though a grainy black and white shot, a young girl's pale face was clearly visible.

Held, with her back pressed against his groin, by a young boy. They were both naked. Though her eyes were frightened, the girl was attempting a pout; the boy's face was in shadow. He poked a finger at the photo. Something about the kids, especially the curly-haired girl, seemed familiar. "They're probably still suffering. So tell me, I gotta talk to 'em."

"You'll have to wait till tomorrow."

"Uh uhh. These're too hot, you shoulda told me about them on the phone."

"You have to wait...we need Child Protection Services representation."

Patrick blinked.

"It's that child. Sydney. Sydney Mayne."

SYDNEY PEERED OUT OF THE DORM WINDOW AND watched Constable Painter march under brilliant moonlight to his vehicle. *Oh no, she's brought in the cops!*

She slid down and crept back to her bed. She paused, breathing quietly, and waited, listening for the regular sighs of her sleeping mates. Satisfied, she made a quick check between mattresses. Sydney inhaled deeply and wormed into bed. The book was still there.

Silver light poured across the line of small beds as she tried to sleep. *Maybe talk to someone about it? But who?*

A single thought spun round in her head, as though she were counting sheep: Get rid of it!

Get rid of it...get rid of...get rid...get...get...

SEVENTEEN

Softly, softly, let us carry on
With our vengeance;
The one who least expects it
Will be its prey.

—CHORUS, ACT 1

The roar and throb of the bike almost overwhelmed the anger, the memories, the yearning.

Almost. But not quite.

As the Pig raced south along the Patricia Bay Highway, Tempest struggled to let the vibrations, humming through her hands and shoulders, jerk the thoughts free. She envisioned them, chattering off her back in explosive bursts, swirling in the crosswinds and spiralling up into the glittering black sky.

Yellow lights flashed overhead, warning her of an upcoming light change at McTavish. She kicked the Pig and the big green bike stuttered and whined as it slowed. Traffic heading into Victoria was light but a pile-up of oncoming trucks and cars, racing for the last ferry, greeted her at the stop line. Relieved she was not ferrying off the Island, she geared up and bolted as the light turned green.

Nothing like a high-performance motorbike to suffuse you with a sense of power, a dizzying taste of thrill. When she cruised, cutting sharply in and out of slower-moving traffic, Tempest Ivory was untouchable and unreachable. The ability to fly, to escape reality's gravitational pull, was at her fingertips, and her anonymity was guaranteed by helmet and shield.

A light dazzled off her side mirror. *Jesus Christ!* Startled from her reverie, Tempest glanced back. Her stomach clenched. Headlights blazed close behind. She punched her foot and the Pig shot forward, bursting through the brightly lit intersection at Mount Newton Cross Road.

Her eyes flicked down to the speedometer. One hundred thirty kilometres an hour. Fifty above the speed limit. About average for her. For a second she remembered how many penalty points she'd already racked up and slacked off on the accelerator, breathing hard. The side mirrors glowed again, suddenly filled with blinding high beams. The trailing vehicle was within thirty feet, suddenly twenty. *Fuuuck!* She geared up and swept the bike right, into the slow lane.

Tires screeched and the headlamps followed. She looked back again. She began to sweat, dampness clinging to her back, fogging her face shield. In the darkness through Central Saanich, the vehicle's lights glared like entrances to hell. *What the...?* Swerving left around a van, Tempest kicked into a higher gear, rocketing through the Island View interchange.

Curving left as the highway hugged the Martindale Valley, Tempest tried to catch her breath, slow her pounding heart, think! She cut the gas, flipped up the shield and gasped as the stinging, icy air penetrated her face and body. Despite the ricochets of fear along her spine, she grinned. This was what dulled the rage: an adrenaline charge electrified by the sickening yet titillating fear of cutting too close to the edge.

The high beams flashed again. They were so near that Tempest could make out the boxy silhouette of a truck's cab, a shadowy figure hunched over the steering wheel. The truck's bumper shot up to the Pig's rear, missing it by centimetres. Her facade of control crumbled, the absurd velocity no longer her choice. The fun dissipated, replaced by terror. In the right lane, a semi-trailer thundered by, gaining downhill speed. Far ahead, the yellow warning lights flashed.

Tensing, she shoved the throttle and swung right. Almost immediately, she cut power. The truck swerved, skidding into the lane. Brake lights blossomed as the driver realized she was now following him. Tempest pulled back, arms aching, fingers numb.

Too late, the driver saw the red lights of the tractor trailer. Tires screeched as the black vehicle skittered. With a metallic *bang!* it rammed into the trailer's flat, gray back. A hubcap popped off and rattled to a stop.

The trailer *whooshed* as the parking brake was applied and light glittered as the driver cracked open his door and jumped down to the pavement.

The Pig ripped up beside the driver's door of the damaged pickup. Without thinking, Tempest braked sharply and jumped off the stalled bike. She sprinted to the old vehicle. Ignoring the dazed man inside, she reached in and yanked out the keys. With a fluid twist, Tempest turned. She cocked back her right arm. A slight grunt and the keys sailed across the highway into a pasture.

The sound of footsteps startled her. She glanced back into the pickup. Terry Brethour's pale eyes, wide with astonishment, stared at her from the cab. He licked his wormlike lips, reached for the door and began to open his mouth.

"Y'all right?" The man's voice came from the rear of the tractor trailer.

Tempest hustled to the Pig, trying to remember what gear she'd left it in. Would it start? *Please, God.* She climbed on, jammed down the gears and punched the start button. The Pig roared to life. Ignoring the stranger's wave, she wheeled the bike around and scooted into the protective darkness of Sayward Road.

Tempest only dropped her guard upon hearing the crunch of crushed stone under the Pig's wheels. As she rolled up her lane to a stop, she found it difficult to swing free of the bike. Her hands and arms, though trembling, wouldn't release, and her damp thighs hugged the leather seat as if she were clinging to a cliff.

Slowly, carefully, she began relaxing her muscles, mentally soothing and calming them until she was able to pry her fingers and legs free. Numbed hands struggled with her helmet, fingers fumbled with the strap. Walking as though she'd sailed in a tempest, she crept slowly into her house and collapsed on her old leather sofa.

Tears came slowly, accompanied by aching sobs and fluttering breaths. When she felt stronger, she reached over and slipped *The Marriage of Figaro* into her tapedeck. Soon Mozart's achingly beautiful notes rose, saturating her living room. Tempest fell back, submerging under the music's tingling embrace.

She awoke to darkness. Her antique mantle clock rattled, then rang three times, its last hollow bong echoing softly. Tempest moved, winced at her stiffness, rose and stretched. At least her ankle didn't twinge any more. Continued sleep wasn't an option. Too many thoughts pressed against her forehead.

She brewed decaffeinated tea, then laughed softly. She wouldn't sleep now, no matter what. She tossed the tea—she found it weak and unsatisfying at the best of times—and made orange pekoe. She leaned against the counter and dug into a tub of Häagen-Dazs Chocolate Chocolate Chip ice-cream until her teeth and forehead ached from the cold.

With a steaming mug—she never used teacups, too small and delicate for her thick fingers—clasped between her hands, she sat and released the thoughts.

First, I'm gonna kill that bastard Brethour. She took a sip, licking her lips with satisfaction. Vocalizing made her feel better, so she shouted it. Then again. Of course, she knew murder wasn't her style, but a phone call to Constable Painter would do the trick. When she sat back and tucked her knees into her body, she felt deliciously pleased and full. She had suspected Brethour's child abuse, now his threats convinced her. She swallowed and felt a bubble of release, Amelia slightly shifting. Much like the release she felt when she cut her wrists...all the tension bleeding away. Replaced by a distorted euphoria, a successful transition, a rebirth.

One thing resolved.

From her exhaustion and giddy sense of relief came an opening of her mind, and unrestricted memories and thoughts slid in quietly like eels into a darkened stream.

The shamrocks.

Tempest blinked. Surely they were just a coincidence? No one else knew, at least no one alive who could speak. But what about St. Patrick's Day? To choose to die on the day honouring the man who liberated Ireland from snakes. *Why, Amelia? Why?*

Just a coincidence. Had to be. Tempest refilled her mug and laced it with cream. She moved to the piano, as though in a trance, and gently picked up the photo of three children. She was relieved Painter hadn't pried further. His fingers on the frame troubled her. No one touched her past.

She stroked the treble clef frame, soothed by the familiar musical symbol. The young faces smiled up at her, the boy's arms protectively thrown round his sisters' shoulders. She touched his smile. Too bad his protection had ended with the photographer's flash.

One coincidence: shame on you; two: shame on me. The shamrocks at Vita's feet. She'd seen that arrangement before. She replaced the frame. Tempest squeezed her eyes shut, working to block the memory.

Sister Gabriel's green eyes glittered through.

EIGHTEEN

Ah, the curse!
—RIGOLETTO, ACT 1

"HigginsTuttyHilliarandMason." The female voice was high and rushed, tumbling the words into a long spew of vowels and consonants.

Patrick blinked. "Is that...uh..." he shuffled papers on his desk, pulling free a yellow sheet. "Higgins, Tutty, Hilliar and Mason, the law firm?"

"Yes." Somehow she made the word shorter than three letters.

Why do law firms always have so many names? he thought, not for the first time. Why not just initials or somethin' catchy like Torts R Us? "Can't make up your mind?"

"Pardon?"

Patrick grimaced and adjusted the phone receiver. "Forget it. Bad joke. I'm looking for..." He glanced at the paper. "...uh, Kim Hilliar."

"Ms. Hilliar's unavailable at the moment, may I take a message?"

It took Patrick a moment to translate the speeding words. "You certainly may. Tell me, how many lawyers you got at Higgins, Tutty, Hilliar and Mason? Quite a mouthful, eh?"

After a slight hesitation, the young woman spoke. "Nine, I believe. Your message for Ms. Hilliar?"

Trying to imagine her reciting all nine names, Patrick replied: "Tell 'er to call Constable Painter at the Sidney and North Saanich RCMP." He recited the number. "Soon as possible, okay?" He paused. " Miss?"

"Yes?"

He couldn't resist. "What're the rest of the names?"

"The rest? This a joke?"

He assured her it wasn't.

"Well...RomaineLangerWestRussellandEiliason. Anything else?"

Still trying to separate the names, Patrick mumbled "No," and hung up.

He quickly dialled again. "Yes, hello? Sister Winifred, please. Constable Painter."

While on hold, he thought of Tempest's hair and creamy skin. Suddenly, a voice was in his ear.

"...trick, is that you?"

"Yes, yes," he replied, shaking away his daydream. "You get in touch with her parents? Outta town? Okay. Child Protection Services're on their way over. I'll be there in a few minutes. Can you make sure Sydney's available?"

"In the middle of the school day? Surely this can—"

"No way. Shoulda talked to 'er last night. Staff sergeant's already on my case. Bye." He hung up feeling slightly guilty. Not from cutting her off, but from how good it felt.

HE FELT EVEN BETTER WHEN HE PULLED UP BESIDE the bright green Kawasaki. Whistling softly, he grabbed the envelope of photos, climbed out and skipped up the steps into the quiet of the Perpetual Soul.

Mother Superior was waiting for him. Wordlessly, she led him down a sunlit corridor into a small anteroom. Sydney Mayne and Dr. Ivory sat side by side across a wooden table. The girl dropped her chin and folded her arms across her chest. Only the tapping of her foot revealed her anxiety. Patrick's heart skipped at Tempest's serious expression. He smiled, but her face remained immobile. All business, are we? he thought. No problemo.

He motioned to Sister Winifred to sit and plunked himself into a stiff-backed chair, laying the envelope on the table. He smiled at Sydney. "Hello Sydney, you remember me? I'm Constable Painter."

The girl's dark eyes moved to the envelope then to Sister Winifred. Uh oh, she thought. Now Old Inferior's brought the police to question me.

"We're just here to talk. No one says you've done anything wrong, okay?"

Sydney muttered something which sounded like "Yeah, right."

"Dr. Ivory's here on behalf of Child Protection Services..." He cocked an eyebrow in Tempest's direction. She nodded slightly. "...and the Mother Superior is here acting for your parents. Seems they're out of town?"

"Surprise, surprise," Sydney whispered. *Oh, why didn't I just leave it somewhere? Anywhere?*

Winifred stared at her like a pint-sized grey avenger. The girl's foot tapped harder.

"It's no big deal, Sydney. Seems you've been in a bit of mischief, eh?"

Sydney clenched her small hands. "Ain't done nothin'."

"No?" Patrick leaned back; the chair creaked dangerously. Sydney's eyes widened. *Maybe if I tell him now, he'll let me off.*

Patrick shifted forward slightly. They spoke simultaneously.

"I didn't mean to keep it," Sydney whined.

"Remember the messages you sent?" he asked.

"Keep what?" Dr. Ivory's voice jumped onto the girl's words.

"Messages?" Sydney screwed up her eyes. "Whaddya mean? You're not here about..."

"Answer Dr. Ivory," Patrick snapped.

Sydney bit her lip and hunched forward.

"Sydney!" Winifred's nasal voice rasped. "The doctor asked you a question. Answer her!"

The child remained mute, her right foot pounding against a nearby table leg.

This wasn't getting them anywhere. Kids. Patrick sighed. He started to lean back, then stopped. "Look, kid," he said soothingly. "I don't know what sneaky little thing you've done and frankly I don't care." The foot stopped tapping. "I'm here about the messages."

"What messages?"

"Quit jerkin' me around. The nasty ones in the chapel coin box."

Relief spilled over her like a shower. *Those messages!*

Dr. Ivory sensed the child's relaxation and watched her closely. Sydney shot a glance at Sister Winifred. "That was before."

"I know," Patrick said, patiently. "I want to know about now."

"Don't do it any more."

"I believe you." He glanced round the room. Tempest nodded, Sister Winifred remained impassive. "We all do. Someone put something in the coin box recently."

"Wasn't me." Her eyes lifted. "Wasn't me!"

"Right. You know who did, though, don't you?"

Her small face beamed, lit by her renewed sense of spirit. It could be all right. "Mebbe. What's it to you?"

Patrick leaned across the table. Sydney shifted back. Tempest patted her hand.

"Listen to me very carefully," he whispered. Sydney's eyes looked like manhole covers. "If you know who recently put something in the coin box, you must tell me. I don't care about the other stuff, okay? Two little girls have died. We don't want any more deaths."

"What's in the envelope?"

Patrick held it enticingly in front of him. "You're a smart girl, you tell me."

"What'll you give me if I do?"

"For heaven's sakes, child!" Winifred's voice snapped. She stood up, paced a couple of steps. "Tell the officer!"

Patrick flicked Winifred a glance that plainly said *shut up!* and slid the envelope onto his lap. The Mother Superior sat down.

"Whaddya want?"

Sydney stroked the table's edge. *What a chance!* "I want her to get off my back." She smiled coldly. "She's always after me."

"That's not true—"

Sydney's eyes moved to the Mother Superior. "I'm not the only one, y'know. Just leave me alone, all right?"

Patrick looked at his great-aunt. Her thin cheeks puffed in and out as she stroked her silver cross necklace. "How dare—"

Tempest stood up, splotches of pink rising on her cheeks.

Winifred paused, cheeks quivering. "All right," she said finally, her voice devoid of emotion.

"Fine. That's settled." Tempest reacquainted herself with her chair. "Now," Patrick asked, "who'd you see?"

Sydney smiled. Patrick was astounded at how disdainful she seemed. She wasn't yet a teen but had all the right attitude.

"Vita."

"Vita Bell?"

She nodded.

"What'd you see?"

"Not gonna punish me, right?"

Patrick threw a look at his great-aunt and held up his right hand. "Scouts' honour."

"Well..." Sydney bit her lower lip. "Amelia'd given her somethin'." She scowled. "Photos, I think. Is that what's in the envelope? I bet it is." A look from Patrick hurried her along. "Anyway, she was scared. I...I asked her to show 'em to me." Yeah, right, thought Patrick. "She wouldn't. Got real upset, crying, ran into the chapel. Said she hadta hide 'em." She grinned, turning to Tempest. "I told her to stuff 'em in the coin box. She really believed, you know? So I said if she paid God, maybe he'd help her." She turned back to Patrick. "Figured I'd get 'em later."

"And?"

Sydney stuck out a short finger across the table

toward Sister Winifred. "She found 'em before I did. So, can I see 'em?"

"SURE YOU WANT TO HAVE A LOOK AT THEM? THEY'RE kinda...disturbing."

Tempest stuck out her hand. "I'm a psychologist, for crying out loud. Course I want to see them."

"Okay," Patrick replied hesitantly, withdrawing the photos from the envelope. They were alone in the room. Sister Winifred had escorted Sydney back to class, muttering to Patrick that she'd never get there otherwise. "Not sure how Amelia'd react to this filth. There's something familiar, but I can't place it. Which is why," he added sheepishly, "I'm glad you offered to look. I want your opinion."

He handed the three photos to Tempest. "Would these cause her to commit suicide?"

"You've got to remember that potential suicides are being bombarded with emotions and controlled by a logic that for you and me seems twist–" *Oh my god!* Tempest stopped breathing. *I don't believe this.* Her stomach clenched, her head whirled. She knew the photos were in her hand, she remembered feeling their glossy surfaces. Why couldn't she feel them now?

"Hey! You okay?"

The constable's voice was muffled. She tried to sit down, then realized she was already sitting. *Family secrets...oh, not again!* Her hands flew to her face. Exhaustion oozed through Tempest as a dye through water. She wasn't sure how much longer she could keep the secrets; the energy and evasion imposed an appalling toll. How she longed to banish her emotional distance and embrace the innocent bliss of spontaneous conversation.

His hand was on her shoulder, warm breath in her ear. "You okay?" he kept asking in a far-away voice.

"I'm fine," she managed to whisper through dry lips. It was a lie.

NINETEEN

If you will not talk about yourself,
At least tell me who my mother was.

—GILDA, ACT 1

"You know the old saying, 'Women sing with their ovaries and men with their testicles?'"

Tempest nodded as Gertie Clement made another tuck in the waistline of Gilda's dress. She was astounded at the physical impact of wearing the costume, the same worn by other Gildas at the Vic Opera. This year's production of *Rigoletto* was a nostalgic revival for the long-established company. Verdi's epic tale of love and deceit had not been tackled for over a decade.

Like most opera and theatrical costumes, Gilda's dress—*long-sleeved, thank God*—was created with a complex array of hooks and buttons to allow for variety of fit. Wardrobe was expensive, with individual pieces costing many hundreds of dollars. Tempest tried to relax, adjusting to the weight—quite a bit lighter than many costumes, some of which added twenty to thirty pounds to the wearer—of the long, flowing dress, and mentally let Verdi's music reveal a sense of Rigoletto's cherished daughter.

Gertie paused, shoved a hand into her smock pocket. "Vitamin C?" she asked, popping several orange disks into her mouth.

Tempest hesitated, immersed in Gilda, then shook her head.

"Too bad...excellent for the voice. As I was saying, the sound has to be rooted in something very concrete," Gertie continued, bits of orange appearing at the side of her mouth. "That's the body's centre. Singing from the heart is twaddle. We emote from our heart, yes, but sing from our bodies, yes?"

Tempest resisted the temptation to stare at Gertie's increasingly orange lips. "Uh huh."

"Have any kids?"

"No. Why?"

Gertie's right hand darted into her coiled mass of grey hair and scratched quickly. "You've got good range. Often comes after childbirth. Turn 'round."

For a couple of minutes, Gertie measured and pulled, her thin fingers moving confidently among the voluminous layers of linen and satin as though playing an instrument.

"Helped your mother."

Tempest blinked. *What? Mother?* "Excuse..." Her voice faltered, pinched by her pounding heart. She swallowed, tried again. "Excuse me, did you say my mother?"

The thin woman nodded, fingers playing with back hooks.

"Stop!"

The grey head snapped up. Gertie's pale green eyes widened behind the thick glasses.

"I'm...I'm sorry. I didn't mean to shout." Her voice

dropped to a whisper. How did she know? "You...you think you knew my mother?"

Gertie smiled, revealing pumpkin-coloured stained teeth. "Course. Took me a while. You changed your name." She shook her head. "Not as sharp as I used to be, but..." she peered up at Tempest, "...knew something about you was familiar...hair, way you move, but it was the voice, *the* voice. Your mother's might've been bigger." She handed Tempest some vitamin C, which Tempest chewed without thinking. "But you've got the same range and colour."

The sweet granular taste of the pills almost choked her. For years, Tempest had somewhat successfully side-stepped her past, an effort both extreme and taxing. For a second she felt like grabbing the woman's narrow wrists and asking about her mother, her voice, how she prepared herself for a role, did she ever talk about her kids? But she didn't. Her self-control, though difficult to achieve, had settled slowly into her persona like curing concrete. Once set, it would take a jackhammer to break.

"You knew her...here?"

Gertie nodded her head vigorously, the coils of silver hair sliding up and down like a twisting snake. "I was her dresser...till the end."

Gertie stopped as though thunderstruck. The tiny woman turned her pale eyes to Tempest. Her voice, when finally found, was hoarse and full of awe.

"This...this dress..." she faltered, fingers reaching for the material, "...she wore it last."

"YOU MUST KNOW WHO HER PARENTS ARE."
"I told you. Vita was an orphan." The nasal voice

paused, followed by a sound like a swallow. Betcha she's eating a jujube, Painter thought. Yellow? No, probably red.

"She came to us as a baby. Illegitimate. In those days, society didn't accept them, the church often helped out. What was I to do? Leave her on the front steps?"

"Of course not. But surely you musta—"

Winifred interrupted her great-nephew. "There wasn't so much paperwork then. We took her in, agreed to care for her. Child Protection Services was relieved, one less to worry about."

"Her name? Where'd that come from?"

"The poor child's dead, Patrick."

"Humour me."

The nun sighed. "I called her Vita, from the Latin *vitalis*, or life. Appropriate at the time..." her voice trailed off.

"And Bell?"

"Oh...uh, sorry...my grandmother's maiden name. Had a nice ring." She laughed harshly.

"Sorry?"

"Said the same thing eleven years ago. Thought it funny then...you know: ring, bell."

"Oh, yeah." Painter shifted in his chair. Perhaps it was just nonsense, but he had a niggling worry about Vita Bell. The coroner had confirmed suicide as the cause of death, but Patrick found it difficult to accept. His instincts were good. Had saved him on many occasions. Like he always knew about an aphid invasion on his Explorer rose just before it became obvious. The child had appeared happy. He'd probed those silver-plate eyes and found nothing. Nothing but excessive blinking and an oddly familiar quiet stare. He scratched his jaw. Maybe the blinking was a sign of distress? A question for Tempest.

"Sure you don't know anything about her parents, her family?" He knew from experience that, once dislodged, this disquiet would continue to rattle round in his mind. "They should be informed."

"I'm, we're her family. That's all I know. Really, Patrick, surely you must have criminals to catch?"

Oh, yes, he thought, hanging up. Never in short supply. Maybe even at a Catholic academy.

"YOU KNEW HER WELL?" TEMPEST HAD CHANGED back into work clothes, preparing to leave. She'd pulled them on like a zombie, her thoughts reeling. *My mom played Gilda! She wore the same dress, the exact same dress.* The bizarre coincidence, the sad irony that playing Verdi's young heroine, her own debut, was her mother's finale, rocked her. She couldn't produce a note if her life depended on it.

"Not so's we'd have coffee or anything, but spend as much time as I do with someone, dear, you hear things, get an understanding."

"You...you know how she died?"

Gertie nodded quickly then lowered her eyes and fussed with straightening a costume hanging nearby. "Must have been hard on you kids."

Tempest nodded, found herself sitting down. "I wish I could be sure."

"Sure?"

"You know, how she died? Why?"

"Your father, didn't he...?"

"He told us she was dead, an accident. Then my brother died." Tears filled her eyes. Tempest blinked furiously. *Get a grip! What in God's name are you doing, bawling in front of a stranger?* Angrily, she wiped them and started to stand up. "That's all I knew for years."

The dresser waved her to sit down. "She had a marvellous voice, just like yours. She'd be proud of you, you know?"

Tempest felt her throat tighten.

"Mind you, she had her troubles."

"What troubles?"

Gertie blushed. "Spoke out of turn, dearie. Your mom was grand, very beautiful."

Tempest nodded. "I remember. We came backstage many times. She seemed different, like a movie star, with the makeup, costume, all the excitement...like someone who resembled my mom but acted totally differently." She paused, remembering the smell of newly painted sets, the hollow sounds of backstage laughter and the glow of her mother's face in the footlights. "Was she popular?"

Gertie snorted. "Too right." She stopped, a look of guilt flashing across her lined face.

"Was there a problem?"

Gertie shook her head.

"Really, I want to know. I...I have to. You're the first person I've met who knew my mother as an artist. That's how I remember her, how I want to know her."

Gertie concentrated on sewing a button.

"Please."

The woman fished out more pills, offered some to Tempest, who gently refused, and chewed vigorously. "You know what this life's like, dearie. High-strung artists, some of 'em with the self-esteem of a gnat.

Playing a romantic part, bigger than life, intense schedule, they all lead to affairs."

"My mom? Was she—?"

Gertie shook her head. "Nobody in the cast interested her. Didn't stop one Romeo." She started to laugh, a dry, whimpering sound.

"What happened?"

Gertie Clement wiped her eyes. "It was classic! He'd been all over her since rehearsals began but she wanted nothing to do with 'im. He took full advantage, see, he was playing Rigoletto. When she'd had enough..." More whimpering laughter. "Did it during dress rehearsal."

"Did what?"

Gertie reached out and patted Tempest's arm. "You'll love this, dearie. You know when you're singing a duet, sometimes you'll agree to stop at the squeeze of your partner's hand so that you'll be in unison?" Tempest nodded. An old singing trick.

"Well, in the first act, during *Figlia! Mio padre*, you know, *culto, famiglia, la patria...*"

Tempest nodded again. The stunning duet between father and daughter, where he effusively claims that she is his religion, family and country and she fervently replies that making him happy is her life's joy, was one of opera's most famous.

"He squeezes her hand as they reach their crescendo..."

"And?"

"She ignores him!" Gertie snorted loudly. "The poor fool shuts his mouth and she keeps on soaring. She couldn't have hurt 'im worse if she'd kicked him in the balls!" Another cackling laugh and snort. "He's left looking like an unprofessional fool. The whole cast

laughed until they collapsed. Boy, if looks could kill..."
She stopped, embarrassed by her choice of words.
Glancing at her watch, she said: "Look dear, I've got
to go—"

"It's okay," Tempest replied, buoyed by her mother's guts. *Sure got mine honestly.* "One last thing?"

"Yes?"

"What was the guy's name, the one who played
Rigoletto?"

A look of surprise changed Gertie's demeanour. "But
I...I thought you already knew."

Tempest shook her head.

"Oh. Quite a coincidence, really. It's Sir Noisy
Nodes himself. Sad case, that. Another victim of the
Irish flu."

"Irish flu?" she asked though her mind rattled with
Gertie's earlier words. Sir Noisy Nodes? *Can't be...not—*

"The drink, dearie. Course the cigars're worse." She
hesitated. "Poor ol' Cy. Never sang after, well, you
know."

"Cy?"

Gertie popped another tablet, then mumbled:
"Cyrus Everard."

TWENTY

The anger you provoke
Could turn against you.
—THE DUKE OF MANTUA, ACT 1

"No, don't be afraid. Hands up, that's it, see how much stronger you feel? How much more air you have?"

Sydney nodded and continued to sing. Her voice was stronger, carrying the notes rather than dragging them.

"Very good, that's very good, Sydney." Tempest stopped playing. The girl's demeanour puzzled her. Though she had dark smudges under her eyes and had yawned frequently, she seemed oddly energized. "Take a break, have a drink of water."

The girl hopped over to the coffee table and slurped into a cup. "I'm better, aren't I?"

Tempest looked at Sydney's flushed face and too-brilliant eyes, certain now that this was her only positive reinforcement. "Yes, little one, you're doing great."

Since the first voice lesson, they'd had two others. Both had gone well, with Sydney discovering more of her voice and self-confidence each time. Today, the girl had arrived promptly, rattling off scales as she skipped through the front door. Tempest now wanted to introduce a song that followed natural speaking rhythms to ease learning, and had an emotional story-line. Something she and Sydney could discuss, perhaps use as a springboard to the girl's current situation.

Winifred was demanding results. When was she going to confront the girl about the fire? Tempest knew she couldn't delay much longer or the Mother Superior would yank Sydney from her and launch at the child herself.

Tempest chose Harnick and Bock's *Far from the Home I Love*, from Fiddler on the Roof. A melancholy tale of a daughter leaving her father and her home for the man she loves.

"I'd like us to try a song now, you game?"

"Yes, yes, yes!"

Tempest began to play the song's slow introduction. "This's a story of a girl who's sad. Ever been sad?"

Sydney hesitated. This wasn't the sort of song she'd expected. Did Dr. Ivory know about the diary? She chewed her lower lip.

"She's sad 'cause she's leaving her family, her home—"

Sydney punched the music stand. It rattled, then crashed to the floor. "No! I won't go, I won't!"

Tempest abruptly stopped playing. "Hey! It's okay." She stood slowly and repositioned the music stand. "Wait a second, nobody's making you go anywhere, it's just a song."

Sydney took a step back. "You...you said leaving—"

"Yes, the girl in the song."

"The...song?"

Tempest nodded, her fingers rippling over the piano keys.

"But she's also happy, blissfully happy. Know why?"
Sydney shook her head.

"She's fallen in love."

Sidney's lips parted in a quick smile. *This is more like it!*

"Remember I told you that we always have a sub-script, like a mental movie going on, when we're singing? That's from using our own memories, helps us bring real emotion to the words.

"So, think of what it'd be like to tell your dad you're leaving home. That you–" She stopped, noticing that the girl had stiffened. Tempest continued to play through the song. "Good! I can see you're thinking about it. Now, think about what kind of clothes you'd be wearing...in this case, probably a skirt and sweater. Does the sweater itch?"

Sydney shook her head. She was suddenly tired, too tired to worry about some stupid girl with an itchy sweater. She leaned against the music stand.

"Okay, that's enough. You look exhausted. Come over here..." Tempest patted the smooth black piano bench. Sydney paused, then stumbled over gratefully. Tempest began playing Chopin's *A-Flat Major Nocturne*.

As Tempest gently caressed the keys, the girl leaned against her shoulder, eyes shut tight.

Finally, Sydney whispered: "If I tell you something, promise to keep it a secret?"

Tempest nodded and kept playing. A couple of minutes later, she carried the sleeping child to her couch, covering her with a brightly coloured woolen throw.

She sat across the room and watched the pale young face, marked by thick brown lashes.

Perhaps the time for truth had come.

"MRS. HILLIAR, WHAT DO YOU MEAN THE NOTE WAS from my mother?" Constable Patrick Painter shifted in his chair, eyeing a piece of paper in his right hand. He glanced about the small station. He was alone save for the dispatcher, tucked away in a far corner.

"*Ms.* Hilliar, Constable. Well, er..." Kim Hilliar hesitated, "exactly that. Your mother brought it to the office. Asked that we keep it confidential. And..."

"Yes?"

"Well, after her death, return it to her husband, Mr. L. P. Painter."

"Her husband? Sure about that?" Constable Painter asked, staring at the yellowing white sheet. Absent-mindedly, he folded it along deeply creased lines.

"Why, yes. I spoke with her personally. She was a lovely lady, wore sunglasses I think, yes. Huge ones." She paused. "She seemed..."

"What?"

"Well, you realize I didn't know the lady but...a bit upset."

"Upset?" Patrick gripped the phone tighter. He'd seen the sunglasses, too. Ignored them. Sometimes after he left home, he'd pick his mother up, take her to Sidney for coffee. She often wore them, rain or shine. On the wet coast, the sun took a hike much of the time. But he never asked. Just like he never asked if the old man knew they saw one another. Painter Senior wasn't mentioned, but his presence loomed everywhere, restricting their conversation and stiffening their posture. "How?"

He heard a slow intake of breath. "I'm sure you realize...client confidentiality...I'm not able to say."

"Come on, Ms. Hilliar," Painter snapped. "My

mom's dead. You saw something, you shoulda report-
ed it."

The dispatcher turned toward him, then quickly
looked away.

"I saw nothing out of the ordinary!"

"But you just said, you said she was upset! Why didn't
you question her?" Why didn't you? he thought, jumping to his feet. Coward! You saw the bruises, the make-
up, but you didn't ask, did you? With an effort, he
released the paper before he completely crumpled it
into a ball and forced himself to sit.

"Don't raise your voice with me, Constable! I'm an
officer of the court, not a social worker. I did my job."

*Job? That's a laugh! That's exactly what I'd done. Taken a
transfer to Fort St. John. Avoided her, avoided him.* God
help me, he thought. I didn't ask. He inhaled heavily.
"You did not! You blew it."

"Pardon?"

"Your job, your precious responsibility to your
client."

Hilliar sighed with exasperation. "What are you talking about, Constable?"

"The letter," he said, regaining his composure. "You
delivered it to the wrong man."

Silence. Then Painter could hear a rush of shuffling
papers. Hilliar's voice boomed in his ear. "Not sure I
know what you mean...here it is. The note, along with
a short explanation from our firm, was delivered
on...let's see, yes, March seventeenth."

"Yeah, but not to her husband."

A pause. "No?"

"No, Ms. Hilliar."

"But Const–"

He dropped the phone, smoothed the paper and stared at the unfamiliar round handwriting with the simple two-initial signature.

Addio...speranza ed anima
Sol tu sarai per me.
Addio...vivrà immutabile
L'affetto mio per te.

V.W.

Italian. He was pretty sure it was Italian. He was also pretty sure his father knew it as well as he did. That is to say: not at all. So why would his mom send it to him after her death? What did it mean? Who was V.W.?

Painter folded it carefully and slipped it into his jacket. Perhaps a singing acquaintance of his could translate.

TWENTY-ONE

And even if you condemn me to death,
You will see again as a terrifying ghost,
Carrying my head in my hand,
Demanding vengeance from the world and God.

—COUNT MONTERONE, ACT 1

The secret was a thick, worn book bound in textured black leather. On the inside cover, the Mother Superior had written: *Property of Sister Winifred, Sisters of the Perpetual Soul, 1981.*

Tempest stared at Winifred's tiny, perfect writing. She knew she should shut the cover immediately and return it unread. Yeah right, she thought, fingering the leather. Once she had confessed, little Sydney Mayne had almost thrown the book at her. As if compelled by her admission, the child added breathlessly that Amelia was being abused by her step-father. She'd overheard 'Melia crying to Vita.

Then, like all those consumed by guilt, full disclosure brought euphoria and with it, immediate renunciation of the troubling matter. The child skipped out her front door, lungs bellowing.

Confirmation of her original fears about Terry

Brethour brought Tempest the first pangs of relief. Now
she had the bastard!

Sydney's conscience was clean; Tempest's was beginning to stain. She leaned against her leather couch and
felt the familiar tingle of risk. Perhaps just a quick glance
before returning the journal. What could be the harm?

The early entries were pretty dull, as Sister Winifred
noted academy expenditures and the comings and
goings of Sisters and students. Each was dated with
sometimes days or months of time between them. Most
of the notations were in point form or just an item and
accompanying dollar amount. Winifred must have
occasionally needed an emotional release, for there
were the briefest of hints of the agonies of a lonely
woman losing herself for God. Tempest flipped forward,
missing chunks of pages and years at a time.

July '84 was red-circled with the words *Mother
Superior!!!* heavily underlined, followed by *mine, finally!!!!* Tempest was touched by the excessive exclamation
points. A sure sign of victory, but over whom? The
church? Religious life? Another nun?

It was as though the appointment freed Sister
Winifred, for at that point, she began to add comments
on critical academy decisions, history and local and
church support. On the odd date she would even
express an opinion about a benefactor or, more rarely,
Catholic educational policy. Though Tempest did not
recognize many of the names, she instinctively knew the
damage some revelations would cause.

About two-thirds of the way through, a name stopped
Tempest's fingers cold. *What? Can't be...* Heart pounding, she flipped back. And stared at the tiny words written under the date December 14, 1983.

LP brought Darcy Winsloe and baby girl.
Couldn't refuse, both desperate.
Child Protection Services?

Darcy? The name burned into her eyes. Baby girl? Her mind emptied with a sickening thud felt down in her solar plexus; her ears roared. Head stuffed between her legs, Tempest pulled in air. *Not possible or...is it?*

When the rushing sound dulled, she arched back and, gripping tightly to reduce the tremor, carefully read the next few pages. Nothing of significance until February 2. Groundhog Day. Tempest couldn't resist thinking: Wonder if Whiarton Willy saw his shadow that year?

Winifred had written:

Winsloe new novitiate: Gabriel.
Baby: Vita Bell, at academy.
LP & CPS OK.

The journal dropped from her unresponsive fingers. *She's alive?* The roar increased, screaming over her like a tidal wave. It was too much. She squeezed her eyes shut, covered her ears, but the clamour continued.

After a long time, Tempest opened her eyes but saw nothing except the words *Darcy Winsloe* and *Gabriel*.

With a gasping shudder, she wrapped her arms around herself and pitched into the belly of the sofa.

With lightning speed, the connections clicked: the familiar green eyes, the startling smile, that stare. Her sister was alive...was Sister Gabriel.

She gulped and a soft giggle rose from her soul. Up from the couch, dancing, feet flying, shouting: "I'm not alone! Darcy...Darcy's alive!"

A niece, she thought. I have a niece! Tempest moaned as the truth slid home. The euphoria died, her feet stopped.

Had a niece. Tempest put her hands to her face, catching the first tears.

Oh my God, she's dead! Vita Bell was my niece and she's dead!

ACT THREE

Whatever is hidden away
Will be brought out into the open
And whatever is covered up
Will be uncovered.

—MARK 4:22

Act Three synopsis, *Rigoletto*

At night, outside an inn, Rigoletto forces his daughter to watch through a crack in the wall. Gilda is horrified to see the duke making love to the assassin's sister. The jester sends his distraught daughter away to disguise herself in a man's attire and leave for another city. The assassin arrives with the initial stirrings of a storm. Rigoletto pays him to kill the duke and departs.

The storm increases as Gilda reappears, dressed as a man. Peering through the crack, she overhears the assassin's sister pleading with her brother to spare the duke. The assassin agrees that if a stranger calls at the inn before midnight, he will kill him instead and hand his body over to Rigoletto. Gilda decides to sacrifice herself for the duke and enters. A tremendous crash of thunder drowns her cries as the assassin knifes her.

After the storm abates, Rigoletto returns to collect the

duke's body. He drags the sack toward the river when suddenly he hears the duke's voice singing *La donna è mobile.* Rigoletto tears open the sack to find the dying Gilda inside. Stricken with grief, he embraces her and they sing a tender farewell. As she dies, Rigoletto cries out that Monterone's curse has been fulfilled.

TWENTY-TWO

I tremble...It is a human body!
—RIGOLETTO, ACT 3

Sister Benedict's beads stopped clicking. They fell clattering from her slackened hand into a mound of shamrocks. Her thick body followed, collapsing heavily onto the hardwood floor. But Sister Benedict's astonished mind hung in momentarily as she processed the horror, thinking for the last time, Oh dear, oh dear, I don't believe what's happening here...oh dear...oh de...

Her final vision—like that of Saint Bartholomew—was of hell on earth. Benedict's spirit escaped her pious body, gingerly skirting the hanging child and her swaying shadow, fleeing the earth and the stone fetters of the Perpetual Soul.

PATRICK WAS ATTEMPTING THE IMPOSSIBLE: TRYING to understand and appreciate opera. At least, that's how it seemed to him sitting up in the nose-bleeders at McPherson Playhouse. Ignorance of Italian was one thing, but what was with the excessive yodelling?

As he'd climbed to his lofty spot, he heard a man backstage humming a tune, something like "dune dune

dune dudadune, dune dune dune dudadune..." Patrick knew he'd heard it before, but where? Was it part of *Rigoletto*? He was certain he'd never heard the opera before. By the time he was seated, he was fascinated with the activities below and quickly forgot the tune.

Forty-five minutes later, he shifted to relieve his aching back. *These chairs were made for kids!* The red velvet seat creaked; the eyes of the cast rose toward the ornate gold-coved ceiling and him. "Oh dear God," he muttered, cringing, shrinking. *Not again!* He had used his police I.D. and a lot of persuasion—these theatre folks took their art so seriously—to gain access to the rehearsal. No respect for the uniform. In fact, for a second, the stage manager mistook him for a supernumerary or extra. The deal: Go heavenward and for Christ's sake keep quiet! At first he'd almost laughed. He was miles from the stage; it and the players resembled dolls. Who'd ever know he was up here?

When early on he accidentally dropped the libretto— a booklet of the words of the opera included with the music he'd picked up at a local classical music store—the resounding thud prickled his neck hairs. He'd heard about the acoustics, but until that second, never appreciated their startling acuity. The singing stopped. Without thinking, he ducked into the aisle and held his breath. It was only after the music began again and he had carefully shuffled into a nearby seat, that he wondered why in heaven's name he had acted like that. Like a truant schoolboy. It was only a rehearsal, after all.

When would she sing? The guy with the hunched back, Rigoletto, was interesting enough but he wanted Tempest. While he waited—he didn't have a clue where the rehearsing singers were at—he flipped through the libretto and began to read the English translation.

Tempest's powerful voice pulled his eyes to the stage. Lying in Rigoletto's arms, she sang with him. Patrick whipped at the pages, trying to catch a word. After a few moments, he gave up and stared, contentedly mesmerized by Tempest Ivory. Her voice filled the hall, caressing the balconies and balustrades, sending a tingle along his spine. Patrick shivered and grinned. *Damn, she's good!* He was no expert, but brilliance in any form was patently obvious, even to the ignorant. He tapped his fingers on his knee. *Maybe this opera stuff isn't so bad.*

The hunchback left and another man, the duke, he figured, appeared, kneeling at her feet. Patrick couldn't help himself. He leaned forward, a little jealous. The young couple's duet was full of friction and passion. They alternated, then sang together. Patrick had to admit the guy was good. The soprano and tenor voices blended, both arching ever higher. He felt himself rising, mentally joining the voices. Yes! he thought, I know this feeling. He blinked, breathless, struck by the intense melody and his own emotional reaction. It was as though Verdi was peeking into his heart, tugging free twentieth-century feelings with nineteenth-century notes.

He recognized the words *Gualtier Maldè*, the duke's pseudonym. He'd seen it in the English part somewhere. He turned the pages, scanning until he found it.

Then the duke sang something. Patrick stopped reading and listened. Tempest repeated it. Something like "adio". Where had he seen that? The lovers went back and forth, singing higher, their voices winding around one another so that you couldn't tell where hers began and his ended. Again and again, "adio, adio"; one voice, two ranges.

Patrick poured over the Italian. In exasperation, he dropped back a chunk of pages. There it was, near the end of the first act: *Gualtier Maldè.* Scanning the Italian, he barely noticed that the duke had left the stage, then Tempest began to sing.

He flipped forward, trying to find Tempest's song when a word bounced off the page: *Addio...Addio...*that was it! In his excitement, he leaped up and reached into his back pocket. The libretto flew from his lap, hit the chair back in front and flapped to the ground.

Tempest froze. The soaring sounds of her last vowels dangled in the air. Patrick held his breath.

A metallic voice crackled, repeating his name several times. Patrick swore and quickly turned off his shirt mike.

A man's gruff voice, it seemed from the depths of hell itself, thundered up at him. "Get out! Get the fuck outta here!"

"Sorry!" Patrick shouted. He grabbed his cap and the errant booklet and trotted to the nearest exit.

"YOU WERE WONDERFUL, JUST WONDERFUL!"

Don't talk, she pleaded silently. Don't. Tempest's mind was overflowing with Verdi's music, Gilda's emotions and Jeff's instructions. Coming down from a performance high, even a dress rehearsal, was a deflating, melancholy experience. One she preferred to face alone.

"Possessed, even!"

Her head began to pound, like the mournful ringing of a muffled church bell. Tempest shrugged out of the heavy dress and stepped clear. The inner music faded. Thoughts that she'd shoved to the back pushed at her. She felt as if she were a split personality. Not hard to imagine, really, as she had counselled a couple. For the first time, though, she understood their confusion, terror and divided loyalties. A part of her just wanted to sing, another cried for her sister, her niece, her past.

Gertie Clement stooped to pick up the costume and neatly hung it in the small wardrobe. They were alone in the tiny dressing room. Echoes of laughter from other cast members seeped through the thin walls.

"It's your mother, she's here, helping you."

"Sssh!" Tempest hissed then winced. "They'll hear you." With an effort, she crossed the small room to tower over the dresser. "No one's to know, remember?"

"I'm sorry, I was just—" Gertie's voice died in her throat; her eyes fixed on Tempest's bare wrists.

Damn! Heat rising in her neck and cheeks, Tempest turned and quickly dragged on her blouse.

"You poor—"

"I'd like to be alone."

The grey-haired woman continued to stare. Suddenly, she clamped her jaw and rubbed her glasses with her thumbs. "I'll be outta your hair in a jiff." She fished a thin hand into her bib pockets, rummaged for a moment, then shoved a variety of pills into Tempest's hand. As she released the young singer's wrist, Gertie gently touched the pink, puckered skin.

Face aflame, Tempest yanked her arm back. "Please, don't."

"I'm sorry, dearie, don't mean to pry–" *That's exactly what you're doing.* "–you're trying so hard, doing sooo well. I just want to help, is all."

Tempest dropped onto the make-up stool. "Just leave me alone...please."

Gertie batted her pale green eyes. "Okay, darlin'. I'm going." She hustled across to the wardrobe and adjusted the hanging dress. "Sure there's nothing I can do? Ask your friend in?"

"What friend?"

Gertie's eyes widened. "Why, the young policeman...couldn't take his eyes off of you." She gently brushed a curl from Tempest's forehead.

"Police?"

Gertie's coiled grey hair bobbed.

"Oh...no. I don't want to see him. Thanks." Tempest finished by directing her eyes to the door.

"Right then, dearie. Seems a shame, the young man came all this way, snuck in, you might saaayy..." She slowed as though struck by a thought. Her hands flew to her mass of hair.

"What's wrong?" Tempest watched through the mirror as the colour drained from Gertie Clement's cheeks.

"Nothing, really."

"Come on. Something's going on."

Gertie popped a couple of vitamin C pills and chewed. Tempest waited, watching her reflection.

The old woman swallowed. "Struck me as a funny coincidence. You having a cop admirer..."

Tempest pursed her lips. "He's not an admirer, but so?"

Gertie stared. "That...that's just what your mom said."

TWENTY-THREE

Oh, men! Oh, Nature!
You made me a vile scoundrel!
—RIGOLETTO, ACT 1

Patrick rubbed his eyes and stood up. His head ached. Two hours spent poring over hundreds of kiddie-porn mug shots. None matched those of the two frightened children posing in the photographs found by his great-aunt. He sighed, realizing that he'd probably have to look at out-of-province photos.

As he piled up the photos, a glossy brochure fell off his desk. Reaching down, he saw that it was the opera information he'd taken from Tempest's home.

Brochure in hand, he wandered over to the coffee pot. Painter nodded at the dispatcher, Wilma Riglin, poured himself a cup and glanced at the small pamphlet. The words *Vic Opera, 1997-98 Season* were enclosed in some kind of symbol. Patrick stared. It was very familiar. But why?

"There's what on the road, ma'am?"

He heard a garbled voice through the dispatcher's earphones. The young woman's eyes widened.

"Sheep?" In mid-swallow, Painter almost choked.

"There're sheep on McTavish Road?"

Grinning, Wilma pushed a coughing Patrick away then pressed her hands against her earphones.

"Where? Near the Pat Bay?! Jus' a sec, please." The dispatcher swung around, hand covering her small microphone.

"Baaaad news," Patrick joked, brochure forgotten on the coffee table.

The gal started to laugh, a harsh, crisp sound like someone crushing potato chips. It always made Patrick hungry. "You're a riot, Pat. Woman says there're a dozen sheep wandering round the highway. Ferry's out, traffic's a mess. She's afraid someone'll be killed."

Patrick handed her his mug and grabbed his jacket.

"Go man, go!"

Patrick turned and grinned. "Never fear, Wilma. You know us Mounties, we always get our ram!"

Her brittle laugh crunched after him down the steps and into his cruiser. His stomach growled.

"SILENCE AND SECRECY, THE DEADLY DUO."

The figure in the bed remained still and mute, except for the uneven mechanical rattle from the ever-present, ever-watchful equipment. Tempest was in avoidance mode. Dodge those stinging probes of thought. Too many startling realities on the horizon...a rediscovered sister, a dead niece, a troubled mother. She'd lecture any patient of hers who dared present this degree of evasion but...physician, heal thyself? Ha! That's a good one, she had thought, driving into Victoria. Her idea of confrontation was shouting at a coma victim.

"More valuable than gold, if used correctly."

Tempest edged closer, angered as always by her trepidation. "Well, you oughta know, right?"

It was just a hospital room, bone-white walls, piss-yellow linoleum, air that seared your throat and eyes. The thing in bed? He was nothing. Hadn't been in over twenty-four months. Still, the sight of his face, his huge hands, made her tremble. Tempest quickly did a little mental math. *Barry the blob of 730 days? How's that for a paternal nickname?*

She lightly touched the chrome bar, shivered at its coolness and drew back.

"What's the bloody point? I come here for answers and what do I get? The EKG humline and catheter drip."

The steel and silicone contraptions wheezed.

She found herself gripping, shaking the bed's side bar. "Did ya know? Darcy's alive! She had a baby, for Christ's sake! Did ya?" Her fists curled. "By God, I bet you did. Would be just like you to know and not care. She had the guts to break free, didn't she?"

Tears filled her eyes. Gasping, Tempest collapsed into a nearby chair. "Why didn't I? Why? Whyyyy?"

Footsteps padded in the hall. She quickly bent from view and covered her face.

The bathroom door was closed. A cloud of moist air draped the mirror, the tub, the toilet. Behind the shower curtain, Tempest was fumbling with the shampoo. A soft whistle startled her. From the hall, Darcy whispered urgently: "Pesty, hurry up! He's comin'." Her sister's footsteps pounded away. No locks allowed. Shampoo stung her eyes as she reached wildly for the towel. Wrapped it around her prepubescent body just as the fresh air tingled her bare legs. His hand reached in, pushing past the curtain. She slipped, almost lost the towel. Clung to it desperately, backing into the faucet. His blue eyes were angry, unable to see through the thick terrycloth.

She leaned back and slowed her breathing. *Pesty.* A nickname she had hated. Now it brought tears. "Why'd you leave me, Darce? How could you?" Her words were barely above a whisper yet they rustled in the still room like fallen leaves.

Tempest closed her eyes and concentrated. *Rigoletto's* opening music rippled from the back of her brain, the tension and threat of Monterone's curse swelling with the rising, skipping violins, the thundering baritone of an angry father and the full orchestra.

Father-daughter conflicts, she thought, pondering the irony. Verdi was famous for them, from *Oberto* to *Simone Boccanegra.* Rigoletto, perhaps the greatest of Verdi's padres, was a classic contradiction: physically deformed, mentally vile but pure in his absolute love for his daughter. *Egli è delitto, punizione son io.* He is crime; I am punishment, Rigoletto sings as he sets a deadly trap for the man fooling around with his daughter. Of course, as the audience knows upon first hearing the curse's distinctive musical motif, Rigoletto will be punished. Only in opera, Tempest thought angrily. She eyed her father, oblivious to the tears tracking down her cheeks.

You're disgusting, you and your sick interests. Destroyed us. I had the bloody pictures in my house...they made me puke. Couldn't bear to look at 'em but couldn't throw them out. My family album...of secrets. Tempest's shoulders trembled; her mouth gaped as deep, jarring sobs shook her. The pallid light from the small window weakened, turned ashen. Her anguish subsided and the music slipped in. She lay back, tasting salt and forgotten memories, and let the rousing sounds comfort her soul.

Her eyes popped open. Did he know about her mom's admirer? She jumped up and asked the inert figure out loud. "Did you know his name? Was she going to leave you? Is that why she did it?"

PATRICK TRIED TO PICK OFF THE DIRTY WOOL WHICH still clung to his uniform. With a step and a reluctant wave, he watched the old tractor bump along McTavish Road. Should've given the old fool a ticket, he thought, shifting a sore butt. The ram whose broad forehead had bruised Patrick's backside more than once slid out a pink tongue and grunted as the trailer rumbled by. The farmer had tried to convince Patrick that the ram was only being affectionate. That had made the young cop more frustrated; last thing he wanted was to be humped by some sex-starved hunk of wool.

His foot slid. Patrick knew before he looked. He'd stepped in it plenty while charging about, trying to corral the dirty dozen, as the farmer affectionately called his lost sheep.

"Sheeit!"

Broad back nestled against the fire truck, his buddy Jack started to giggle. "Gotta watch your step, Paddy boy."

Patrick glared at the volunteer fire chief and began wiping his boot in the wet grass.

Herding sheep's no simple task, ask any shepherd, he thought. In a tight clot, the shaggy beasts will wander anywhere their skittish, dim-witted nature will lead them. Add two hundred vehicles hell-bent on reaching Victoria a minute sooner than the last trip, and you've got the nasty makings of road mutton.

After an hour of darting, pushing and scaring, the three local men and two young brothers from

Washington state managed to shove the last bushy butt into the farmer's wooden cart, much to the amusement or anger of half the passengers from the mid-afternoon sailing of BC Ferries' *Spirit of Vancouver Island*. The old man was so contrite over his runaways that Patrick didn't have the heart to give him a citation.

Patrick's microphone crackled.

"Painter. What's up?"

"Finished countin' sheep?" Wilma Riglin's voice boomed.

"Very funny."

"Before I forget, two things, kind of a coincidence. Numero uno: you got an urgent message from some lady doctor, uh, Ivory, Dr. Tempest Ivory. Real picky that I get it right. Says she's got proof about Brethour, whatever that means. Says to pick 'im up. Believe that nerve? I'm not surprised, by the sound of her voice. Boy, is she loud. Numero duo: you'll never guess whose prints are on those photos the nun found."

Patrick waited, his nose wrinkling suddenly. He glanced at his boot. Looked clean.

"Dunno," he replied, distracted by the smell.

"You're the detective!"

He smelled his hands. A bit shitty, but nothing fresh. He rubbed them across his butt. The stench swelled. *Oh shit.* "I give, okay?"

Wilma's laugh crunched through the mike. "Gave ya the clue up front. Terry Brethour."

Patrick whistled under his breath but before he could think it through, Wilma's voice burst through again. "But that's not the reason for the call..." Her voice faded then blasted his ears again. "Sorry...li'l busy at the mo. Painter, you still there?"

"Wilma, out with it!"

"Okay, okay...keep your shorts on. The Staff wants ya at the academy, PDQ."

Patrick tossed a wave to the American brothers and quickly thumbed his nose at Jack. He almost replied: What? Winifred's lost another kid? but choked it off just in time. Instead he waited until he was settled in his cruiser to ask her what had happened.

Her voice dropped. "Another suicide."

Jesus H. Christ.

TWENTY-FOUR

Ah, if only I could catch
The traitor who thus disturbs me!
—THE DUKE OF MANTUA, ACT 1

"Lord in Heaven, rejoice, for your daughter is coming home. Jesus is love, amen, amen. Jesusislove, amen."

No one heard the delighted whispers. The hallways of the Perpetual Soul echoed only the soft voices and heavy footsteps of the coroner and her crew as they meticulously examined the dead child and the thick leather belt from which she dangled. A slight figure paused in the shadow of a door, savouring the final, sweet moments of death, of transcendence....the child's still-warm body, her peacefulness, the wondrous power found in straddling two worlds. Physically on earth yet spiritually gone to God. The excited murmurs continued as thin fingers played a black rosary. "Rejoice! Almighty, all-merciful, open your arms to her."

Quietly, the figure disappeared.

"Same as before," Dr. Edwina Harwicke told Patrick. He was still numb from eyeing another grotesquely bloated young face, but worked hard at listening. "Right down to the bloody shamrocks."

The assistant cut down the child, careful not to disturb the knot. If necessary, it would be examined by the forensic knot expert in Vancouver. With Harwicke's help, he gently placed her into a small body bag. Even so, the heavy plastic sagged around its diminutive contents. Harwicke nodded sharply and her assistant zipped in the tiny face and brown hair and pushed the trolley down the long hallway. Sydney Mayne left the Perpetual Soul for the last time. Following a well-worn route tread before her by Amelia Penderghast, Vita Bell, and now, Sister Benedict.

The coroner sniffed cautiously. "You smell something, Constable?" She motioned to the trolley. "And I don't mean her."

Patrick kept his face relaxed and shook his head. He hadn't had time to change so he'd done his best with a towel from the cruiser.

"Smells like...animal dung," she said slowly, moving into the hall.

Dr. Harwicke motioned to Patrick. He pulled his eyes from the rolling trolley and joined her, carefully keeping his distance.

"You been playing at being a Mountie?"

"Huh?"

She touched her nose. "Very sensitive. Trying out for the Musical Ride?"

"Uh, no...nothing like that. Long story...didn't have time to change."

Harwicke smiled slightly. "No problem. Had to be sure. Might contaminate the scene."

She pursed her lips, back to business. "Something's terribly wrong at this school, Constable."

He nodded. "That's an understatement."

The coroner's eyes widened.

Patrick hurried to add: "Kids must be super-stressed or something. I always found school to be a drag but..."

"No. It's not the girls."

Patrick stared at the coroner. "Whaddya mean?"

"Nothing I can put my finger on—and I'll know more after the autopsy—but I hate the long arm of coincidence. I just don't buy it."

"What're you saying? That Sydney was...what—?" His voice fell to a whisper. "—murdered?"

Harwicke scratched her eyebrow. For the first time Patrick realized why she always looked a little puzzled. Her hair had the rich gloss of the horse chestnuts that littered lawns in the fall but her brows were as light as summer wheat. The colour contrast was just jarring enough.

"Not saying anything at the moment...other than I'm bloody concerned." She yanked off a pair of rubber gloves and raked long fingers through her hair. "I'll give Staff Sergeant Lalande a call. In the interim, pay attention. Something's wrong here. We've got to find out what. Oh, and change those pants! You smell like a barnyard."

PATRICK FLIPPED THE SWITCH; THE LIGHTS ROLLED and the siren wailed. About time he was doing something other than chasing sheep. Since Terry Brethour wasn't considered dangerous, Lalande was letting him go after the bastard alone. Suited Painter just fine. *You never know when a perp'll trip or something. My word against the accused. Who're they gonna believe?*

The RCMP cruiser flew along Pat Bay as the afternoon traffic skittered out of its way. He drummed his fingers in time with the *whoop, whoop* of the siren and thought about Tempest's call. He wished he could have spoken to her face to face, something was not right. Somewhere during the conversation, her voice, though choked with emotion, had lost its thunder. It was replaced by a rawness that scorched. Of course, she was blindsided by Sydney's death. But was that it? Nearing Victoria, he mentally replayed some of their conversation.

"I told you," she had shouted as soon as she heard his voice. "That bastard, Terry Brethour, abused her."

"I know you thought so, Tempest, but now you have proof?"

"Yes, yes, yes! Sydney, Sydney Mayne—she's coming for singing lessons—told me. She gave me...well, never mind that...Sydney told me that she overheard Amelia tell Vita that her dad touched her, hurt her."

Sydney? Patrick thought. Oh, God...she doesn't know.

"Said Amelia was crying, mentioned something about taking pictures."

Patrick paused, not sure how to tell her.

"You're gonna arrest him, right?"

"Uh, look, Tempest—"

"Whaddya mean, look?" Her voice cut him off. "We've got proof, bring the bastard in!"

"It...it's not that simple."

"For Christ's sake, it's as simple as ABC. What're you waiting for? You don't believe me? You don't believe Sydney?"

"Look—"

She kept on. "Just ask her. She'll tell you. She—"

"Tempest!" Patrick shouted. Wilma spun in her chair

to shush him. He lowered his voice. "It's not that simple, Tempest. Sydney..."

"Yes?"

"She's...well...she's dead."

"Dead?"

"I'm sorry. I just came from the Old Soul. She–"

There was a slight pause. "Like the others?"

"Yeah. Poor kid hung herself."

A longer pause, then a whisper. "Were...were there
shamrocks?"

That was it! Her voice had changed at that moment.
"Yeah, just like the others."

A strangled noise, then silence.

"Why?"

Click.

A dial tone answered.

THE PIG DROVE ITSELF, HARD. RACING ALONG WEST
Saanich Road as if chased by Beetlejuice himself.
Tempest just hung on, her hands and toes moving
mechanically, pumping gasoline and changing gears.

Dear God, she prayed, it can't be. Please, please, it
can't be! I'll never, never forgive myself.

The bike wheeled onto the academy grounds, sliding sideways on the gravel. Her arms and knees flexed
and balanced automatically; the bike shimmied, then
spurted upright.

Surrounded by towering coniferous trees, Tempest
killed the engine and threw the green machine to the
ground. Pulling off her helmet, she jogged up the stone
steps of the Perpetual Soul.

She was oblivious to the spring smells of cedar,
newly mown grass and freshly turned earth, and to the

welcoming yawn of the academy's heavy front doors.

Tempest saw only her brother's still figure and smelled only the dying shamrocks laid gently at his dangling feet.

TWENTY-FIVE

If there is a mystery about you...
Let it be revealed to me...
Let me know my family.

—GILDA, ACT 1

"Ya can't prove nothin', man." Terry Brethour sucked at a home-made cigarette, then spat bits of tobacco as he exhaled in Constable Painter's direction. "Ya got what, a dead witness? Ha! That'll get you far in court, especially after Renfield."

Patrick glanced at the glistening bits of brown peppering his right shoulder. Mixed with the yellow wool fluff and sheep dung, his uniform was beginning to resemble a nearby field. Of course, the bastard would know about Renfield.

He glanced around for a place to sit. As usual, the small living room was a jumble, wrinkled clothes and dirty dishes being the main decor. He draped his jacket over an understuffed chair. What the hell, he thought, and dropped onto the newspapers.

August Renfield, a local high school teacher, had been arrested 18 months earlier for sexual harassment. The allegations came swiftly on the heels of another scandal, in which a three-year-old boy was abused and killed by his foster parents. The community's rage against Child Protection Services and the police had been unprecedented. A very public, very messy inquiry found that CPS knew of symptoms of abuse toward the boy but hesitated to act. Tapes of 911 calls revealed two from concerned neighbours, which were followed up by the police but abandoned from lack of proof. At CPS, commonly known as McFamily, the file had been shuffled from case worker to case worker, each more overloaded than the first, until the boy died.

Stung, the police were quick to arrest Renfield. Too quick, it turned out, as his young accuser eventually recanted under pressure, confessing that she was angry with the forty-something phys. ed. teacher for cutting her from the soccer team. Too little, too late for Renfield. Though he was reinstated in his position of fifteen years, whispers continued to chase him. A year later, his wife took their two sons and moved to Alberta. Renfield's lawsuit was still pending, the RCMP still smarting.

The staff sergeant had anticipated Brethour's stance, had gone over the possibilities earlier with Patrick. The young constable could've slapped the cuffs on him right then and there and brought him in to the detachment for questioning, would've two years ago. His fingerprints were all over the kiddie-porn photos. That meant something. The guy was definitely into robbing the cradle. But with Sydney Mayne dead, all they had was Tempest's third-hand knowledge of actual abuse. Not enough to risk a man's reputation, at least not any more. Course, it would've been easier if Terry didn't know that.

Whether the sometime roofer would have stayed in custody was anybody's guess. A good lawyer acting fast might have had him released within the hour. Lalande didn't like to lose, so he had instructed Painter to play it by ear, bait him a little, see if he'd talk. Patrick mentally added scaring the bejeesus outta the belligerent jerk if necessary.

Of course, that plan collapsed as soon as Alice Penderghast opened the door. She demanded to stay and her vacuous blue eyes were fixed on him as though he might ignite at any moment. Her blank stare quickly irritated him and he had to control an urge to clap his hands to see her blink.

"Not the same as Renfield, Terry. The girl told Dr. Ivory that you abused Amelia." Alice Penderghast blinked. She nonchalantly reached into a pocket of her oversized sweater. Her fingers gripped the cool casing of one of two rolls of film. She now carried them with her everywhere. "Any court in Canada would take the word of a professional psychologist over yours. Any friggin' day."

Brethour licked his red lips. "Think so, do ya?" He dragged the last bit of nicotine out of his cigarette then ground it out on the scuffed coffee table. Just one more burn among dozens. Patrick glanced at Alice. Her eyes remained on him but were no longer blank. "Well, I don't. No one's gonna believe ya, not after Renfield." He scratched his sweaty armpit and sniffed. "Smells like shit in here. Whatchya been up to, woman?"

Patrick froze.

Brethour scratched again. "Gimme a smoke."

Amelia's mother didn't move. Patrick wasn't sure she heard the order.

Brethour reached across the battered couch and shoved her hard. "Hey! Earth to Alice. I said gimme a smoke."

Alice's right hand slipped out of her pocket as she tried to stop herself from falling. A small black film tube popped free and bounced to the dirty carpet. Patrick and Brethour reached simultaneously.

Alice cried: "No!" as Patrick scooped it up.

He was about to hand it back to her when Brethour lashed out: "Where'd you get that, you bitch?" He slid across the couch, right hand raised.

"Stop!" Patrick barked, drawing his baton with his free hand.

Brethour hesitated, then moved to strike.

Patrick lunged, slammed the stick onto Brethour's back. Terry Brethour whirled, lips a pale rose, and howled.

Alice screamed. Raking her hands through her hair, she crouched in the corner of the sofa.

"Nobody move!" Patrick thundered. "You," he pointed the stick at Brethour, "get over there and shut up!"

"I'm gonna sue you, you fat-nosed bastard!" he said, but slid across to the chair. "You broke my bloody shoulder."

"Now, let's everyone calm down, okay?" The last thing Patrick felt was calm but he figured if he said the word, he'd feel it. He didn't. He took a couple of deep breaths and, with an eye on Brethour–who raised a middle finger–shoved his baton back into the loop on his belt.

"That's good, real good." He sat down. "Now, Alice, what's on the film?"

"THE MOTHER SUPERIOR'S NOT AVAILABLE. WHAT do you want? I'm next in charge."

"I need to see Sister Winifred," Tempest said. "Please, Sister Eileen, it's very important." What she really wanted to say was: Get the fuck outta my way, woman!

Eileen's eyes widened. "You might as well speak to me." She gestured over her shoulder. "She's speaking with the bishop. He's sure to replace her. I warned him the place is a disaster! Sydney's parents are arriving tonight, several others have pulled their children from the school. We have to bury Benedict; fine time to have a heart attack." She shook her head. "Something must be done around here."

"I don't care if she's talking to the bloody pope, I'm going in."

Tempest brushed the woman aside and marched down the hall, listening. A couple of seconds later, she heard a muffled nasal voice behind a thick, wooden door. Ignoring Eileen's protestations, she entered without knocking. Turned and shut the door in the older nun's face.

Startled, Winifred looked up. Her eyes narrowed. "Yes, yes, your Eminence. I–"

"Hang up," Tempest commanded.

Winifred stared, her mouth agape.

"I said hang up, or I'll do it for you."

"Don't be–"

Tempest punched down the switchhook.

Winifred blinked, her face turning purple. "Who do you–"

"–think I am?" Tempest completed her sentence. She leaned over the desk. "I'll tell you who I am. I'm Darcy Winsloe's sister."

Winifred's dark eyes bulged. "Dar–"

"That's right. Sister Gabriel's sister. And you know what else?"

Sister Winifred remained still. Her hollow cheeks puffed in and out like an exhausted jelly fish. A dial tone beeped from the receiver. Tempest took the instrument from the nun's small hand and dropped it on the switchhook.

"I'm Vita Bell's aunt. And I want to know why she was killed."

TWENTY-SIX

A man fears nothing on earth
When he is defending his children's honour.
—RIGOLETTO, ACT 2

All eyes were on the small black tube. Terry Brethour was sucking another cigarette, tongue darting across his thick lips in between drags. Alice Penderghast's tea-coloured hair stood on end, slicked up from her hands' natural oils.

Patrick was thinking, trying to figure out what he held in his hand and how he could use it to nail Brethour. He decided to go on the offensive. Ignoring Brethour, he repeated his question to Alice.

She blinked a few times, then played with her hands. Terry opened his mouth but shut it quickly after a look from Patrick.

"Come on, Alice. You know what it is. I can see it in your face."

"Not a word," Terry snarled.

Patrick whipped his head in Terry's direction. "You, shut the fuck up!" He fiddled with the film case's lid.

"Don't!"

"Why not? What's so special 'bout this film?"

Alice's watery eyes slewed toward her boyfriend but she remained silent.

To hell with this! "Doesn't matter really, 'cause we'll all know once the police lab develops it." Patrick rubbed his nose. "Just thought you might wanna help. You know, a little good faith goes a long way in court."

"Whaddya mean?" Brethour asked.

Patrick kept his eyes on Alice. "Simple. You help us solve a crime and catch the criminal, we'll help you. Understand, Alice?"

Alice Penderghast looked like she'd never understand anything again in her life. Patrick felt sorry for her. Knew that she never meant to put Amelia at risk. But she had. From her dull expression of resignation, he was certain that she knew it. He deliberately baited her.

"You knew Amelia was being–"

"Enough!" Brethour snapped. "Anyone's gettin' a deal is me. I know somethin' you want. You get me a deal, I'll give it to ya."

Still Patrick ignored him. The more he focused on Alice, the greater the chance Brethour would blow.

"Sure you don't want to talk, Alice?"

"You deef or somethin'?" Terry rubbed the fuzz above his mouth. "Look, man, you got kiddie-porn photos, I know where they come from."

Slightly surprised by the subject change, Patrick faced the pale-eyed man. "You, perhaps? Your prints're all over them."

That shook Terry Brethour. His tongue slid over his lips. Patrick suppressed the urge to rip the pink triangle out of the scrawny guy's mouth. Finally he blurted: "No way. Not me."

He stared at his hands, stained with roofing tar. "I

might've touched them, yeah, but that's not important." He looked up. "I know where they come from. Whatchya gonna do for me?"

THE SILVER CROSS FLASHED IN THE HARSH GLARE OF the table light.

Wonder she doesn't rub it raw, Tempest thought.

"Killed? Who said anything about being killed?"

Tempest ignored the question. "How'd she get here?"

"You mean—"

"Darcy, Sister Gabriel."

Winifred sighed heavily. "You may as well sit down."

Tempest obeyed. She knew she had to face Darcy. Soon, but not yet. There was something she must know that only the Mother Superior could tell her. Though the nun's response would guide her, she feared the inevitable ghastly result.

"It's a long story—"

"I've got time."

The nun unscrewed a glass jar, shook out a couple of jujubes and quickly chewed. Tempest refused her offer, so Winifred filled her palm and slowly ate the rest of the colourful candies, one by one.

"Can we get on with it?"

Winifred gulped, then swallowed a red one. Another sigh. "All right." Her grey eyes narrowed. "Why do you think you're Sister Gabriel's sister?"

"I don't think, I know."

Winifred's expression remained blank.

"Her name's Darcy Winsloe, right?"

Winifred nodded.

"Well, my real name's Tempest Winsloe. I...I changed it for personal reasons."

"You have proof?"

"Of course I do! Now, how'd Darcy get here?"

"Why should I tell you?"

Tempest snorted. "Because I have the right to know! And I can bloody well bet that her coming here wasn't strictly by the book." She watched the Mother Superior's expression harden. "Yeah, I thought so." She paused, gathering courage. "I...I'm also afraid."

Winifred pursed her lips. "Afraid? Afraid of what?"

Tempest hesitated, almost changed her mind. Forced herself to think of Vita Bell's red curls and huge eyes. So much like her own. *Come on, Pesty, here we go.* She locked onto the nun's slate-coloured irises.

"Another death."

TWENTY-SEVEN

Tell the truth...
—RIGOLETTO, ACT 1

"You got those photos from Dr. Ivory's place, Dr. Tempest Ivory?" Must be some mistake, thought Patrick. Then something flashed, a faint memory. He tried to grab hold but all he could snag was a flimsy connection to Tempest.

Terry Brethour smirked. With his scrawny face and paltry whiskers, he looked for a moment like one of the street people hanging around Victoria's Inner Harbour. One thing was different: Patrick felt sorry for the street people.

Maybe she's got them for research. Yeah, that's possible.

"No more, 'less you cut a deal." Brethour leaned back and lit another cigarette. Alice Penderghast was silent, her eyes glazed. Arms crossed, she rocked slightly.

"I've got no authority to cut deals. We'll have to go to the station, talk to the staff sergeant."

Brethour exhaled and blue smoke drifted over Patrick. He held both his breath and the desire to blow it right back. "Better be good, man. There's a lot more where those come from." Terry picked tobacco from his teeth. "Worth a ton in the right hands–" he grinned. "Or the wrong?"

"MURDER?" SISTER WINIFRED ASKED IN A CHOKED voice. She swallowed. "No one said anything about murder."

"That's because no one realizes it."

"You do?"

Tempest nodded slowly. "I'm not absolutely positi–"

"Then why in heaven's name have you barged in here saying exactly that? Really, Dr. Ivory! Very unprofession–"

Tempest interrupted her right back. "Don't judge my professionalism," she snapped in a voice as cold as the nearby waters of Patricia Bay. "I'm not responsible for the death of three innocent children."

For a moment, the Mother Superior was speechless. "And..." Winifred sputtered. "And I am?"

Tempest fought the rage, jaw grinding to keep it under control. If only she weren't so tired. Her head ached. "This's getting us nowhere. We...we've got to work together or..."

The Mother Superior gripped her silver cross. The two women eyed each other across the oak desk for a long time. Tempest, who had had plenty of practice outstaring her patients, felt her advantage. A surge of nausea made her dizzy. The nun broke first, glancing down at her candy jar. She gobbled a handful, chewing several at once. Realizing that she was starving, Tempest cautiously chewed a yellow one, then grabbed a fistful, craving sugar.

"My cousin, Leo Painter, brought them," Winifred

finally said in a calm voice. "He was desperate. I never asked, but he had his reasons."

"Painter? Any relation—"

The nun nodded gently. "Father. He and I are first cousins. They came one night, Leo, your sister and her new baby." Her lined face softened. "Such red hair! Like a sunset off Coles Bay." Winifred's mouth hardened. "Things were different then. Why, your sister was a child herself! Leo told me she'd run from an abusive home, spent time on the street. Had the baby in an alley. Alone."

Tempest's stomach tightened. She could smell the loneliness and dampness; her throat felt raw. She needed water.

"He told me she had nowhere to go. Had refused Child Protection Services' help." Winifred dropped her head. When she looked up, her grey eyes were drowning. "He...I...I always wanted a baby. Darcy was a wreck, both physically and emotionally. She wouldn't speak, couldn't care for herself, much less the child." Tears streaked down the fine lines in her face. "I followed the Lord's words: 'And now abideth faith, hope and charity...but the greatest of these is charity.'"

She rummaged in her sweater and removed a handkerchief. Blowing her nose, she added: "Charity begins at home. Well, my home is the Perpetual Soul."

The queasiness curled over the young psychologist. She closed her eyes, stomach churning. Jujubes mixed with insomnia. Her stomach muscles contracted, bile rushed into her throat. Coughing, she begged for water. Winifred jumped up and disappeared into an anteroom. She reappeared moments later with a full glass.

Tempest drank greedily.

God, what a nightmare!

She couldn't, wouldn't believe. Tempest Ivory, née Winsloe, dug deeply, summoning the remains of her courage and asked one of the two questions she most feared.

"So Darcy knew that Vita Bell was her daughter?"

TWENTY-EIGHT

Ah, heaven did not take all from me!
—THE DUKE OF MANTUA, ACT 2

Local opera star dead

The Victoria opera community joins a local family in mourning the loss of Vivian Winsloe. Winsloe, age 35, was found dead in her Metchosin home on March 17 by her husband, Barry Winsloe, chief superintendent of the Victoria School Board. The cause of death has yet to be released.

Mrs. Winsloe, a professional soprano, was a well-known and popular member of Vic Opera. She had been recently chosen to understudy the role of Gilda in Giuseppe Verdi's Rigoletto.

Mrs. Winsloe is survived by her husband and three children, ages 12, 10 and nine.

Victoria Observer, March 18, 1978

Patrick rewound the microfiche and rubbed his eyes. He'd spent the better part of the afternoon at the *Observer*, whipping through the newspaper's microfiched archives. Shamrocks had been on his mind ever since he had heard the change in Tempest's voice. Should've looked into it earlier, he now admitted to himself, given that the first child died on his patron saint's day and there were shamrocks at the scenes of the other deaths. Maybe the plants were symbolic. But of what?

Earlier, he'd checked his gardening books at home. Skipping the part on growing conditions and propagation, he hadn't learned much, other than that the small plants belonged to the *Leguminosae*, or clover family.

A short detour to the Sidney-North Saanich library was more fruitful. Though small, the library boasted a solid reference section, and he quickly skimmed the encyclopedias, jotting down the relevant information.

Patrick reached for and reread those notes. Not much new, if he'd given it any thought. He'd always known that shamrocks were considered a good-luck charm so it made sense that this was the reason the little three-petalled plants were chosen as Ireland's national emblem. Not so. They were symbolic, chosen because St. Patrick, legend had it, used them to illustrate the dogma of the Holy Trinity.

Holy Trinity...three girls' deaths...Catholic school...any connection?

So began his search, checking back through every St. Patrick's Day until he saw the seventeen-year-old headline about the death of a local opera star and whistled. That had been enough to hook him.

Wonder how she died? He'd have to look further.

He glanced again at the printout on the results of Sister Gabriel's fingerprint check. Darcy Winsloe. *Coincidence? Yeah, and I'm Constable Benton Fraser of the Royal Canadian Television Police.*

He leaned back, thinking about Sister Gabriel. Fingerprints didn't lie. Not a common surname. The young nun had to be what, late twenties? He reread the last paragraph of the article: *ages 12, 10 and nine.* No names or sexes. If Vivian Winsloe died in 1978...he grabbed a calculator and carefully punched in some numbers. Her kids would be anywhere from twenty-eight to thirty-one.

Then, he studied the note sent by his mother. Italian? Verdi was Italian. *Damn!* He'd forgotten to bring that libretto booklet.

His eyes fell on the most exciting piece of information. The note in Italian was signed by V.W. *Vivian Winsloe!?*

He shoved in another microfiche cassette and scrolled ahead, past a lead story about three Sidney men who escaped death when a twenty-ton crane flipped on its side and plunged into Tsehum Harbour, to March 20, 1980. Another brief article on Vivian Winsloe. He scanned quickly until part of a sentence sent shivers down to his toes: *The cause of death has been verified as suicide, though no note was found.*

Patrick stared, unseeing, at the screen. *Suicide? Vivian Winsloe committed suicide? On St. Patrick's Day? Bloody hell!*

Idly he scrolled forward, slipping into the next week. The results of a coroner's jury inquest into the drowning death of a local native barely caught his attention. His mind was still churning when a familiar name jumped out from the screen. Patrick reared back in his chair, almost toppling. A woman at a nearby video terminal shot him an angry stare. Heart thumping, throat parched, Patrick ignored her to study the blue screen in front of him.

It was then that he read of the suicide death of thirteen-year-old Nathan Winsloe, son of Barry and Vivian (deceased).

And of the bouquet of shamrocks found at the boy's feet.

"WELL, DID SHE?"

Sister Winifred looked like a gnarled snag of cedar, bleached a colourless grey by the pounding Pacific surf. For once, the silver cross which gleamed against her ashen skin remained untouched.

Tempest hesitated, not surprised by the nun's reaction to such a simple question. This was how it often happened with her patients. A seemingly innocuous statement or query triggered an unpleasant connection, launching them into an emotional tailspin. Following her training, the young psychologist did the most powerful thing she could. She kept quiet and waited. Darcy's younger sister was in no hurry to hear the answer.

"I...I don't understand," Winifred finally whispered.

"Simple question. Does Darcy, excuse me, Sister Gabriel, know that Vita Bell was her daughter?"

"I understand the question." A bit of the Mother Superior's feistiness returned as her nasal voice grew louder. "I don't understand its significance. Sister Gabriel was told that her daughter was adopted by a family up Island. That was the original plan, but..." A small hand darted to worry the cross. "Poor girl's never been very stable, but she seemed to find strength and relief in her religious training. Many do, you know. Even today, some women are attracted by the life of prayer, drawn to the simplicity and solitude. By the time she took her vows, Darcy Winsloe had disappeared." She stared evenly at Tempest. "As a psychologist, you'd know more about why than I."

Tempest refused the bait. "Did she ever ask about the baby?"

Winifred shook her head. "It was as though that part of her never existed. I was a little worried when Vita started school–" A brief smile. "–she still had the red hair, but Gabriel never gave her a second thought."

Tempest drew a long, shuddering breath. *She didn't know! Thank God, she didn't know.*

The nun's brows knitted. "Why's this important? You think your sister needs to know the child's identity? For what, mourning?"

It was Tempest's turn to shake her head.

I must be mad, she thought, unwilling to examine the conclusion that had plagued her since the first death. *It's only a plant, gotta be some bizarre coincidence.*

"I'd like to see my sister. Alone."

TWENTY-NINE

Woman is wayward as a feather in the wind.
—THE DUKE OF MANTUA, ACT 3

The rhythmic beat of violins and reed instruments filled his head. The black truck swerved, streaking into the right lane. Jesus! Patrick thought, whipping the wheel left. The half-ton skipped back into the fast lane, accompanied by the baleful blare of an eighteen wheeler roaring past.

The music! That's it!

Heart pounding against his seat belt, Constable Painter gripped the thick plastic on his steering wheel and squealed off the Pat Bay Highway. The truck lunged down into the pastoral beauty of Martindale Valley and came to a shuddering halt beside a field of trumpeter swans. Huge white and grey bodies rose as if one, wings like fighter jets beating the charcoal skies. For a moment, the giant birds' bugle-like call soared with Verdi's tale of deception and obsession.

What is that word? Mobiey? Patrick punched the backwards skip button on the CD player. The song began again. *I'll be damned!* He slammed the steering wheel. It was the song he'd overheard at the

McPherson Playhouse. More importantly, it was the one song his father had hummed on his sixteenth birthday.

Da da da dadada...da da da dadada...da...da...da dadada... They were sharing a rare moment together, tinkering with the old man's Plymouth, when his mom called her husband to the phone. "Don't worry," he said. "I'll give it to someone else." But something happened. As Patrick watched, his father's famous military bearing slipped as he asked the dispatcher to repeat the address. Leo Painter's eyes seemed to shrink, collapsing into angry clouds. The scar glowed against his heavy, flushed cheek. When he hung up, he was gruff, pushing by his son.

Patrick paused, remembering a father on the verge of tears. Unthinkable! He never told his mom. Not sure why. Something in his father's blank face and softened shoulders had stung him.

Of course, Leo Painter didn't come home for the big meal; the pork tenderloin congealed in the fridge alongside a weeping Caesar salad. Even the green beer—first time it wasn't milk—warmed and went flat on the spotless counter. His mom kept saying, "He'll be here, hon." But they both knew it was a lie.

By nine, he and his mother were so weary of the unanswered angst and unrequited silence that she went to bed. Patrick downed the three glasses of tepid beer, grabbed the lemon meringue pie—his mom's special mile-high version—and pitched it at the garage door. No matter what time he came home, the ol' bastard's headlights couldn't miss the splat of yellow and white.

Patrick stared at the swans, some circling slowly, a couple already touching down. His father's musical tastes ran to big band if they were ever chased, a far cry from opera. He glanced at the libretto and the CD, discovering that the song was called *La donna è mobile*. Mobile. That's what he was hearing.

Punching the CD player again, he read the translation of the famous tenor aria. Watching the munching birds, he listened to the whole song over and over, memories like a cold wind prickling up his spine at every beat.

Woman is wayward as a feather in the wind. He who trusts her or foolishly gives her his heart is always wretched.

Change the female pronoun and it'd sound just like Leonard P. Painter.

"GABRIEL'S EXTREMELY FRAGILE." SISTER WINIFRED slid from behind the desk to bar the doorway in the time it took Tempest to breathe. She'd never seen anyone move that fast, not since envying a young Darcy's slippery speed in avoiding her father's pinch. "You must let me talk to her first, prepare her."

"No way." Tempest marched over and stared down at the smaller woman. A one hundred and seventy-eight pound threat. "She's my sister and I'm gonna speak to her alone." Gone were her fears of confronting Darcy, replaced by a protective fury, roiling to keep this liar from further poisoning her sibling's mind.

With a thick arm, she shoved the Mother Superior aside and stomped down the hallway. Winifred recovered quickly to whine at her heels.

"Darcy!" she bellowed, using the projection which vaulted her voice into the distant rafters of the McPherson. "Daaarrcyyy!"

Faces popped out from doorways, most startled, a few angered. One glance at the bulky figure thundering over the hardwood floors was enough. Mouths were shut tight but eyes stayed wide open as the Sisters of the Perpetual Soul witnessed Tempest Ivory's whistling wake.

One face was different. Lit by a smile, a fleeting expression which grew into a look of pure joy. Sister Gabriel's eyes glittered in the dusky light.

"Pesty," she whispered, arms outstretched. "I prayed you would come to me."

All disturbing thoughts evaporated as Tempest felt, for the first time in thirteen years, the warmth of her only sister's embrace.

"Darcy, it's you, it's really you," she whispered, tears cooling her cheeks. "Thank God, I'm not alone."

THIRTY

If I am evil, it is only because of you!
—RIGOLETTO, ACT 1

"Who's Vivian Winsloe?"

Leonard P. Painter hesitated in mid-gulp. Ignoring his son, Painter swallowed hard, then tossed the dregs over the side. "Guess you're gonna arrest me for polluting."

Patrick had found him at home, aboard *The Paintbox*. For once, the workaholic was at rest. The younger man climbed aboard, but leaned against the gunwale. "No need. Got lots of other causes."

Painter Sr. leaned forward. Patrick felt his stomach muscles clench. His father stopped, then rubbed his scarred cheek with a broad hand. "What's that supposed to mean?"

"Means you know a lot more'n you're saying."

"Oh yeah?" He snorted and struck his knee. "What, like this here boat's used for smuggling?" Suddenly, he stood, holding out hands the size of small hams. "Ya got me dead to rights, copper."

Patrick held his breath.

"I'll come quiet." He laughed gustily but his eyes never left his son's face.

"Very funny. What about Vivian Winsloe? Her committing suicide a joke to you?"

The hands curled into fists. Patrick shifted his weight forward, ready to move. His father surprised him by dropping his arms and plunking down.

"Don't know any Vivian Winsloe, all right?"

"No? Then why'd Mom send you one of her notes?"

The grey-haired head snapped up. Leonard Painter's black eyes fixed on his son's. "What? A note from Vivian?" The eyes narrowed as the older man realized his mistake. "Didn't get any note," he finished gruffly.

Patrick stepped forward and eased into the deck chair across from his parent. "So you do know her."

The older man toyed with his mug.

"What do they tell you?"

Puzzled, Leo looked up.

"The tea leaves." Patrick pulled in a sailful of salty air, then followed a hunch. "Do they tell you where Vivian's suicide note is?"

The mug dropped to the deck with a thud, rolled to its right and split into pieces.

Bingo.

Neither spoke. Recognizing his advantage, Patrick fought his urge to talk, to cut the heavy quiet strung between them like rigging. To wipe the look of startled pain off his father's ruddy face.

His father inhaled heavily, seemed to gain strength from the biting air. "Fuck off," he whispered. His hands curled again. He glanced at them as though surprised they existed, then used them to stand upright. "Fuck right offa my boat 'fore I bust those peas you call balls!"

Patrick scrambled up, knocking the chair over. Got ya, ya bastard! he thought. "You knew her, didn't ya? You must've."

"Told you. Don't know any Vivian Winsloe. Now, get offa my boat!"

Patrick didn't know why, but as he sidled toward the gunwale, he began humming *La donna è mobile.* "Da da da dadada, da da da dadada, da da da dad–"

The ruddiness leaked from Leo Painter's cheeks, leaving the Scar of Bravery glowing like a new moon. Patrick's breath shrivelled under the anguish which stalked across his father's face.

The staggered words came haltingly, thickly, as though spoken in a trance. "How did...Where?" He collapsed into a chair, dropping his head in his hands. "Oh my God."

Why can't I hate you? Christ! An image of his mother snapped into his brain, feeding his anger. Patrick shook his head, uncertain of his next move.

The question popped out before he thought about it. "How'd you meet Darcy Winsloe?

His father's head remained down.

"She's the nun at the Old Soul I told you about, remember? The one you brought in years ago. Happens to be Vivian Winsloe's daughter. Funny coincidence, huh?"

Muffled sounds from behind the thick fingers.

"What'd you say?"

The hands fell away slowly and a much older Leo Painter gazed wearily at his son. "She was fifteen and had just given birth in an alley. Needed help."

"You took 'em to Aunt Winifred?"

A slight nod.

"What happened to the baby?"

Leo's strong shoulders collapsed into a deep sigh. "Adopted, up Island somewhere. I never asked."

"Why not?"

He spread his heavy hands out front. "What'd I care? The girl and the baby got help. End of story."

"Girl or boy?"

Painter Senior looked puzzled.

"The baby...boy or girl?"

"How the hell should I know? Was all covered up." He paused, remembering.

"Yeah?"

Leonard Painter shook his head.

"Come on! What?"

A brief smile lifted the lines on his father's cheeks. "The damnedest thing, the kid had hair the colour of a sunset."

"I DON'T KNOW YOU."

"What?" Tempest felt as though she'd walked into an arena; the warm glow of their earlier embrace shrivelled by the sudden cold. "I...I don't understand." She stared at the thin young woman, trying to ignore the chorus of noes pounding in her head. "Darcy, you...you called me Pesty."

A nasal voice interrupted. "I told you she was fragile. Please, Dr. Ivory, she's had a shock." The Mother Superior led Sister Gabriel to sit at a nearby hall bench. "She needs rest, surely you can understand."

"Rest?" Tempest replied blankly.

"I'm sorry," Gabriel said softly, eyes downcast. "Severing oneself in the name of God is painful." She looked up. Tempest felt as though the familiar green eyes bored right through her. "Feelings don't count. Loneliness helps us realize the need for Him."

She's mad. Oh dear God, she's mad!

"Darcy," she hesitated. No reaction from the young nun. "Sister Gabriel, tell me about Vita, about Sydney."

Gabriel toyed with her rosary. "Gone to glory." Her sudden smile, startlingly pure, haunted Tempest. "Death doesn't exist, only life."

Is it possible she doesn't know?

"It's just a portal to another–"

Tempest felt the pricklings...of horror...of truth.

"I've told you, she must rest." Sister Winifred walked in front of the young psychologist. "I'm asking you to leave, Dr. Ivory."

"But...but she's my...she..." Tempest's powerful voice trembled. One can assail years of physical abuse and fear but the emotional wounds rankle. The resulting rage was returning, fuelled by excitement, discovery and despair. Her head rang like the academy's bell.

Soon, she would lose control.

"Darcy, please!"

She reached for her sister but was rebuffed by Sister Winifred. A flash of anger jolted the young woman and she almost struck the tiny religious. With a tremendous effort, Tempest regained her self-control.

"You don't understand, you fucking idiot. She's my sister. She needs my help!"

Gabriel slowly stood and began walking away.

"No! Wait!"

"Leave us now!" The Mother Superior's voice snapped like a whip. "Or I'll call the police!"

"All right, all right! Darcy," she shouted at the retreating figure, "I'm coming back. I can help."

THIRTY-ONE

Like a thunderbolt hurled by God,
The jester will know how to strike you.
—RIGOLETTO, ACT 2

"Tempest, darling!"

She leaned back, surprised by the alcohol blast.

"Bit early, Cy, even for you?"

Cyrus Everard, ever the professional, kept the show going right along. "Something wrong, my child? Curtain call order not to your little liking?"

The sequence of curtain calls, generally hammered out during the final dress rehearsal, provoked more enmity than Middle East land disputes. The last curtain call was the place of honour, traditionally reserved for the prima donna, except in cases where there was a male title character, like Faust or Don Giovanni. Tempest hadn't given it a moment's thought, but now realized sadly that the honour would go to the actor playing Rigoletto.

Everard was still talking. "Jeffrey's little quirks driving you crazy?" He started to laugh, deep voice rumbling. "Crazy!" He tossed his salt-and-pepper hair. "That's a good one, eh, ma p'tite shrink?"

"Quit the grandstanding. Gonna let me in?"

The deep-set brown eyes blinked dramatically. "Of course, darling prima donna." He extended a satin-covered arm with a Shakespearean flourish. "Do come in."

She refused her coach's offer of a drink and dropped into his heavy leather chair. Cyrus raised his eyebrows— the seat was his favourite—and made a production of settling into a nearby wicker rocker. She was pleased to see him shift as the rocker's wooden cross pleats dug into his back. Just as they'd irritated hers for months.

"Did you have an affair with Vivian Winsloe?"

Everard barked harshly. "What?" A flash of yellow teeth. "Never one for small talk, eh, my little canary?"

Tempest held her tongue. She'd seen fear and recognition flash behind the round glasses.

Cyrus took a long pull from his glass and carefully licked his lips. "What li'l bird told you that?"

"Forget the bird crap, Cyrus, answer the question."

"I think I'll have another drink." He stood up, arched his back. "Sure you won't join me?"

Tempest shook her head.

"Pity. Somehow I feel we're both going to need it." Cyrus strode across to a nearby sideboard and liberally sloshed whiskey into his glass. He dipped a long, yellow-stained finger then licked it sensuously.

"Who's Vivian Winsloe?" he asked with a straight face.

"Uh uh. Not playing, Sir Noisy Nodes."

"Ah! So that's how it is." Everard perched on the rocker. "You tell that bitch Gertie she's a li'l shit!"

He sighed dramatically and removed a cigar from his breast pocket. "She was a singer. So what? Long time ago."

"You had an affair?"

To her surprise, he sniffed the stogie and shook his head.

"I don't believe you."

"Really? Why ask, then?" Cyrus Everard smiled thinly. "You think it does my reputation any good to deny it? Even fifteen years later?"

He hummed softly, a tune Tempest couldn't quite make out. "Ha! At my age, that's all there's left, darling. Sex in the past, real or imagined."

He paused, then hummed louder.

Tempest waited for the connection. Bizet! *The Flower Song* from *Carmen*. Poor Don Jose, another man blinded by love.

Finally, Cyrus downed the remaining alcohol in a quick gulp. He shuddered. "Such a tragedy." The rough voice cringed in a whisper. "She was the only one."

"FAREWELL, YOU ALONE ARE MY HOPE AND SOUL."

Leo Painter hesitated in tying *The Paintbox*'s lead line to the heavy dockside cleat.

Patrick continued to read. "Farewell, my love for you will never change. Signed V.W." He glanced at his father. "Sorry, should read it in Italian but my accent sucks."

The big man was erect, staring at his only son, mouth agape.

How do relationships change? Not with a bang but a whimper. Patrick watched the man he had adored as a child, had desperately wanted to emulate. Part of him still did, goddamn it, but after that St. Patrick's Day, the lives of the three Painters had slipped and slid out of control in the slow, inexorable twist of a loose nut.

"Where'd you...?" The voice was a horrified whisper. The ex-police officer hunched, as though kicked in the stomach.

"Recognize it, huh? Thought you would, you see— hey!"

The blow was unexpected, low to his legs. Patrick whirled and grabbed with his free hand.

His father yelping. Fingers clutching grey hair.

Searing pain to his kidneys. *Aaoww!*

He dropped, arms raised in defence.

Tearing sound. Half the sheet gone.

Father's face in his, angry, scar blazing.

"Gimme that, you bastard!"

Right fingers wrenched, paper freed. Ragged breathing. *Mine or his?*

Pain stabbing his index finger. *Jesus!*

"You goddamned piece of shit!"

Blinded, scrambling to his feet.

Lunging, left hook.

Painter Senior's black eyes rolled, his neck snapped back. More uneven breathing.

Patrick cradled his injured hand in his left palm, teeth clenched, sucking in air.

"It's broken." He glanced up under black bangs. "You broke my bloody finger."

His father hesitated, then slowly moved toward him.

"Lemme alone!"

The big hands were gentle, oddly comforting. "Come on, Paddy boy," his father said in a strained voice. "Take you to the hospital."

THIRTY-TWO

I want to confess only before you...
—GILDA, ACT 2

"It was so Italian, passion at its very core. I thought she felt the same." He removed the round spectacles and looked at Tempest. "*La vita è così.*"

His brown eyes seemed dull and shrunken without the magnification of the thick glasses. She saw the faint spiderwebs which caressed his eyes and forehead. He really loved her! she thought.

"Oh, it could have been like other affairs." A quick grin. "I've had my nips. Ask anyone."

I'll bet you have, you old goat.

He sipped thoughtfully, eyes hooded. "But it wasn't. Ever lost in love, ma p'tite?"

What could she say? The truth? He'd either laugh at or pity her. She couldn't bear that, nor would she explain that you can't lose what you've never had.

"Yes," she replied confidently. After all, she was an actor, as well as a singer.

"Ah!" he leaned forward. "Then you know what I mean. Vivian was my Isolde but alas, I wasn't her Tristan." Tempest nodded, familiar with opera's version of Romeo and Juliet. "She..." he hesitated, then replaced his glasses.

His eyes shone like puddles. "She was brilliant! Botticelli face, voice of an aroused angel..."

A pause. He studied her.

"Hair...hair the colour, why..." Cyrus scratched his beard. "Just like yours."

Cyrus Everard stared at Tempest as though seeing her for the first time. His eyes widened and he almost dropped his glass.

"That's it!" he shouted, slamming the glass on a table. "All along something 'bout you's been niggling at me. The voice, the hair...couldn't put a finger on it. But now I see." He stretched a long yellow finger at Tempest. "You're just like her!"

She nodded. "My mother."

It's finally out.

Cyrus gasped. "Your...your mother? Vivian? But your name?"

"I changed it." She eyed her coach defiantly. "Can you blame me? After...after what she, what my brother...oh hell!"

Still too painful to verbalize. The social stigma of suicide had been her daily torment, from the schoolyard taunts to the teachers' and parents' fears and subsequent rejection. Their contempt wasn't enough. Tempest inflicted far greater damage on herself.

She wiped at tears and shook her head, discouraged by her own failure to cope. As always, vanquished by the millstone of hopelessness. *Such a loser, Pesty. Those who can, do; those who can't, counsel.*

"There, there..." He reached out a hand, then retreated, unsure. "It's okay, okay."

Cyrus's pathetic attempts to console her made her giggle. Suddenly, she threw back her mane of red curls and roared.

Startled, her coach stared for a moment. Then he, too, grinned and began to laugh. A deep, rumbling gurgle that seemed to come from the earth below.

After a while, they both caught their breath and chuckled sporadically. Finally, the room was quiet. Each thinking of a lost love and its resulting lifelong pain.

"You loved her?"

Cyrus unwrapped a cigar and began playing a lit match around its base. "*Addio, vivrà immutabile, L'affetto mio per te*," he quoted with a gush of smoke.

Farewell, my love for you will never change. Tempest nodded, recognizing the phrase from Verdi's passionate duet between the duke and Gilda.

"And she...?"

A bitter snort. "Loved another."

Tempest nodded. "My father."

Everard's grey head jerked back. "No, my child. Another man."

"What?! You sure?"

"Of course! Think she'd reject *me* for your father?"

A vision of a dark-haired bedridden figure popped into Tempest's mind. Other memories–pot-flinging arguments and uncontrolled sobbing–slipped in as well. She cut them off firmly. "Guess not."

"Damn right. Lookit me!"

Tempest examined his face, the long aquiline nose, even features and penetrating eyes. He had been a stunningly handsome man. Had been.

"I know I look like shit now, but once, Tempest my

dear, I had 'em eating outta my hand." He rubbed the precious palms. "All but one."

"Who was he?"

Cyrus puffed harshly. "No idea. She wouldn't say."

"You're sure? Did she say anything about him, anything at all?"

From behind a cloud of grey smoke, he replied. "Naah."

Another puff.

"Come on, Cy. She musta said something."

"Well...I think she mentioned something 'bout his job."

"Job?"

"Yeah. Painting, I think."

"Painting? You mean walls and stuff?"

"How the hell should I know? Didn't wanna have anything to do with him." He took another drink. "Prob'ly some fag artist who sketches dead meat."

A STRANGER HAD COME HOME THAT MORNING.

With a rattle of the front door. Clink of keys dropping, followed by a frustrated bellow. Pissed, the man stumbled in with the sun, bringing anything but warmth.

The boy's eyes snapped open. Hands digging at his shirt. A struggle. Patrick, sixty pounds lighter, soared off the bed and into the wall. One crack with the back of the man's hand and Patrick's right cheek imploded. Tears and blood flowing, Patrick scrambled free, found his voice and started screaming. The sounds seemed to arouse the man. He shook, like a big, wet dog, and looked at Patrick, as though for the first time. Tormented black eyes unfocused, swollen with tears.

Spittle dragged across his dark chin. For a fleeting moment, the young man saw a flicker of love, even shame, then something darker flooded in. His father turned. His mother backtracked out of the way.

The stranger fell into bed and a long, fretful sleep.

"SHE DIED ON MY SIXTEENTH BIRTHDAY."

Leonard Painter glanced at his son, slumped against the window of his truck. Patrick's eyes were closed, nostrils pinched in pain as he cradled his bandaged right hand and remembered.

It had been a quiet night at the San Pen hospital. Painter Senior made a big deal about drawing number one on the patient pick-a-number machine, but Patrick hadn't even smiled. A young intern had quickly approached. He took one look at the angle of Patrick's finger and said, "That looks special. How'd you do it?"

Keeping his eyes away from his father, Patrick replied, "Got it caught in rigging." He felt, rather than heard, Leo Painter sigh.

Within an hour, Patrick's finger had been X-rayed, set and placed in a finger splint.

Now, as Leonard drove his son home, the questions began.

"Never forget that day," Patrick continued, bolstered by painkiller confidence. "Turning sixteen's a big deal, y'know. You promised you'd be there, but no, you left for some stupid case and that night a real bastard came home."

Leo shifted gears. "I know," he whispered finally. "I know."

Patrick opened his eyes. "Don't care who it hurts. Three little girls've died and I'm not sure how or why anymore." He shifted gingerly. "Only connection seems to be shamrocks and Winsloes. I know Vivian Winsloe committed suicide, I've read the newspaper accounts and, as you know, her last note. Mom sent it to you. Why?"

His father sighed, downshifted, then gunned the motor. Patrick lurched forward and swore. The truck roared along Madrona Drive, twisting with the narrow curves.

"You wanna know?" Leo slammed on the brakes and slid around a corner. The truck skidded to a stop. He shoved the gearshift into first and yanked up the emergency brake. "Okay. You're gonna know. Your mother's dead, guess there's no point in avoiding it anymore."

He clenched the fat steering wheel. "I killed her."

THIRTY-THREE

Yes, vengeance, terrible vengeance,
Is my soul's only desire...
—RIGOLETTO, ACT 2

The Pig couldn't go fast enough, even if it had the wings of a Stealth Fighter. Tempest Ivory's curled wrist strained, burying the speedometer's needle in the depths of the red zone. Teeth chattering, arms buzzing, the vibrations were intoxicating. The dizzying speed demanded absolute concentration, exactly what Tempest sought. A kilometre an hour less and she might think.

Think of her mother, her brother, her sister. Ponder how all three were linked to suicide and shamrocks.

As the pavement whirled under her feet and the trees streaked past, she strained to see beyond the patch illuminated by her headlight. In a flash, she realized that she had been doing this forever. Peering ahead while the world skittered by, trying to figure out what lay in front. Always needing to be prepared, never able to accept life as it arrived.

Essential if you had to camouflage yourself to try to fit in. To renounce your family and continually struggle with an ill-fitting identity. To hide psychological wounds and physical disfigurement. To not give a flying fuckola.

She thought of the three dead girls. Her breath came quicker. Her face shield began to fog. How she empathized with Amelia Penderghast's desperation! She glanced down at her own disfigured wrists. The scars were Tempest's personal testament to such abject despondency.

Tears flowed freely now, she swiped at them and her shield. All she could see was a brilliant red sunset.

Vita. Her red hair, her only relative. What sort of aunt lets her niece die?

She heard Sydney's voice, charmingly weak, then gasped as she recalled the new confidence in those dark brown eyes, now permanently shut.

Tempest shed both tears and miles for a long time.

Finally, nearing Keating Cross Road, she'd had enough.

Pesty, old girl, time for a change. Can't live your whole—or for you, your depressingly fragmentary—life terrorized by the past.

"Get on with it!" she shouted into her face shield, a phrase she commonly used on recalcitrant patients. The Pig's whine sharpened as she jammed on the gas.

Old maps used to characterize uncharted territory with a blood-curdling phrase: beyond here there be dragons.

Secure on her trusted steed, Tempest Ivory was about to do a Saint George.

THIRTY-FOUR

But now everything is gone
The altar is overthrown!
—RIGOLETTO, ACT 2

"You...you killed her? But the papers said—"

"To hell with the papers!" Leonard Painter drew a painful breath. "I...sure as I knotted the belt, I killed Vivian."

Patrick leaned against his seat, shaking his head slightly. *I don't believe this. Maybe I'm hallucinating.* He blinked and looked at his father. The elder Painter's face was drawn, his black eyes sunk into his head like sewers.

Must be the drugs, Patrick thought desperately. Must be.

"You don't believe me." Leo's wide hand struck the steering wheel. A heavy thump reverberated in the small cab. "Well, by God, you're gonna!"

His eyes, now glowing like reflected pools of oil, fixed on his son's face. "You were right. That day, your sixteenth birthday, was a nightmare." He rubbed his facial scar and continued in a whisper. "Oh God...I...I didn't know, couldn't believe it was her."

"You were having an affair?" It suddenly became obvious, the late nights, the arguments, the growing tension between his parents.

"Yes, but..." His voice choked off.

The searing combination of medication, pain and truth numbed the young constable. Patrick felt disoriented, like he was in another galaxy, some kind of Star Trek time-space continuum. Maybe Scotty would beam him up any minute. Lord, he hoped so.

His finger began to throb in earnest. He shifted his right hand. "But what?"

Leo turned away, staring at the lemon grid of daffodil fields.

Patrick waited. As a distraction from the pain, he studied the tall flowers and forced himself to count the long, narrow rows. When he reached thirty-eight, his father spoke, his voice as flat as the surrounding acreage.

"I didn't love her. It...it was–" He bit his lip then continued. "Just an affair, y'know? She was beautiful, I...I wanted her, but..."

"But what?" Patrick heard himself repeat.

"I wasn't gonna leave your mother."

"Why not?" The words popped out. "You never cared for her."

His father reared back, raising his right arm. Patrick remained immobile, too tired and confused to be afraid. "Course I did! I loved your mother. We were happy, really happy until..."

Patrick knew the answer. He'd tasted his father's bitter jealousy all his life. "Till I was born."

The words just dropped between them, neither willing to give support.

"It was just a bit of fun, that's all," Leo said. "At least I thought it was, till she started talking about leaving her husband. She'd already told him! She started pressuring me to tell your mom." He swallowed. "The day before she...died, I'd told her it was over."

He reached for the keys and the truck's motor roared to life. As he shoved the shift into gear, he said, "She died 'cause o' me." The truck spun through a U-turn. "How'd you think that made me feel?"

Like the shit you are, Patrick thought, but said nothing. He concentrated on the pain, the only sensation that seemed remotely real.

"SISTER GABRIEL, HAVE YOU ANYTHING TO CONFESS?" "It's good for the soul, isn't it?"

"Yes," replied Sister Winifred in a soothing tone usually reserved for funerals. She leaned across the desk. "Do you have need of the confessional? I could call Father–"

"Don't bother," snapped a voice in the hallway. Sister Eileen hurried into the Mother Superior's office. "I've just spoken with the bishop," she said, her chest swelling. "He wants to see you immediately. About time, too, girls dying every which way."

"People are hungry about death," Gabriel said in a soft voice that gave the British-born nun pause. "To know what to believe."

Eileen and Winifred exchanged a slow glance. Dear Lord, Sister Winifred thought, the poor thing's daft.

"It's nothing to be afraid of." Gabriel's eyes were glowing, focused on a point somewhere in the garden. "I know. I–"

"Thank you, Sister Eileen," Winifred said, deliberately ignoring Gabriel. "I'll be with him directly. I just—"

"Now, Sister."

Winifred started from her chair. "Sister?"

Eileen rubbed her hands together. "He's asked me to act as interim Mother Superior."

"You? Interim Mother!" Winifred slumped down. "No. He can't, he...wouldn't!"

Eileen just smirked.

So that was it. Thirty-two years of dedication to Christ down the pious drain. A religious didn't just take her vows once, she had to retake them mentally again and again. Winifred had experienced difficulty lately in accepting those sacred words and their consequences. She looked into Gabriel's wild eyes and knew she would take them no more.

God forgive me, she thought, automatically crossing herself. When her hand reached her left shoulder, she hesitated. Did she still believe? She didn't have the answer.

Sister Winifred was only certain of two facts: that Sister Gabriel was mad and that she was responsible.

THIRTY-FIVE

And you, snake,
You who laugh at a father's grief,
Be damned!
                        —COUNT MONTERONE, ACT 1

"Were you surprised?"

"Surprised?" Everard's raspy voice carried the unmistakable drawl of alcohol.

"By what Vivian—my mother—did."

Her coach pulled at his silver beard. "You mean..."

Oh for heaven's sake, spit it out! "Suicide!"

Everard's eyes widened.

She paused, then lowered her voice. "Yes. Were you surprised that Vivian Winsloe committed suicide?"

He got up deliberately and poured himself another three fingers. With a toss, the liquid flew down his throat. "No."

"No? You mean...you expected it?"

"Good God, no!" his voice boomed. "Never! I was...horrified."

"I can't understand it, you know?" Tempest began to pace the large, carpeted room. "I've been trying for years—I'm a psychologist, for Pete's sake—yet, I can't see why. Why she'd kill her–" She gulped. "If she were unhappy with Dad," she shivered, "Lord knows she had her reasons, she could've left, taken us with her. She was singing Gilda, she was in love. She...she had every reason to live."

She stopped. "What? You winced. What's that all about?"

"Nothing! Nothing, just an old man's aches and pains."

Tempest shook her head, started walking. "Uh uh. Something twigged. What'd I say? She was in love?"

"Stop that stomping around."

She ignored him, moving more slowly. "She had us? She could've left him?"

"Sit down, child. You're giving me a headache."

"She was singing Gil–wait!" Tempest marched over to her coach. "She...she wasn't?"

Everard hands covered his eyes. "Sit down. Sit down!"

She sat and waited.

When he dropped his hands, Cyrus Everard looked up. "You're so like her!" He smiled sadly. "It...it hurts."

"It hurts?" she mocked his pain. "Big hairy deal." Tempest fingered a curl. "Get over it. I've had to. Now, tell me, was she singing Gilda?"

Everard sighed. "Guess Gertie'll tell you anyway."

"Tell me what?"

He removed his glasses and began rubbing them with his thumbs. "I had 'er replaced."

"You what?! On what grounds?"

He refused to meet her gaze, eyes fixed firmly on the spectacles. "On the most basic grounds of all: she rejected me."

Tempest was speechless.

It didn't matter. There was nothing like a delayed confession to free the tongue. Cyrus Everard was ready to talk. "After she...I, uh, spread a rumour, said she was too temperamental, that we couldn't work together. Got the Opera to dismiss 'er due to artistic differences."

He smiled wanly. "It wasn't difficult. I was the star. When she...died, I blamed myself. The play was abandoned, never performed since." He fondled his glass.

"I found another lover."

He paused.

Tempest felt empty and exhausted.

"It's almost funny. Like *Hamlet*."

"What?" she asked automatically.

"It's as if *Rigoletto* cursed us all."

THIRTY-SIX

Be quiet, your tears are useless;
You know now that he lied...
—RIGOLETTO, ACT 3

He felt a surge of nausea. Squeezing his eyes shut, he lost himself in the hum of the tires and the slight rocking of the cab. Immersed in the soft glow of pain and painkillers. Like being in the womb, he thought sleepily.

A memory of sunlight streaking her coffin jolted him awake. He shivered; his eyes snapped open. She's dead, he whispered to himself, surprised at the anger rippling up his spine. No longer in denial, Patrick Painter had evolved into the third stage of grieving. Someone had to pay for his loss.

He didn't search far. Less than twenty-four inches away, his father sat stiffly at the wheel of his son's truck. The note.

"How'd Mom get Vivian Winsloe's note?"

His father's hands tightened on the wheel. He geared down, took a corner with all tires squealing. Patrick slammed against the door and yelped.

Leo Painter upshifted and the truck shot along the

narrow lane. "Didn't know Vivian Winsloe left a note. No mention of it in the papers."

He hit the brakes and the vehicle crunched to a stop in front of Patrick's tiny home.

Leo yanked free the keys and opened his door. Patrick didn't move. His father had never been in his house, never would be, yet unerringly, he had known to avoid the dead end and follow the complicated switchbacks and lanes right to his son's drive. How did he know?

"You're right. I've read the papers. No note found. But—" Leo stopped his descent to the wet grass. "—Mom sent the note—where is it, by the way?"

His father patted his shirt pocket.

"Signed by V.W., words taken from *Rigoletto*." He reached across and shoved his father with his left hand. "You were there, damn you! Called first to the scene! You were humming *La donna è mobile* for weeks before her death."

"La donna what?"

Patrick shook his head, fury at his mother's death spilling into his words. "Don't give me that shit! Y'know what I'm talking about." He began humming the opening bars to the duke's aria, each note punctuated with rage.

His father's face turned white; he slouched back into the cab and dropped the keys on the dash.

"You took that note, didn't you? Didn't you!"

The grimace of guilt was enough.

"You...you tampered with a crime scene, took evidence...jus' to save your sorry ass."

"Damn right I did!" his father snapped. "Wasn't gonna let some whore ruin my career. I saw the note, panicked...knew it pointed to me—"

"Whore?! Jesus, you're a bastard." Patrick turned away, wondering who the man beside him was. He breathed through his nose for a long time. "It was in Italian. How'd you know what it said?"

An ugly flush crept up Leo's face, exposing the scar. "She sang it to me, told me what it meant." He slouched over the steering wheel. "Never meant to interfere with the scene. Christ, Paddy! She was hanging...no sign of struggle. Don't mind tellin' you, I was that surprised. Viv really loved her kids, y'know, but it was obviously a suicide. I was right; coroner said so. Once I'd taken it, couldn't put it back. I wanted to, dear God, but..." He picked at the plastic covering the wheel. "So I hid it."

Patrick ran a finger along his hand splint. The pain was mounting, he wanted to be alone, to sleep, to forget. But the anger kept flickering. "So, what happened? Mom found it?"

Leo nodded. "Bout a year later." He smiled thinly. "She had me by the short and curlies, never let me forget it. She knew what it'd mean to my career if it ever came out."

He laughed harshly. "Gotta give the ol' girl credit. Sent it back to me, like she promised."

Patrick grabbed the keys, then struggled with the door latch. With an effort, he edged out. He gazed at the tar sky, punctured by brilliant pinpoints of light.

"No, she didn't," he said, walking to his front door. Fumbling with the key, he pushed open the door.

Patrick turned and awkwardly tugged from his pocket Vivian Winsloe's original letter.

"She sent it to me," he said softly and closed the door.

"TELL ME HOW YOU DISCOVERED GABRIEL'S IDENTITY and I'll let you see her."

Sister Winifred's damage control was in full force. The bishop had confirmed Eileen's statement, she had been removed as Mother Superior of the Perpetual Soul. His Eminence had suggested–the Church's euphemism for an offer a religious can't refuse–that she move east and dedicate herself to a convent in Eastern Quebec. Not as the Mother Superior, mind you, nor as a teacher, for there was no parochial school attached.

As she waited for Dr. Ivory's response, the small woman pondered the irony of her life. I thought I'd arrived somewhere, only to find that it's only somewhere, not the end that I'd hoped. Is that end serving God?

She didn't think so. Her dismissal had stripped Winifred not only of her pride, it had peeled away the last layer of her belief in her religious vocation.

Winifred started, realizing Dr. Ivory was speaking. "I'm sorry, what were you saying?"

Tempest pursed her lips. "I said it's none of your business."

"Really?" Winifred fingered her cross. She had to move fast. Obviously Dr. Ivory was unaware of her new plebeian stature. Any minute Sister Eileen would barge in and ruin it. "It is if you have my personal property."

Tempest played dumb. "Your property?"

"Don't trifle with me, child! There's only one way you'd have found your sister." She stood up and leaned across her desk. "You have my private journal. I want it back."

Tempest couldn't care less about the journal. She meant to give it back ages ago. All she wanted was time with Darcy, alone. "You'll leave us alone?"

"Return the journal now, I'll give you my permission to spend as much time as you like alone with Sister Gabriel."

"Deal," replied Tempest, said, the book in her raised hand.

In her haste to control the diary, Winifred practically wrenched the young woman's arm from its socket.

THIRTY-SEVEN

When I have finished the task before me
We can leave this dismal place.
—RIGOLETTO, ACT 2

Marching along the hardwood halls, she would have ignored the whispering from a small clutch of Sisters if she hadn't heard the soft voice clearly say, "Sister Winifred's out, the bishop himself said so."

She paused, recognizing one of the older nuns. "Excuse me," she asked Sister Louise. "What was that about the Mother Superior?"

Suddenly quiet, the nuns exchanged glances.

Sister Louise frowned. "Well, it's official, so I suppose it's all right." A couple of the women smiled. Encouraged, Louise continued in a low voice, "Sister Winifred's no longer the Mother Superior."

"What?"

Louise nodded. "She's being relocated to Quebec. The new Mother Superior is Sister Eileen."

"Eileen! But she's such a..." Tempest hesitated, struck by a thought. Winifred had no authority to forbid her from seeing Darcy! She was about to inquire further when something caught her attention. She wheeled and began walking toward the staircase.

"Doctor? Dr. Ivory, where're you going?" Louise called after her.

Tempest disregarded her, drawn suddenly by a beautiful sound.

Though untrained—the breathing and control were weak—the unknown soprano had an astonishing purity and range. She found herself singing the vespers softly in accompaniment, pulled toward it, almost forgetting her distressing task.

She skipped up the winding steps, transfixed by the music emanating from a small open room near the landing.

For the first time in days, Tempest wasn't thinking of her mother's death. Instead, she envisioned her parent alive, singing to a standing ovation while she and her siblings, tingling with goosebumps, watched from the wings.

She walked into the room. The ethereal voice stopped.

"You?" Tempest stared at her sister. "That was you?"

Gabriel remained silent but her eyes glowed.

In a rush of emotion, Tempest threw her arms around her sister. "You sound just like her! Just—"

She hesitated. Gabriel's arms hung limply. Tempest flushed and moved back. "Just like Mom," she finished weakly.

"Mom?" Gabriel's expression was blank. "I don't remember Mom."

Tempest froze, as though blasted by a winter wind. "You don't? Uh, d'you know me, Darcy?"

Gabriel blinked then laughed. The brittle sound made Tempest's teeth ache.

"Darcy, remember me? Tempest...Pesty."

Sister Gabriel's gentle face lit up. "Pesty! Yes, yes, little Pesty." She hugged Tempest briefly. "I've missed you."

"Me too. I–" Oh, there's so much I want to ask you, Tempest thought, eyes fixed on her older sister. What happened when you left? Who was Vita's father? Did you miss me? Even think of me?

There wasn't time. At any moment she would be turned out, perhaps denied the chance of seeing Darcy again. The Church could do that, she was certain. Sister Eileen would take great joy in keeping the Winsloes apart.

"Darcy, listen! There's not much time. There's something I have to know." She wanted to ask about the girls, their deaths, but felt a compulsion to understand her mom's. "Remember when Mom died?"

Sister Gabriel frowned.

"You remember? Please, concentrate!" Tempest held her sister's hands. "March 17th, 1978? You were there! You..." she gulped, "...you saw."

"'Without freedom to sacrifice one's life in death, there can be no freedom toward God...'"

"Bonhoeffer?" The name popped out. Tempest recalled studying Dietrich Bonhoeffer and his ground-breaking work on ethics. She had found his sentiments too religious to be of interest.

Gabriel nodded. "You agree?"

"I'm sorry," Tempest blinked. "I don't understand."

"That suicide is the ultimate act of self-justification?"

Tempest dropped her sister's hands. "Are you saying Mom's suicide was justified?"

Gabriel frowned again.

"Darcy, listen carefully. Did Mom leave a note?"

The young nun began looking around the wood-paneled room. Spying a mirror near the door, she took a couple of steps and touched the glass. "Where's the note, he asked?" she whispered. She turned to her sister and raised her eyebrows. "Where's the note?"

"Don't do that!" Tempest snapped. "You always did that, acting stupid, making Dad crazy." She shook her sister. "It's just a ploy. I know all 'bout it. Studied it. Creative stupidity, Jorgensen's term for coping with abuse. You think you're achieving some control."

Gabriel's body rocked without restraint. The green eyes were lifeless.

Tempest dropped her hands. "Look, I'm sorry. It's just...oh hell!" She backed off. "Think, please! I've found out some things about Mom, things that worry me."

No reaction.

Tempest kept babbling. "She was having an affair, did y'know? With some artist, a painter or something–" she stopped, thunderstruck, remembering Gertie's comment: "Struck me as a funny coincidence. You having a cop admirer."

A cop! A painter– She paused, astounded by her intuitive connection. *Jesus Christ, she wasn't having an affair with an artist. She was getting it on with Patrick's father!*

It took Tempest a few seconds to hear her sister. "No," Gabriel was saying, lucid again. "Didn't know about any affair. Think he knew about it."

"Who?"

"Dad."

"Dad knew she was having an affair?" Voices reverberated on the stairway. "Think Darcy, think. This's important." She crossed in front of her sister and shut the door.

"There wasn't any note."

Oh, for crying out loud! "That's what I'm asking!" Tempest shouted.

Gabriel cocked her head. "So did he."

"What? Who?"

"'Man is free to accept his life or to destroy it.'"

"Forget bloody Bonhoeffer." Tempest's right hand lashed out and struck Sister Gabriel.

A white imprint of Tempest's fingers rose on her sister's cheek.

"Oh, Jesus! Darce, I'm sorry."

Gabriel looked in the mirror, stroking her jaw gently. "Leonardo," she smiled slightly. "Just like Leonardo."

The voices grew louder.

"Who the hell's Leonardo?"

Gabriel spoke to the looking glass. "A painter, of course."

Creak of the door handle.

"What the—oh, for heaven's sake! Who said there wasn't any note?"

The door flung open. Sister Eileen marched in. "You," she pointed to Tempest, "are no longer welcome." She saw the mark on Gabriel's cheek. "Dear heavens! What happened?"

Gabriel smiled serenely. Tempest's heart sank.

The new Mother Superior fixed her wide blue eyes on Tempest. "You...you struck her! I'll have you arrested for assault. Now get out!"

Tempest ignored her. "Darcy, please! Who?"

"Leave her alone."

Eileen's strong hands gripped Tempest's arm and she began propelling the young psychologist to the door. Though the nun equalled her in pounds, Tempest had the weight of fear on her side. Resisting, she pleaded with her sister.

With a sad expression, Sister Gabriel said, "Our Father."

THIRTY-EIGHT

Up there in heaven, next to my mother...
I will pray for you forever.

—GILDA, ACT 3

The light was brilliant, hurtful. She tried to shield her eyes but found her hands were frozen. The noise increased, thundering percussion rolling with strident strings. Her ears rang but she couldn't protect them. Her eyes burned with tears. An enormous sense of sadness crushed her and she felt her body fold, collapsing into her solar plexus with a G-force weight.

Breathing was agony. Better not to bother. Best to give up, let the sound and light agony lash her. As she let go, a single, pure note bled through the cacophony. She twisted, strained to hear. The note, a high C, continued to trill, gaining in strength and projection. Soon, the music muffled all other sounds and softened the light. Her body flexed, reaching for the glorious vocal.

It stopped. Still arching, she blinked. A figure appeared, obscured by a shimmering halo. The superb sound renewed.

"Darcy?" She wasn't sure if she spoke the word.

A flash of green eyes, then the figure slipped back, swallowed whole by a burst of orchestral vibrations.

She shouted, but was voiceless. She wriggled, desperately tried to follow, yet remained immobile.

Bellowing her sister's name, Tempest awoke. Startled by the reverberations, she fell back, sweaty and exhausted.

"Darcy," she finally whispered. "Goodbye."

A RINGING SOUND. THROBBING PAIN. HE MOVED, then whimpered. His eyes opened. His bedside clock read 7:12 a.m. Memories of his father, their fight, the hospital. Patrick groaned and stared at his bandaged hand. How could a finger hurt so damn much?

He stumbled out of bed, into the tiny bathroom. Spotted the Tylenol Threes, popped a couple. Changed hand positions but the finger pounded in every one. Running his good hand across a tickly chin, he shook his head at his mirrored image.

"What've you got to say for yourself?"

The mirror remained mute.

"Bloody fuckin' useless," he said, creeping back toward his bed.

The night had been long, an endless succession of pain, tortured thoughts and fits of sleep. He'd never been at ease with his father. Now he wished the old man were a stranger, someone whose dirty secrets he could ignore.

The phone rang, startling him, and he bumped his injured hand against a dresser.

"Aaaoooww!" he cried, biting back tears. Ignoring the phone, he carefully reclaimed his mattress.

The ringing stopped. He breathed heavily, waiting

for relief. Thoughts of his mother crept into his mind. How she must have suffered! To suspect, no, to know her husband was bedding another woman. To hold the proof in her hands! His mother was fastidiously clean. Would she have worn her ubiquitous rubber gloves when she carefully folded and placed the note in an envelope for the lawyer?

The ringing began again. He ignored it. Old phrases, hurled by his parents, returned. Now he understood her disgust, her sense of failure. *Jesus, Mom, why didn't you tell me?*

Of course, he knew why. She'd tried not to colour his understanding of his father. Patrick gritted his teeth. *What a waste! I already thought the worst of the bastard.*

In about fifteen minutes, the finger stopped throbbing. He moved it gingerly and though it ached, the discomfort was tolerable.

Patrick reached across the bed and fumbled with the answering machine. It whirred and clicked, rewinding for a long time. As he waited, he pondered his mother's suspect use of the note. Blackmail. A nasty word for a nasty business. He thought he could empathize with her thinking of it, but his mother's actual threats disturbed him. He didn't like to think about it.

Finally the answering machine stopped humming and began playing the messages. All three were from Wilma Riglin.

She'd left the first late the day before. It was short, just informing him of the receipt of the rest of his fingerprint results. "One thing's kinda interesting," she said. "One of 'em has changed her name. Jus' a sec." There was a sound of shuffling paper. He leaned forward, waiting. Suddenly, the young woman's crisp laugh filled his ears. "Uh, sorry, the Staff's jus' drawn a bead on the computer." Her voice faded. "If you'll just hang on a sec, sir, I'll get the program loaded." The volume increased. "Sorry, Paddy, here...let's see...yeah, this's it. Dr. Tempest Ivory. Real name: Tempest Winsloe. Thought you'd wanna know."

Patrick fell back against his pillow. Tempest was a Winsloe?! But that meant—"

His thoughts were interrupted by Riglin's voice, this time very anxious.

"Hey Paddy, you there? Come on, answer! We got trouble—" The voice changed, suddenly muffled as though speaking to someone else. "—right, call's already made—Paddy, pick up!" Riglin's voice shifted again. "I'm just leaving him a message." The line went dead.

He reached for the phone when Riglin's voice boomed again.

"Paddy? For crying out loud, man, where are you? There's trouble at the Perpetual Soul—"

He didn't wait to hear the rest. Jamming off the machine, he quickly dialled the detachment.

Riglin was frantic. "Called you twice! The Staff's having kittens. Whatchya been doing? You're on duty."

"Sorry, long story. What's up?"

"Just received a 911...fire at the academy. Sounds serious, I'm calling everyone in. Firefighters've been called."

"Jesus H. Christ!" he shouted. "On my way."

He slammed down the phone and reached for his uniform.

THIRTY-NINE

A tempest in the heavens!...
A murder on earth!
—RIGOLETTO, ACT 3

She choked on the last swallow, thin cheeks ballooning in their attempt to capture air. Wiping spittle from her lips, Sister Winifred blinked slowly and stared angrily at the small leather book.

Darkness still curtained her windows. She'd spent the night pacing, drinking and muttering aloud, once in a while fingering the weathered pages of her diary. Upon each she had painstakingly recorded her life at the Old Soul, dutifully summarizing both successes and failures. Strange how one of her greatest achievements, the saving of Darcy Winsloe and her baby, had led to her biggest failure. She was no longer the Mother Superior of her beloved academy.

She reached and, careful to avoid the lit candles scattered about her desk, plopped the vodka bottle beside the jujube jar. For once, the chewy morsels held no appeal. She was unused to alcohol, hadn't even sniffed the potent liquid–save a sip or two at the altar–since she was a teen. She giggled half-heartedly at the irony.

Decades without liquor's wonderful warm glow; what good had teetotalling done her?

She rubbed her eyes but couldn't remove the gritty feeling. The creed that had brilliantly and rigidly guided her life had now failed her. As had her faith in God. A stream of tears marked her hollow cheeks. Winifred felt abandoned and alone, understanding for the first time the naked agony Jesus must have felt on the cross, forsaken by his father.

She yawned several times, overwhelmed by exhaustion. Closing her eyes, Winifred's fingers reached for the open journal. She was unconscious before her arm touched the wooden desk top. She didn't feel the candle nor notice as it toppled onto her diary. Within seconds, the page for December 14, 1983 was scorched and the words *LP brought Darcy Winsloe and baby girl* began to curl and blacken.

SOOTY BANNERS OF SMOKE CURLED OUT OF THE domed windows and tiger-tail flames licked the copper bell tower. Tempest tried to swallow, but her throat was parched. She'd seen the dark mushroom cloud climbing above the Peninsula's horizon and had kicked the Pig into a race with the west wind. She roared by every vehicle on West Saanich, ignoring the horns and jabbed fingers. A hooting clamour chased her and she reluctantly released the gas to allow a red boxcar of a fire engine to thunder past.

An unimaginable chaos of sounds assaulted her ears as she spun round the final corner. Gunning the Pig down the drive, she deeked under the yellow caution tape which roped off the land around the Perpetual Soul and slid the Kawasaki into a stall.

The usually tranquil grounds were in pandemonium as the crews of several volunteer fire engines battled the blaze. Jets of water roared from thick black hoses as the yellow-suited firefighters pummeled the third storey. Dozens of students, small chests heaving from the smoke, hovered just outside the tape under the frantic watch of the Sisters of the Perpetual Soul and several RCMP officers.

Tempest scanned the anxious crowd. Patrick Painter was near the perimeter, holding a little girl, her pale face covered by a plastic oxygen mask. His eyes widened in recognition. No sign of Darcy. She ran to the nearest Sister who had her arms around three young students. "Sister, have you seen Darc–I mean Sister Gabriel?"

The nun looked at her with wild eyes. "Gabriel? No, we're still trying to get an accurate count."

"I saw 'er," a young voice broke in.

Tempest glanced down at the pig-tailed child. "Sister Gabriel? Where?"

The girl brushed ash from her eyes. "Running up the tower stairs."

The nun released her charges and grabbed the child's arm. "Tower stairs? Don't be foolish. No one goes up there."

"Did so," whined the girl.

The sound of breaking glass jarred the crowd and several girls screamed. The pig-tailed girl began to cough.

Tempest took a shallow breath, spat out soot and shouted, "Where's Sister Winifred?"

The nun quickly crossed herself. "She hasn't been seen, either. The firefighters are inside but, ohh, dear Lord, just look at the flames! No one can survive that."

Tempest jogged to a puddle, dipped her scarf in it and wrapped the moistened fleece around her neck. Entry through the front door was impossible as a duo of firefighters struggled up the steps, barely restraining their pulsing hose. Remembering a narrow staircase, she sprinted round the edge of the crowd, holding her breath until she reached the back. More firefighters and police. Her injured ankle throbbed slightly.

Retching, she rubbed her eyes, searching for an entry. Someone bellowed, then a spray of water drenched her. A policewoman marched toward her through the haze, mouth moving. Tempest shook her head, waving the woman back. Then she saw it.

A single open doorway, a pulsating hose trailing. She wound the scarf around her face and dashed into the building. Billows of smoke stung her eyes and lungs so she shut her lids and mouth and, using her arms for direction, crept blindly up the stairwell.

On the first landing, she stopped, coughing uncontrollably. The windowless stairwell was as dark as a winter night. Tempest shifted the scarf and blundered up the next flight. The temperature increased. As she shuffled around a dog-leg turn, she reached for the railing.

With a gasp, she wrenched back her hand, fingers singed. Moaning, she leaned against the warmth of the wall and began yelling her sister's name.

A thumping from above startled her. The smoke gusted and through the temporary clearing a figure appeared, a fireman with a body slung over his shoulders.

Through his clear face mask, she saw him swear, then mouth the words, "What're you doing here?"

Tempest blinked away a torrent of tears and peered at the body.

FORTY

If you go away...I will be left here alone...
Do not die...or let me die with you!
—RIGOLETTO, ACT 3

The head hung down, face out of view. Tempest held her breath. Though only tufts of silver hair remained on the singed scalp, she knew that Sister Winifred was no longer of the Perpetual Soul.

"Anyone else up there?" she shouted, her voice laced with gravel.

Head and face enshrouded, the fireman shook his head. With his free gloved hand, he gave her a push, then motioned down to her.

Her throat and eyes burned, each breath hurt. For a moment she paused. This's insane, she shouted to herself. Get the fuck outta here. Nodding, she moved to let the man and his burden pass. Just as she was about to descend, Tempest thought she heard a sound, a voice. Darcy?

Concentrating, trying to eliminate the scuffle and clang as the firefighter edged down, she held her breath and listened with all her might.

A cough, then the resonance of a soprano.

"Save yourself!" she whispered, though the firefighter had been swallowed up by the smoke and, braced against the melting heat, mounted the next step.

"Daaarrcccyyy!" With a voice as raw as shredded skin, she trumpeted her sister's name. She climbed what seemed like Mount Everest at night, slipping and falling on several occasions, slamming both elbows and re-spraining her ankle. The scarf disappeared. She kept moving, one hand over her mouth. Finally she stumbled into something solid. Feeling about, she realized it was a fixed ladder. The smoke receded. She touched a metal rung and hissed as it scorched her palm. Gritting her teeth, she began pulling herself up. Every couple of rungs, she hesitated, then listened, certain someone was singing.

Finally, her hand lifted automatically but there were no more rungs. She pitched onto her chest. Rolling over, Tempest yelled again and was rewarded by the sound of a voice. The wall of smoke had dissipated, just a few ghostly tendrils waved through the air. Glancing at the leaded windows and octagonal room, she realized that she was in the bell tower. A rush of sweet, fresh air swept over her and she swallowed greedily, then gagged. Overhead dangled a heavy rope and the Perpetual Soul's massive bronze bell.

A bizarre memory from her opera history studies jumped into her head: Giuseppe Verdi hid with his mother from skirmishes between French and Austrian forces in the bell tower of a church, whose organ he later played. She blinked the digression away. Through a broken pane she could see, at a distance of about fifty feet, the flames leaping into the sky, battling a hissing, white stream.

Other than broken windows and wisps of smoke, the tower was untouched by the fire. A cough startled her.

"Darcy!" she whispered, clambering to her feet.

Her sister was sitting on a window ledge, leaning out. She turned quickly, emerald eyes wide in fright. Tempest raced across to her and grabbed her by the shoulders.

Ashen-faced, Darcy wrenched free and almost lost her seat.

"Noooo!" screamed Tempest.

"Don't touch me!"

Tempest reared back but croaked, "Come on, Darcy! Come on!"

Her sister violently shook her head. "The fire's my sign. Just like St. Patrick's Day. I knew what I had to do. I'm not afraid of dying," she yelled.

"You're not going to die." Tempest bent forward. "Take my hand!"

Again, Darcy shook her head and shifted her hips. "Get back!"

Tempest heard screams and glanced down. A hundred tiny white faces stared up, mouths agape.

"Please, take my hand! We've got to get out of here."

Using her fingers as levers, Darcy pushed herself off the sill and stood on the sloped roof. A wail rose from the onlookers.

"You don't understand. I'm not afraid...I'm being transformed, resurrected!" she cried. "I helped Vita and Sydney, now it's my turn."

"No!" Tempest struggled to mount the window sill.

The crowd gasped.

"Don't worry, Pesty," her sister whispered. "You have to die before you can live again."

Called to glory, Darcy Winsloe leaped eagerly into her final journey.

"No!" Tempest flung herself over the ledge, grasping for her sister. "Darcy, noooo!"

FORTY-ONE

He is Crime, I am Punishment.
—RIGOLETTO, ACT 3

Someone had taken a cheese grater to her throat. Not content to mutilate just her vocal cords, the bastard had used her chest as a loading zone. At least, that's how it felt to Tempest as she lay in hospital trying to master a new but essential trick: breathing without movement. She gasped lightly, a long way from being a maestro.

When she had finally awoken after the accident, she'd looked up into the indigo blue eyes of an elderly doctor. He had told her that her cracked ribs would heal in about two months, her throat in a couple of weeks.

"I hear you're a singer," he'd said as he prodded another rib.

Gasping, she nodded.

"I love blues, Billie Holiday, Johnny Coltrane, you know?"

This time she just blinked, shedding tears of pain.

"Young cop outside says you're in the opera." He

laughed dryly. "All that caterwauling, can't say as I like it." Another chest poke. "Hate to break the news, but you won't be singing anytime soon."

She tried to scream. Then quickly wished she hadn't.

"None of that," the doctor commanded. "No talking, no moving. Just rest and breathe easy. Got it?"

She got it...in quadruple time. A day later, as she lay practising her superficial breathing, tears again welled in her eyes. Her sister's face, glowing with an insane fever, mesmerized her. "Darcy," she whispered, tightly closing her eyes until the ghostly image receded, replaced by an abstract of orange and black.

Refusing to relive her sister's death, Tempest let her mind click through memories, anything to keep from stalling. The haunting music of the curse in Rigoletto crept in. She embraced the distraction.

I'm not going to sing Gilda, she admitted with more tears. It was too much. To be given such a chance only to have it rescinded before she could prove her worth.

In her mind, she sang the role of Gilda, from her dramatic entrance to her final, poignant duet with Rigoletto. Concentrating on the words, the music, the pronunciation and emphasis on each syllable kept her from seeing and hearing Darcy. Until Gilda's last line where the young woman bids Rigoletto farewell, then dies, fulfilling the curse on her father.

Or was it the curse of the Winsloes? Beads of sweat rolled off her forehead as she embraced the pain and the irony. She had lost her mother to suicide, then her only brother...now her sister—twice. Aware of the magnetic tug of suicide, Tempest remembered the light, the rush of bliss, the lightness and soaring sounds. She was afraid that she, too, would succumb.

She gave in to the tears, to the trembles and shudders, biting her tongue against the agony. Reveling in the grief.

"WANNA DRINK OF WATER?"

She started to shake her head, then froze, caught by a searing pain across her ribs. She motioned toward her throat with an unsteady hand.

Patrick winced. Seeing Tempest looking whiter than the impossibly white bed weakened his knees, but she looked a helluva lot better than the limp, sooty sack Jack had hauled out of the Perpetual Soul. He reached to pat her hand. Seeing the scars, he hesitated, dropped his hand.

"You look great," he said, pulling a chair near her bed.

Tempest rolled her eyes.

"No, really." He shuddered. "You should've seen yourself. Man, I thought you were a goner."

The word hung between them like an unanswered question.

Patrick flushed. "Uh, I'm real sorry about your sister."

Tempest's fingers curled into ivory fists.

A nurse popped her head in and told Patrick, "Five more minutes."

"Ten."

She glanced at Tempest then nodded. Patrick turned back to the bed.

"Look, I know you're in a lotta pain and all, but...I wanted to show you something. Might make you feel a li'l better." He reached into his pocket and pulled out one of the photographs Terry Brethour had stolen from her home. Seeing her fists, he held the photo in front of her.

"No," she croaked, body jack-knifing. Gently, he pushed her shoulders. She groaned and fell back, eyes wide and full of questions. "It's okay, it's okay. Got this and a box more from Brethour. He confessed to the B and E at your place, something about tripping over the box or some such bullshit. Ended up carrying it off."

Carefully, she raised her right hand and took the photo. Her brother and sister stared back at her, their young bodies intertwined. Tempest laid the picture face down on her chest and closed her eyes.

All Patrick wanted to do was stroke her curls; instead, he waited, watching the photo rise and fall with her tortured breathing.

After five minutes, her eyes opened and she motioned to his finger splint.

"Oh, got it caught in a door."

She raised her eyebrows.

"Honest." He picked up the black and white picture and began stroking an edge. "You know 'bout Brethour abusin' Amelia. Seems these photos gave the bastard some ideas. Amelia found 'em, wanted help but didn't know how to get it. She must have brought 'em to school, maybe hoping to show a teacher. Anyway, Sydney convinced her to put 'em in the chapel coin box."

He inhaled, then let the air out slowly. "What I'm trying to say is that we've got the photos. No one's gonna see 'em."

He couldn't prove it but she may have smiled.

"You wanna tell me who took them?"

Before she could respond, the nurse returned. "Time to go, Officer."

"Okay, just another minute, please?"

"Dr. Ivory's exhausted—" she stopped as Tempest reached toward her. "All right, a couple more."

Patrick thanked the nurse and waited until she left. He smiled. "Sorry," he said pointing to her throat. "Stupid question." He stroked his nose. "Look, uh, there's something else I wanna tell you."

Tempest shifted slightly, then grimaced.

He glanced into the hallway to make sure no one overheard. "It's about my dad and—" he lowered his voice, "your mom."

She frowned.

"They...they were hav—"

He paused as the nurse swept back in. "Time's up, Officer. Out!"

Tempest tried to speak but managed only fractured whispers.

"See?" the nurse declared. "You've upset her. That's it." She took him by the shoulders and none-too-gently shoved him out the door.

"Wait a sec," he cried and wriggled free. He turned back to the bed and reached into his pocket. "This's rightfully yours," he said, placing Vivian Winsloe's suicide note in Tempest's hand.

Her eyes darkened with a question.

He glanced at the nurse. "From your mom. Sent years ago. Got picked up by accident, never delivered."

AFTER THE NURSE GAVE HER ANOTHER SHOT OF Demerol, she read the familiar lines for the hundredth time and softly stroked the initials. It didn't make sense. Patrick would eventually tell her how he got the suicide note, maybe how it disappeared. But the real

puzzle was how it got there in the first place. No salutation, just a few lines from an Italian opera...not the
sort of note her mother would have left.

She remembered her sister's reaction when she
asked about the note. Darcy had looked into, then
touched a mirror. "Where's the note, he asked?" she
had whispered. When Tempest had pressed her, just
before Sister Eileen took her away, her sister had
replied, "Our Father."

Our Father! Tempest had automatically thought that
Darcy meant God, but what if she hadn't? What if it
were: Our father? She lay back, breathing lightly,
thinking, her eyelids growing heavy.

She was planning to leave him. Tempest knew her
dad. He couldn't bear the failure, the humiliation.
He'd do anything to protect his image, to keep them
all under his control.

What if he'd killed her, faked her mother's suicide?

Her chest throbbed. She rubbed her eyes. "The bastard!" she whispered, unable to contain the yawns. *The
fucking bastard.*

Maybe mom didn't abandon us at all, she thought,
welcoming the sleep.

FORTY-TWO

She is dead!
Ah, the curse!
—RIGOLETTO, ACT 3

Except for a few lime-green fingers of moss, the two tombstones hadn't changed. She had spent a lifetime jealous of her brother's courage to die and furious at her sister's desertion. Tempest eyed the stones sadly, touched by the blast of sorrow gripping her heart. They were just names and dates etched in marble, like the hundreds of others decorating the Holy Trinity graveyard. Of course, these two names, soon to be joined by a third, had one thing in common: the surname of Winsloe.

"None of you should be here," she murmured. *That fucking bastard.*

The little graveyard was deserted. The few attendees at Darcy Winsloe's final exit had gone long ago. Tempest had barely heard the funeral rites, couldn't remember the faces of the other mourners. Déjà vu from almost two decades before.

Inhaling, Tempest reached out to touch the stones. Her chest ached, but the pain no longer kidnapped each breath. She kept her eyes averted from the fresh mound to the left of her brother's grave.

"You okay?"

Startled, she lurched forward. He grabbed her, careful to grip her shoulders. Her breath came in short, wheezing gasps. "I'm sorry, I didn't mean to frighten you."

Gritting her teeth, Tempest pushed him away and leaned against her mother's tombstone. Despite the sharp pain, she began to laugh lightly and swear ever so softly.

Patrick stared at her. Finally, as she held her chest and ignored the tears streaming down her face, he asked, "What's so funny?"

"It's so stupid," she panted, voice still hoarse.

"What?"

"This—" she coughed then made a face. "is the first time I've gotten any support from my mom in years."

He watched her, uncertain whether to laugh or cry. So he handed her a tissue and waited.

After a long time, she blew her nose.

"Walk you out?"

She shook her head and watched a seagull wheel overhead.

"Okay," he said reluctantly, "if you're sure you're gonna be all right."

Her face told him that she would never be all right again. He swallowed, wondering if she had ever been all right. He said goodbye and turned to leave.

"Patrick?"

He spun on his heel.

"Thanks...for telling me about the photos."

"No problem." He looked her square in the eye. "Your dad?"

She closed her eyes and nodded.

Patrick let out a heavy sigh. "Thought so. I'm...I'm sorry, Tempest." He took a step closer. "Just between you and me, can...can I ask you about your sister?"

Tempest glanced at the mound and nodded.

"What'd she say, you know, on the roof?"

She leaned hard against the stone. It felt cold, damp and very strong. "She...she wasn't making much sense." He waited, eyes unwavering. "She was ill, needed help." She paused and swallowed. "Said something about dying to live again."

"The girls?"

She kneeled down and grabbed a handful of fresh earth from her sister's grave. Cool, damp, very fragile.

Darcy's eyes, brimming with insanity.

Rubbing the dirt through her fingers, Tempest replied, "Bet you'd like this stuff, looks very healthy."

"Bit too much sand, pretty common round here."

She flashed him a puzzled look.

"Poor in nutrients, gotta add stuff like mushroom compost"–he realized she wasn't listening– "manure..." he finished lamely.

She wiped her hand. "She...said St. Patrick's Day was a sign, like the fire." The soil dribbled free.

"Sign? Sign of what?"

"Transformation, resurrection...I don't know," her husky voice trailed off.

A pair of gulls screeched. Patrick watched the birds soar for a while.

"You think Amelia...?"

She winced. "I think Amelia took her own life. St. Patrick's Day was just a coincidence."

"It triggered your–" She turned away. He let the sentence hang.

Just as he was going to leave, her harsh whisper stopped him. "Ever ask your dad about my mother?"

"You know!"

Tempest nodded.

"But how?"

"Your dad's a thief and adulterer, mine's a child abuser and a murderer." She gave him a sad smile. "Go home, grow something in your garden."

His face blanched. "Murderer!"

"Can't prove it, but..." she coughed.

"What're you going to do?"

"Do?" She laughed bitterly. "He's a fucking vegetable, rest of my family's dead. I'm gonna do what I've always done."

"What's that?"

Tempest Ivory blew a soft kiss to all three graves and walked away.

"Be alone."

He watched her walk away, her broad back a facade of strength. She hesitated at the small white plaque, drawn by its restful words. Tempest gulped as a shudder rippled over her shoulders like the west winds rustling the Garry oaks overhead.

"One is Nearer God's Heart in a Garden, Than Anywhere Else on Earth," he whispered at her side.

She blinked. "Lord, I hope so," she murmured finally, and slowly moved away.

"Tempest?"

She paused at his soft call but didn't look back.

"I've got some perennials—hollyhocks, daisies, fox-glove—nothin' special, but they'd do really well in your yard."

He watched her shoulders rise and fall, like the faint hope he nursed.

"Could I bring 'em over sometime?"

She didn't say no.

NICOLA FURLONG

was born in Alberta, Canada, the sixth of eight children, and raised in Saskatchewan, Ontario and Prince Edward Island. She lives in Sidney on Vancouver Island, British Columbia. Her first mystery novel, *Teed Off!*, features professional golfer and coroner Riley Quinn. Furlong's passions are chocolate, mysteries and more chocolate.